THE CONSTANT LOVERS

A Richard Nottingham Mystery

Chris Nickson

Severn House Large Print
London & New York

This first large print edition published 2013
in Great Britain and the USA by
SEVERN HOUSE PUBLISHERS LTD of
19 Cedar Road, Sutton, Surrey, England, SM2 5DA.
First world regular print edition published 2012 by
Severn House Publishers Ltd., London and New York.

British Library (

Nickson, Chris.
  The constant l
Nottingham n
  1. Nottingham
  2. Constables
  (England)--Hi
  and mystery s
  I. Title II. Ser
  823.9'2-dc23

  ISBN-13: 9780727896490

Severn House Publishers support the Forest Stewardship Council™
[FSC™], the leading international forest certification organisation. All
our titles that are printed on FSC certified paper carry the FSC logo.

MIX
Paper from
responsible sources
FSC
www.fsc.org FSC® C013056

Printed and bound in Great Britain by
T J International, Padstow, Cornwall.

And now every night at six bells they appear
When the moon is shining and the stars they are
clear
These two constant lovers with each other's
charms
Rolling over and over in each other's arms.

Traditional broadside ballad

One

Richard Nottingham crossed Timble Bridge as the bell in the Parish Church chimed seven. The morning air was July warm, and the low water in Sheepscar Beck slipped quietly over the rocks. He stopped for a moment, feeling a gentle joy in life. For a few small minutes at least, everything could be right with the world. No crime, no anger, just the sound of the stream and the quiet chatter of birds up in the trees that shaded the bank.

All too soon, once he walked past York Bar and up Kirkgate, Leeds would envelop him and life would return. The noise and the full, heady stink of the city would rush in like a wave. Once again he'd be Richard Nottingham, Constable of Leeds. After such a long winter of cold, ice and deaths, this summer of 1732 was exactly what people needed, placid and peaceful. He lingered, loath to go, his hands resting on the wood of the trestle, letting his thoughts wander. Finally he turned, pushed the fringe of hair back from his forehead and walked into the city.

As he passed the Parish Church his eyes flickered to the graveyard, immediately picking out the spot where they'd buried his older daughter, Rose, in February. The grass grew thick and green over her bones; next spring the earth would have settled enough to put up the headstone that waited in the mason's yard.

He carried on past the White Cloth Hall where the wool merchants would be adding to their fortunes later in the day, and the jumble of houses, new and old, that lined the street, to the jail at the top of the street. He unlocked the heavy wooden door, opened the window to release the stifling heat that already filled the room, and settled at his desk.

Spring had been quiet, just small crimes and the minor everyday violence of life. But as June arrived they'd caught a thief. It was fortune, sheer good luck rather than skill that had reeled him in. The man had been dead drunk at the Rose and Crown, and his tools and the carefully packed gold coins had tumbled from the pockets of his waistcoat when Nottingham tried to rouse him.

The trial had been short and the sentence the only one possible. A week later the man had been taken up to Chapeltown Moor in the back of a cart and hung from the gallows. The event had drawn a good crowd, pulled in by the spectacle and the glorious weather. For a short time it had almost felt like a fair, with jugglers and fiddlers and a hastily printed broadside, everything building to the climax of the noose.

But in the end it had proved to be a poor business. The man had been heavy and no sooner had he been put to swing, the cart leaving him jerking and dangling, than his neck had broken. It was over in an instant.

The hundreds gathered hadn't been happy. They'd been drinking, anticipating the cheap enjoyment of long minutes of suffering and it had been snatched away from them. For a short time they swayed on the edge of mayhem and riot and the Constable had tensed. Then the hangman had cut down the body and they'd roared towards it, pulling at clothes and hair, women rubbing their babies against thick dead fingers for luck.

Once the dangerous moment passed he'd been able to leave, walking back to the city, bowing his head obediently to the aldermen and mayor as they passed in polished coaches or on sleek horses, chattering away earnestly about markets and profit with no mention of the life that had just ended.

And now it looked as if some false servants had come to Leeds, taking work and then robbing their new masters – a service lay. Just the day before, Morrison the chandler had reported that the maid who'd been with him barely a week had vanished. Five shillings had gone with her, along with three fine lace handkerchiefs that belonged to his wife. There'd been a similar incident a fortnight earlier, this time a male servant who worked for a merchant. He'd only been employed for three days and had run off with ten shillings in coins and some silver plate.

Nottingham had barely sat down to write his daily report when the deputy arrived, breezing in on his long legs and tossing his battered old hat on to the chair.

'Morning, boss.' He was smiling, happy. John Sedgwick had grown into his position, a long way from where he'd started out as a rough, raw lad, lanky and awkward, all too aware of the pox scars across his cheeks. He'd blossomed to become an ideal deputy Constable, resourceful, persuasive, and willing to put in the long, aching hours the job demanded.

'Did you talk to Morrison?' Nottingham asked.

Sedgwick shrugged. 'According to him it was his wife who hired the girl. She says the lass knocked on the door one day looking for work. Claimed to have arrived from Knaresborough.'

'And she took her on just like that?'

'It was lucky timing, her maid had left the week before. And there was a reference, evidently. But Morrison's wife doesn't remember the name on it. Of course.' He snorted.

'Any description?'

'Nothing worth having. She sounds like half the girls in Leeds – dark hair, small, quiet and polite. Went by the name of Nan, but you can wager good money that's not what she's really called. Morrison thinks she might have had blue eyes. From the look on his face I reckon he'd been hoping to tup her.'

'Do you think he did?'

'Just wishful thinking, most likely.'

They knew no more about the male servant. Dark hair, obedient, middle height; he could

10

have been anyone. It could be a pair working together, or there might even be more of them. The last time they'd had this problem, three years before, it had been a gang of five, three women and two men, and they'd proved slippery to catch. The Constable sighed.

'Put the word out. She'll probably try to sell the lace somewhere. I'm going to check the market.'

The trestles for the cloth market lined each side of Briggate, the main street of the city, winding all the way from Boar Lane down to the bridge over the Aire. Each Tuesday and Saturday morning the clothiers brought their goods in from homes, the dyed lengths they'd woven that were the product of weeks of work, and with the brief tolling of the bell the business of buying and selling drew underway.

Nottingham walked slowly down the street, as amazed as ever at the silence of the transactions. The merchants and factors would move from table to table, inspecting the quality and comparing the dyes against the swatches in their pockets. As soon as they found what they wanted, all it took was a few whispered words. A matter of seconds and the bargain was sealed.

He'd lived here all his life, but the ceremony of it all never ceased to surprise him. It had all the sanctity, the quiet holiness, of church. It was the lifeblood of the city. At each market thousands of pounds quietly changed hands. There was more wealth here than most people could imagine.

The Constable exchanged greetings with some of the merchants. They were dressed in light suits of good worsted, advertisements for their products, waistcoats flowing long and gaudy to their knees, hose brilliant white in the sunlight, shoe buckles shining silver and gold to flaunt their riches.

In his old work coat, stock untied and breeches worn shiny, Nottingham offered a contrast. They had their periwigs, short and lovingly powdered or full-bottom and glossy, while he kept his hair long and pulled back with a ribbon on his neck. They had the money and the power in the city. He kept them safe to enjoy it.

Within ten minutes more than half the boards were empty, the material moved away to be carried to warehouses later. Then the clothiers would lead their packhorses back out to the villages across the West Riding, coins jangling in their pockets, ready to start weaving all over again.

He stopped on the bridge, arms resting on the wide stone parapet. The river was sluggish, as lazy as the weather, bubbles showing where fish rose to snap at flies. He listened to its soft burblings for a few minutes, watching the water as it meandered.

Finally he pushed himself away and back into the tumult of Leeds. There was still plenty of work to be done. He strode back up Briggate, the noise from the inns loud and merry now most of the business had finished.

The merchants were smiling, money spent

carefully and much more to be made later. Nottingham had barely turned the corner on to Kirkgate when a shout and running footsteps made him turn.

The man was panting, ancient boots dusty and a sheen of sweat on his face. 'Are you the Constable?' he asked breathlessly.

'I am.'

'You'd better come quick, then. There's a dead lass.'

Two

'Where?' Nottingham asked urgently. The man was bent over, hands on his knees, trying to catch his breath.

'Out at Kirkstall Abbey,' he answered, pushing the words out.

'That's not Leeds,' the Constable told him.

'Aye, master,' the man protested, wiping his face dry with large hands, hair plastered against his scalp, 'but they don't know what to do. So they told me to fetch you.'

Nottingham considered. Leeds was the largest town in the area. Sometimes they sent for him from the neighbouring villages if a crime was too great for them.

'Come down to the jail,' he said finally.

He sat the man down, poured him a mug of small beer and watched as he gulped it down quickly, followed by another.

'What's your name?' he asked.

'Luke, sir. Luke Edgehill.'

'You ran all the way in?'

'Aye.' He grinned with pride. 'That's why they wanted me; I can run.'

He was a young man, maybe eighteen, long, dirty blond hair damp and stringy, skin coloured

14

by the sun and the wind. Tall and wiry, with guileless blue eyes, he looked directly at the Constable.

'What else do you know about all this, Luke?'

'Not much, sir.' He scratched at his scalp. 'One of the farmers found her by the old abbey this morning when he went to look after his sheep. She'd been stabbed, they told me.'

That certainly sounded like murder, Nottingham thought with a sigh; no wonder they wanted him there. But the abbey was a good three miles away; walking there and back would take too long.

'I'll ride out there,' he offered.

'Thank you, sir.' Edgehill stood. 'I'll go back and tell them you're coming.'

Through the window Nottingham watched him lope easily up Kirkgate then disappear into the crowds.

At the ostler's he selected his usual horse, a placid animal that he'd come to trust over the years. He never felt comfortable so far off the ground, but at least this beast didn't leave him fearful. Slowly he headed out along the road from Leeds, past the end of Boar Lane, where the houses gave way to fields and cottages that hugged the river.

Sheep grazed on the higher ground, and further down the crops were growing fast, ripening into rich colours. The heady scent of flowers, lavender and honeysuckle and others he could not name, clung in the air as he passed, clear and pure after the reek of the city.

15

By the time he reached the abbey sweat had soaked his shirt, making it stick against his skin. The old buildings, now just suggestions of what they'd once been, lay on a broad strip of ground between road and river. Only the church still had a sense of majesty, the nave a triumph of arches, the crumbling tower clawing towards heaven.

The abbey had once been important and wealthy; it had owned most of the lands around Leeds and beyond until King Henry took everything. That was what Ralph Thoresby had told him long ago, and Thoresby had known all about the history of Leeds. To Nottingham it was nothing more than an attractive ruin. He'd walked out here a few times on Sundays with Mary back in the distant days when they were courting.

In the bright light it looked like a painting sprung gently to life. Trees gave shade, the river flowed gently a few yards away. But close by one of the ruins, now little more than a few heaps of weathered, shapeless stone, a small group of men had gathered. He dismounted, feeling the tight ache in his thighs, and walked the horse over, pulling off the tricorn hat to wipe at his forehead.

'I'm Richard Nottingham, the Constable from Leeds,' he announced. 'One of you sent for me?'

'That were me.' A thickset man moved forward, his bearded face set in a dark frown. He was in an old shirt and breeches, sleeves rolled up over weatherbeaten, hairy forearms. 'Didn't know who to get.' He gestured at a grand house

16

partway up the hill. 'Master's gone for a week, so I sent the lad who works here to fetch you.'

'He said you'd found a girl dead.'

'Aye. She's back there, other side of the refectory.' There was a restlessness about the man, shifting uneasily from foot to foot as he talked, his gaze moving around. Shock, the Constable guessed, and fear. Seeing a body often left folk that way.

'Why don't you show me where she is?' he suggested.

The man walked away without a word. A black and white dog that had been lying in the shadow of a tree rose and followed him.

'What's your name?' Nottingham asked him as he tried to keep up. It was simple, human talk, trying to put the man at his ease.

'Tobias Johnson.' The man offered a broad hand for the Constable to shake. 'I look after the land for the master. We graze the sheep here.'

'When did you find the girl?'

Johnson stopped to calculate.

'Mebbe two hours ago. Bit longer, perhaps. I'd been working a few fields away and came back through here. The dog smelt summat, started whining.' He reached down and patted the animal. 'He dun't do that usually, so I thought I'd better look. She were just over here.'

They rounded a corner, the fragment of wall that stood thick and taller than a man. The girl lay on the ground, curled close to the stone, almost touching it. Against the lush, even colour of the grass her skin seemed eerily pale, the deep blue of her dress glistening. A knife handle protruded from her back, blade buried all the way to the hilt.

Nottingham squatted by the body, turning her slightly to look for any other wounds. She'd been a pretty girl, with long, pale hair. The dress was made of high quality material with a pattern woven in; there was nothing cheap about the fabric or the stitching. He glanced at the weapon: polished rosewood, the fittings shining brass. It was all money.

A few hours ago, a day, maybe a little more, whoever she was, this girl had still been alive. Slowly, tenderly, he laid her back down and rose to his feet, knees cracking.

'When were you last here?' he asked Johnson.

The farmer looked off into the distance, picturing his movements.

'Late yesterday afternoon,' he answered finally. 'I'd been down to Kirkstall Forge with a couple of scythes for mending. I came back up the bank. I'd have seen her if she'd been here then.'

Nottingham thought. It was a long stretch of time, but this was open land, not like the city where people were always around.

'You didn't hear anything last night?'

'Nothing.'

Johnson gave the corpse a last sad look and hurriedly strode off out of sight, the dog close at his heels. The Constable found him around the corner, standing silently, packing tobacco in a clay pipe.

'She's nobbut a lass,' he said mournfully.

'Who'd do that to someone like her? Leave her like that?'

'That's what they pay me to find out,' Nottingham told him. 'Have you seen any of her clothing? Anything at all?'

'Nowt,' Johnson answered. 'Just her, like that.' The Constable could see that the man's hand was trembling, clutching tight on the brittle pipe stem.

'Have some people look around,' he suggested. 'There might be something.'

'I will,' Johnson agreed.

'Do you have a coroner out here?' Nottingham said. Outside the city boundary, this was beyond the writ of Edward Brodgen, the Leeds coroner.

'Usually the master does it, but he's gone, like I say.'

'Have his deputy pronounce her dead. Can you find someone to bring her to the jail?' he asked. 'I'll need her there.'

'I'll get Elias and his cart. He does all the hauling round here.'

'Cover her properly,' Nottingham warned gently. 'We don't want all the world staring at her.'

'Aye,' Johnson agreed, his voice barely more than a whisper. 'Aye.'

'And if you find anything, bring it to me. Anything at all. It could be important.'

He walked away, leaving the farmer to his thoughts, and mounted the horse for the ride back to Leeds. His spine hurt from the constant, jarring movement, and he looked to the dis-

19

tance, happy to see the outline of the city, the roofs and spires that meant home.

Like it or not, it seemed that looking for the girl's killer was going to be his job. She obviously wasn't local to Kirkstall; someone would have known her immediately. Nor did she have the air of the country girl about her. Her skin was too white, too smooth; she'd never spent much time exposed to the sun. When they brought her to the jail he'd look at her hands, but he was willing to wager there would be no calluses.

She came from money. Everything about her said that. Very soon someone would report her missing and then he'd be under pressure to find the murderer. The mayor, now in the last months of his office, would carp and command. Never mind the poor who died from violence, this would come first.

But there was nothing more he could do until he inspected her body properly. He hadn't paid attention to see if she wore any rings, or had marks on her fingers from them. There would be a few things she could still tell him, even in death.

He sighed, willing the horse back to its stable so he could plant his two feet on the ground. The heat had grown during the morning, and even the small breeze simply stirred the warm air around.

Soon enough, though, Leeds was around him, the noise and press of people, the full, awful summer perfume of the city filling his nostrils.

Strangers often found the place unnerving, roaring loud, busy and crowded, but the familiarity of it all comforted him. Smiling, he walked back along Boar Lane, glancing up at the buildings, the inviting scent of ale seeping from the open door of an inn.

Sedgwick was waiting at the jail, the remains of a beef pie on the desk in front of him, his coat thrown across a chair. Nottingham poured a mug of small beer and drank eagerly.

'Any joy with the thieving servants?' he asked.

'No. I've told people to look out for the lace handkerchiefs. I don't think there's anything else we can do for now. If this lot have any sense they'll have moved on by now and be trying it somewhere else.'

'How many criminals have sense?' Nottingham asked. 'We've got something bigger now. We have a murderer to find.'

'Oh?' Sedgwick fixed his stare on the Constable.

'They called me out to Kirkstall. A girl stabbed at the abbey.' He poured more beer and drank. 'From a quick look at her, I'd say she's from quality.'

Sedgwick made a sour face. He knew what that meant.

'Someone's going to be bringing her in later. Once we know a little more I'll tell His Worship.' The mayor would need to be informed.

'If we're looking for a murderer we could use someone else to help,' the deputy pointed out.

'I know.'

21

Until the spring they'd had someone, a young cutpurse named Josh who'd turned into a promising Constable's man. But he'd left, and Nottingham couldn't blame him for going. His girl had lost their baby and died, and Josh had been beaten bloody by a pair of thugs. There'd been precious little to keep him in Leeds.

Since then he'd talked to a few prospects, but there'd been no one to equal the lad they'd lost. He'd had intelligence and energy, he listened well and was used to being invisible, unnoticed. Finding someone that good was hard, but the Constable wasn't going to settle for less.

'I need to find the right person,' he said. 'You know anyone?'

Sedgwick shook his head. 'None of the men are up to it. They'll do what you need if you prod them but nothing more than that.'

Nottingham grinned. 'Maybe we'll be lucky and solve this one in a day.'

'Aye, and maybe someone will have left me a fortune in his will.' The deputy stood and stretched loudly, his arms extending almost to the ceiling. 'Do you want me to check the Hall later?'

Every Tuesday and Saturday afternoon un-dyed cloth was sold at the White Cloth Hall. Like the morning market on Briggate it was held in near silence; only the sound of whispers and footsteps echoed around the stone wings of the building. There was never any trouble, but they went when they could, just to walk around and remind people that the law was watching.

'Yes, I suppose we'd better put in an appearance,' Nottingham answered. 'I'll wait here for the body.'

Left alone he slipped next door to the White Swan for a fresh jug of ale and a pie from their kitchen. It would be at least an hour before the carter arrived with the corpse and he'd no intention of going hungry while he waited.

The mutton was stringy but the gravy was rich and spicy, soaking deep into the pastry. The ale tasted refreshing, cool from the deep, dark cellar where a stream ran through the earth. He sat back on the bench, resting his head against the wall, and closed his eyes.

Tomorrow his family would all be together. Emily would have the day off from her post as a governess in Headingley, and walk into Leeds to be with them. Mary would be cleaning the house now, although it was already spotless, ready for their daughter's arrival.

The girl seemed to have settled happily into her position. There was a new air of gravity and maturity replacing the wild ways of last autumn when she'd seemed uncontrollable. She loved the two young girls in her care, and responsibility agreed with her, smiles and sharp eyes replacing the bleak silences of winter.

But that season had been a bad time for them all. After Rose had died, slipping away to a wraith in just a week, their lives had simply crumbled. Slowly, painfully they'd managed to look ahead. And now, with Emily gone, he and Mary were gradually becoming used to life alone again, cast back on themselves.

It had been a tenuous easing back to old familiarities and intimacies. They were finding each other again, reminded of the pleasure of each other's company once more. With the good weather they'd taken to walking together, just as they had when they were younger, letting their grief evaporate in the long, warm evenings.

The grating squeak of a cart turning the corner on to Kirkgate roused him from his thoughts and he glanced through the dust on the window. The man had made good time from Kirkstall. He gulped the last of the ale and rushed into the street.

The carter had stopped in front of the jail. He was a squat, bearded man, dressed in breeches and shirt, an old leather apron bulging over his large stomach, sleeves rolled up to show brawny, tanned arms.

'Got summat for you,' he said, gesturing idly at the bundle in the back of the wagon. The girl had been covered with a dirty sheet, but there was no mistaking the fact that a body lay underneath. 'I'll help you get her in.'

She was an awkward load, but together they managed to ease her through to the cell the city used as a mortuary.

The carter wiped his hands on the apron. 'Nasty business, that.'

'Do you know who she was?' Nottingham asked.

'No.' The carter answered. 'Not local, though, I can tell you that.' He paused, head tilted to one

24

side. 'Oh aye,' he remembered, 'I've summat else to give you. Come with me.'

The Constable followed him out to the cart. The man reached under the seat and brought out an object in an old sack.

'The knife,' he explained. 'We had to take it out to wrap her. Bugger of a job it was, too. The blade was twisted and caught, didn't want to come.'

He climbed up to the wagon and flicked the reins lightly. The horse started to move. The man didn't bother to look back.

Removing the sheet, Nottingham could see her properly for the first time. The flies had gathered around her mouth and nose and he had to keep brushing them away. Already there was the smell of decay about her, sickening and sweet like overripe fruit.

She was smaller than he'd first thought, no more than five feet and dainty, with the easy slimness of youth. Eighteen, he thought, possibly twenty, but no older than that. She had blue eyes and even features, a girl who was pretty, but with looks that stopped shy of beauty.

He lifted her left hand, turning it over to examine the palm. It was exactly as he'd thought; the skin was soft and pale, she'd never had to work in her life. Her fingernails were clean, not bitten or worn to the quick. He held up the ring finger to the light, noticing a paler band of flesh, the sign of a wedding ring taken from her. There was a small, faint scar, shaped like a C, in the triangle between her thumb and forefinger.

25

Her feet were tiny, the toes all straight, with no indication they'd ever been forced into shoes that didn't fit. Finally he pushed her on to her side and exposed the wound in her back. The maggots were already there, tiny white creatures crawling and feasting around the gash. He flicked them away with a fingernail, bending to look more closely. There was just one cut, and judging from the position it would have pierced her heart.

Gently he laid her back down and closed her eyelids. There were small bruises on her upper arms as if someone had held her too tightly, keeping her helpless. So perhaps there had been two of them, he thought, one to hold her still while the other stabbed.

Nottingham ran his hands over the dress, feeling slowly along the seams for anything that might be hidden there. Moving down, his fingertips touched something, a pocket cleverly concealed in the fabric. He opened it carefully and took out a piece of paper, folded several times into a tiny square. He opened it up and held it to the light. A note in a man's handwriting: *Soon we'll be together and our hearts can sing loud, my love. W.* Was that just a keepsake she kept close to treasure or something hidden for a reason, he wondered.

He stood back, staring down at the fragile body. Someone had loved this girl, raised her, seen her go when another wedded her. She'd come from a family with enough money that she'd never wanted for anything. People would miss her very soon.

At the desk he picked up the sack and shook out the knife. Blood had dried on the edges of the blade in veins like rust. It might have been made for cutting meat in the kitchen, but it had still cost someone deep in the purse, an expenive weapon for a killing. This didn't look like a random murder by thieves. If it had been, they wouldn't have left her where the body would be found so easily. There was more going on here.

He sat back, steepling his fingers under his chin. Girls of quality didn't disappear in the West Riding. Especially wives. Today, tomorrow at the latest, he'd have word that someone was frantically searching for her. Then he'd have a name and he could start seeking the person who'd done this.

The easy, languorous mood of early morning had vanished and in its place Nottingham felt a growing tension. From long experience he knew that most murders were solved quickly; the more time went by, the harder his job would become. Half a day had passed already since she'd been found. He needed to know who she was.

He was still wondering, half expecting someone to arrive and give the girl a name, when Sedgwick returned.

'Hot out now,' he commented, shedding his coat to show large patches of sweat darkening his old, darned shirt. 'Starting to get close.'

'Any problems?' Nottingham asked.

'Nothing. The heat must be making them lazy.'

'Just wait until later. Saturday night, plenty of drink and the temperature – there'll be trouble enough.'

The deputy nodded his agreement, pouring the last of the small beer.

'Did they bring her in?'

'A little while ago.'

'And?'

'She grew up around money, no doubt about that. And she was married, by the look of it.' He pushed the knife across the desk. 'Take a look at that.'

Sedgwick hefted the blade, balancing the handle on his finger. 'That's what killed her?'

'Yes.'

'That's not cheap. So either the killer's rich or he panicked a little.'

'The carter said the blade had caught in the bone. They probably couldn't pull it out. There must have been two of them. Someone else was holding her; there's bruising on her arms.'

'But we've no idea who she was?'

'None at all. Go and take a look at her, see if the face is familiar.'

The deputy vanished for a few moments and came back out shaking his head.

'Then we'll have to wait until someone claims her,' the Constable continued. 'Go on home, John; they'll be keeping you busy tonight.'

With a bright grin Sedgwick drained his cup, gathered up his coat and left, vanishing into the warmth of the street.

Three

No one came for the girl that day or the next. Emily arrived home as the Sunday morning bells at the Parish Church rang eight; she'd set off early from Headingley, her shoes covered in dust from the road. She carried herself with pride and confidence these days, Nottingham thought with pleasure as they all strolled together to morning service.

Later he heard the laughing burble of voices from the kitchen as she prepared dinner with Mary, the scent of cooking meat making him hungry. It was good to have the family together, however briefly it might be. He enjoyed having his wife to himself, to rediscover why they'd fallen in love and do it all over again, but this ... it brought a different, deeper contentment.

Emily was full of tales of her charges, Constance and Faith. She cared about the girls, that much would have been clear to a blind man, her eyes smiling whenever she talked about them. He listened, basking in her joy, thinking of her when she was small and still in apron strings herself, then a little older and gawky, her head always in a book.

In the evening he walked her back into the

city, her arm daintily crooked in his, the late warmth rising from the ground.

'Are you happy?' he asked as they crossed Timble Bridge and began the gentle climb up Kirkgate.

'Yes, I am, papa.' Her answer was heartfelt. 'I love the girls, and the Hartingtons are very good to me. I sit with them at dinner, and they listen to my opinions.'

'Then you'd better make sure you're not too free in what you say,' he advised.

She blushed. 'I'm always very careful, papa.' She paused, and he could tell she was looking for a neutral topic. 'They took me to see the oak last week.'

'The oak?'

'The big oak tree on the main road in Headingley. People say it's been there for hundreds of years. Mr Hartington explained how important it used to be, how people met there to govern things long ago.'

He smiled. Thoresby, the historian, had told him about the old shire oak years before, but he'd never paid much attention. In those days he'd been too busy surviving the present to concern himself with the past.

They parted at the jail, and he waited by the door until she vanished up Briggate with a wave. Grown up and gone, off into her own life. He smiled and unlocked the door.

He expected a note from Sedgwick, saying the body had been claimed and giving her a name, but there was nothing. He could smell her corpse, rotting by the hour in this weather, the stink of her decomposition clawing at his throat.

The Constable was surprised, and worried. By now, surely, someone must have missed her and come looking. She couldn't have lived too far away. Then his mind fell to the practicalities. The way her body was turning, if no one arrived tomorrow they'd have no choice but to put her in the ground, to tip her into a pauper's grave before she became too rank.

There was something wrong, skewed, about all of this. Why would someone leave her at the abbey where she was going to be found? Who wanted to kill her and leave her that way? And the biggest question – why was she still nameless? It was as if someone wanted her to be a mystery, to tantalize.

It could have been her husband who'd killed her, he mused. If that were the case, no one would report her missing for a time. It was easy enough to spin tales to cover a wife's absence. He gave a sigh; until he had information, everything was just a guess. He pulled a ragged old handkerchief from his breeches, put it over his mouth and glanced around the cell door at her face, so empty and lonely in death.

She was buried the next day. They could do nothing else; the foul stench of her filled the jail. Once she'd been carried out, it still took hours for the air to sweeten enough so they didn't gag when they breathed.

On Tuesday morning, as Nottingham sat with his quill, scratching at the paper to ask for more money from the city for the night watch, the door opened and a man entered cautiously, glancing around as if not sure he should be there. He cleared his throat, clutching his hat in his hands, blunted fingernails scratching at the felt of the brim as the Constable looked up at him.

'My wife's disappeared,' he said.

Four

The Constable was instantly alert, sitting up sharply at the desk.

'What's your name?' he asked.

'Samuel Godlove,' the man answered. He looked to be in his late forties, comfortable in his coat and stock, his face wind burnt and his eyes like next year's hope. A farmer, Nottingham judged from his appearance, but definitely a prosperous one, dressed for a visit to the city. The material of the coat was expensive, the cut that of a fine tailor, his face glistened with a fresh shave, pores wide, a full-bottom wig of the best chestnut hair hanging far over his collar. But for all he might be worth, there was no authority in his bearing. He looked like a man who was fearful of life.

'Sit down, Mr Godlove.' The Constable gestured at the chair. 'Your wife's disappeared?'

The man perched on the edge of the chair, shoulders pulled in awkwardly close to his body. 'Yes,' he said hesitantly. 'I expected her back yesterday, but she never arrived.'

'She didn't send word?'

'No.'

The man's eyes darting nervously round the

room. This wasn't going to be easy, Nottingham thought.

'Where had she gone?'

'To see her family. She gets lonely out where we live, there's not much for her to do. She wanted some time with her mother and father. She went Thursday last. She was going to surprise them.'

'And where are they?'

'Roundhay,' Godlove answered. The Constable knew it vaguely, farming land a few miles to the north east of the city.

'Where do you live?'

'Near Horsforth. I have a farm...' He let the words tail away, as if he didn't want to reveal too much.

Horsforth wasn't far from Kirkstall, Nottingham mused.

'Have you seen her parents?' he asked. 'Did she leave there?'

Godlove looked up at him, his eyes wide and moist.

'I was worried. I rode over late yesterday. They said she'd never arrived.'

The words hung in the air. Nottingham sat up straighter and rubbed a hand across his chin. The farmer looked lost, trying to blink the tears away.

'What's your wife's name, Mr Godlove?'

'Sarah.' He said the word tenderly, lovingly, a caress as much as a sound. 'We've only been married a year.'

The Constable kept his eyes firmly on the

man's face. There was no dissembling here, just a tumult of grief and confusion. Godlove was a lost man.

'How old is she?'

'Eighteen.' Even as his skin flushed, Godlove raised his head higher, as if daring the other man to question him about age.

Nottingham just waited, not rising to the bait.

'What does she look like?' he asked kindly, although he suspected he already knew the answer.

'She's small,' the man said, raising an arm to indicate her height. 'Fair hair, blue eyes. A lovely girl.' He smiled. 'Too thin, though. I keep telling her she needs to eat more.'

'Was she wearing a wedding ring?'

Godlove looked at him quizzically, not expecting the question. 'Yes, of course. She always wears it, she's a married woman.'

'Does she have any marks? Is there anything that might make her stand out?'

'No,' he replied.

'No scars?' Nottingham prompted. 'Nothing at all?'

'Just a little one, here,' the farmer said after a few moments' thought. He showed his left hand. 'Almost like a circle. You'd hardly notice it. And she can't take the sun. The last couple of months she's had to have a parasol and a bonnet every day to keep it off her. She burns very easily. It's painful.'

Nottingham was silent. So now he had a name for the corpse. He didn't know what private sorrows the man was carrying, but he knew he was going to add to them.

'Mr Godlove,' he said, 'I'm sorry. I have no comfort for you.'

'What do you mean?' Godlove's voice rose in panic and confusion.

'Someone who matches the description you just gave me was found dead at Kirkstall Abbey on Saturday.'

'What?' The farmer's head jerked up as if someone had pulled him hard by the hair. Words tumbled from him. 'No, it can't ... but ... no ... Kirkstall?'

The Constable nodded his head sadly. 'The body had the same scar. I'm sorry, she'd been murdered.'

The man slumped forward, pushing his chin against his chest for a few seconds. Nottingham watched him breathe slowly, trying to regain control before he raised his head again, eyes full of pain. 'I don't understand,' he said simply, adrift now in a country he didn't know. 'You said she's dead? And someone killed her?'

'Yes.' Godlove stared at him, and he knew he had to give the man the truth. 'She'd been stabbed.'

'Why?' he asked, uncomprehending, barely murmuring the words. 'Why?'

'I don't know. I didn't even know who she was until you arrived.' He paused, wondering how to phrase the next part. 'We had to bury her yesterday. The heat...'

He watched Godlove but the man was too

stunned by his wife's death to take in the fact.

'Murdered?' The word came out in wonder and astonishment.

The Constable stood up and began to pace, the sound of his boot heels hard on the flagstones. He needed the man's attention. He had a name for the girl now, but he needed more, everything he could learn, and he needed it as quickly as possible.

'Mr Godlove,' he said. 'How was she travelling? Did anyone go with her?'

The farmer roused himself slowly, as if he'd only heard the words from a far distance. It took him a few moments to collect his thoughts.

'I'm sorry.' He gave a weak, polite smile that did nothing to cover his torment. 'She decided to ride. I have a carriage, but the weather was good and she had a horse she loved. It wasn't that far.'

'Who went with her?'

'Her maid.'

'Was she on horseback, too?'

'No,' Godlove said after a short while, 'she wouldn't get on one. She was scared of them.'

'What's the maid's name?' Nottingham persisted. So now there was someone else to hunt.

'Anne.'

'What does Anne look like? How long has she been with you?'

'She came with Sarah when I married her.' He was unfocused, drifting away. 'She's just a girl, plump, ordinary. Not especially pretty, but not ugly. I—' He started to speak, then stopped. The

37

Constable waited but he didn't continue.

'And what are your wife's parents called?'

'Lord and Lady Gibton,' the man answered.

Nottingham's heart sank; it was all he could do not to grimace. The death of someone wealthy was one thing, the murder of an aristocrat was another altogether.

'I want to take her home. I want to bury her properly,' Godlove announced with surprising decision.

'Of course,' the Constable agreed quickly. 'I'll have the parish arrange it.'

'She was stabbed, you said?'

'Yes.' He opened the desk drawer and took out the knife. 'Have you ever seen this before?'

Godlove shook his head. He was pale, looking wearied and far older than his years.

'Can I get you anything?'

'No.' The man stood, head hanging down, and the Constable knew he'd have no more information today. 'I'll ... Can you...?'

'I'll see she's brought out to you.'

'Thank you.'

Godlove left slowly, going out into a day the Constable knew he would never be able to forget.

Nottingham sat back and sighed loudly. With nobility involved he needed to inform the mayor. He waited a few minutes, trying to imagine how he might phrase things, then walked to the Moot Hall. The building dominated Briggate, sitting two storeys tall, square in the middle of the street, the stocks outside the arched

38

front, the road flowing on each side of it like a river. On the ground floor the butchers' shops were a stink of meat spoiling in the heat, the thick buzzing of flies like a curtain around them that reminded him of the insects heavy around the girl's body. Nottingham entered through the heavy doors, leaving most of the sound outside, then walked up the polished steps and along a corridor where a thick Turkey carpet muffled his footsteps.

He knocked on the wooden door and waited for the command to enter. Edward Kenion was behind his desk, as the Constable knew he would be. In less than two months he'd pass the chain of office to his successor, and he already looked as if he'd be glad to be relieved of its grievous weight.

Kenion's clothes might have been crisp, the cut and the material of his coat a subtle sign of his wealth, but the dark shading under his eyes showed the toll of long hours and responsibility, and his belly bulged further than before against the rich brocade of his waistcoat. It was a thankless job, Nottingham knew that, an ill reward for service to the Corporation. Some men paid a fine rather than take the post.

'What is it, Nottingham?' he asked sharply, barely glancing up from his papers.

'I sent you a report about the girl out in Kirkstall.'

'Aye, I remember. You didn't know who she was.'

'I do now. Her husband was just at the jail. He

39

has a farm out towards Horsforth. Probably an estate, from the look of him.'

Kenion looked at him wearily from under bushy eyebrows. 'Is that it?'

'No. He said the girl's father is Lord Gibton.'

The mayor threw down his quill. 'Bugger. Do you know who he is?'

Nottingham shook his head. He'd never heard the name until a few minutes before.

'God knows how long ago or why, but one of our kings made Gibton's ancestor a baron,' Kenion explained. 'Along the way one of them lost all the estate and most of the money. About all they had left was the title and a little bit of land. They scraped by, from what I heard, poor by the standards they'd known before.' He waved his hand. 'A year or so back they got some money from somewhere. Now you'd think they always owned half the county from the way they act. He's bad enough but his wife is even worse, a shrew. This means I'll be hearing from them soon.' He sighed. 'I hope you can bloody well find his killer fast, Constable.'

It was half wish, half command.

'Sarah Godlove,' he told Sedgwick when he returned to the jail. The deputy was there, practising his writing with a small piece of chalk and some slate. Nottingham had taught him his letters, preparing him for the role of Constable some day in the future.

Sedgwick cocked his head.

'That's the name of the dead girl. Her husband came in.'

40

'Rich?'

'He is,' Nottingham answered. 'But it's worse than that. Her father's a baron. I've just been to tell the mayor.'

'Fuck,' the deputy muttered.

'Except they haven't had much wealth for a long time. They've just come into money, evidently.'

'Poor nobility?' Sedgwick snorted. 'Pigs fly too, do they?'

The Constable smiled briefly. 'That's the story, anyway. You'd better have her exhumed and take her out to the husband tomorrow. He's out at Horsforth. See what you can find out from him.'

'What did he tell you, boss?'

'She left on Thursday, going over to see her parents in Roundhay. It was meant to be a surprise visit. She was on horseback, had a maid with her. She never arrived.'

'So where's the maid?'

'I wondered that, too. Gone, apparently.'

The deputy looked thoughtful.

'What is it?' Nottingham asked.

'Nothing, really. Had the maid been with them long? It could be the service lay gone wrong.'

Nottingham shook his head firmly.

'According to the husband, the maid had been with the girl a long time. I'm going out to Roundhay tomorrow to see the Gibtons. We should know more after that.'

'How did the mayor take the news?'

'I think he'd have been happier at his own

41

funeral. He doesn't seem to care much for Lord Gibton or his wife.'

It was brushing twilight when Sedgwick returned to his room. There was dirt on his hose from where they'd opened the grave, and he could still feel death cloying in his mouth.

It had been hard to watch the coffin pulled up from the earth, the sense of eternity disturbed. And harder still to hoist it up on to the cart, then cover it, ready for the morning and the journey out to Horsforth.

Lizzie was waiting, a warm smile from her his welcome. She set the mending aside, pushing the needle into the fabric, and came over to kiss him. Down on the pallet bed, James turned over and burrowed back into sleep.

'How's he been?'

'Up and down,' she said. The boy had a summer cold, but they both knew it took so little for things to become worse. To live without money was to always walk on a knife edge. 'He's slept a few times today.' She reached down and ran her fingers lightly across James's forehead. 'I think he's over the worst of it, he seems cool enough now.'

Lizzie had been a whore he'd known from his work. They'd shared jokes on night-time corners, her laughter genuine and infectious. She'd offered herself to him a few times, and once or twice, when things had been bad at home, he'd accepted. After Sedgwick's wife had run off with a soldier, she'd turned up at his door,

42

wondering who'd look after his son.

She'd been living with him since the previous autumn and he was still surprised at the joy it brought him every day. He looked forward to coming home, to the feel of her lips on his, to the pleasure in her eyes when she saw him.

He picked up some bread and began to chew.

'John?' Her voice was tentative, unsure, so unlike her that he turned.

'Do you think I'm a good mother with James?'

'Of course I do,' he told her, meaning it. She loved the lad properly, giving him ample care and attention. He'd blossomed with her, revelling in life, playing on the riverbank as she watched, discovering mischief, all the things he should be doing. He reached out and took her hand. 'Why are you asking?'

She smiled shyly.

'Well, it looks like you're going to be a father again.'

Five

He loved this time of day, the soft minutes between waking and sleep when his mind could wander freely. Mary's head rested on his chest, her hair loose and tickling his cheek as she slept. The window was open wide and from the woods in the distance he could hear the restless hoot of an owl.

Earlier they'd walked out past Burmantofts, taking a stroll in the quiet evening. It was a good way to put the cares of the day behind him, a chance for restful conversation. He understood that their new situation, just the two of them, was hard on Mary. She was alone all day, tending the house and the garden, feeling the emptiness and the silence of the place. When he came home she drank in his company, eager for words, a touch, a soft smile, the pleasure of talking.

He stroked Mary's shoulder through her shift and felt her stir slightly. Years before, he recalled, they'd discussed all the wonderful things they'd do once the girls had gone. Now that time was here and they were groping their way into it. Yet Mary was already gazing ahead to the day he'd retire.

'Richard,' she'd said as they passed the old burgage plots, heavy now with fruit and flowers and herbs, 'we'll be able to spend all our time together. We can do things.'

He smiled at her, happy to hear the eagerness that seemed so girlish. After Rose's death in the winter he'd watched helplessly as some of the light leave her. Now it seemed to have returned, her eyes twinkling as she dreamed of the future.

'We'll have precious little money,' he'd pointed out. It was true; the city would grant him the house and a tiny pension – if he lived that long. He took her hand and tried to stop her thoughts. 'Besides, that's a long time off yet. Let's just enjoy what we have now, shall we?'

She laughed, pulling him down the lane towards home.

He gazed at her later as she let down her hair then untied the mantua dress he'd bought her in May. It was second-hand, the blue faded to the colour of dawn sky, but she loved wearing it. She slipped into bed, curling around him with a kiss. Thoughts of the young man he'd once been touched him, his curious, cautious shyness, the sense that the world could fall at any time. And he realized he loved her more now than he had back then. A different love, less ardent maybe, but stronger than youth.

Nottingham set off early for Roundhay, taking the gentle horse from the ostler and following the road that ran out by Sheepscar Beck. He could see people already hard at work in the fields but there were precious few travellers at this hour; all he encountered was a pair of riders and they were going into Leeds.

He passed a small sign guiding travellers to Gibton's Well. He'd heard of the place, that the waters there were supposed to be beneficial. For a while it had been fashionable and some of the merchants and aldermen had come out with their wives, all hoping to be healed of their aches and pains by its waters. None of them had ever looked much better.

He continued up the gentle slope, the vista spreading out green before him, sheep grazing in large white flocks.

By the time he reached Roundhay village the sun was well risen, the warmth rounding on his shoulders and leaving his throat dry. He stopped at the alehouse, letting the horse drink from the stone trough while he went inside for a mug of small beer.

It was nothing more than a ramshackle cottage with a bench and two barrels of ale resting on trestles. The woman who served him was small and old, her back bent, lines cracking deep on her face.

'Do you know Lord Gibton?' Nottingham asked.

The woman chuckled. He could see her gnarled knuckles as she poured his ale.

'Oh aye, Lord,' she said mysteriously, took a clay pipe from her apron and lit it, blowing smoke up to the low ceiling. The Constable waited and she continued, her voice rough and gravelly. 'Allus had their airs, they have, thought they were better than everyone, although the family's lived almost like the rest of us longer than anyone can remember.'

She made a half-hearted attempt to wipe the table, brushing a few stale crumbs on to the earth floor with her hand, happy to continue the gossip.

'What happened to their money?'

'All sorts of tales,' she said dismissively. She leaned forward, bringing the smell of ancient sweat and foul breath. 'I'll tell you what most folk round here say, though. Long time ago, they owned all this land but lost it at cards.'

'Do you believe that?'

She shrugged. 'All I know is they got some money again and they're back living like royalty.' She spat towards the empty hearth.

'How long ago did that happen?' Nottingham asked.

She stopped to consider, counting back in her head.

'About eighteen month back, something like that,' she answered finally. 'Not too long before that little lass of theirs got wed.'

'Sarah?'

'Aye, only one they had. They'd had some others, but they all died. Some of them as babbies, some older. Doted on that girl, they did, couldn't do enough for her. Married her into wealth, from the way she dresses when she comes back.'

'Does she come back often?'

47

The woman paused and thought. 'Every month or so, I suppose. Hard not to notice her, way she prances around the place on her horse.'

'So where did this all new money come from?' he wondered.

'They *said* they'd inherited it,' she said, rolling her eyes, every word oozing doubt. 'I reckon it was that farmer paid for Sarah. Cost him enough if it was, mind.'

'What?' He couldn't believe that. He knew well enough about the dowries many women brought to marriage, anything from land and coin to a small chest of sheets, but he'd never heard of a man paying to wed a girl. 'Where did you hear that?'

'Summat folks have said here and there,' the woman said with a small air of defiance. 'Makes sense enough. There's no one to leave brass to the Gibtons.'

He considered the idea. Who'd sell their daughter that way? But the more the thought lingered, the more he had to admit that it could happen. With the rich, everything was wealth and power, however they could obtain it.

'Where do they live now?'

'Moved out the village.' She clicked her tongue at the idea. 'They used to have a cottage close to the crossroads but they left that. It was a pretty enough place, too, bigger than most. If you want to find them, go along the old Roman road, the one that goes to Moortown. There's a house about half a mile down, set back behind some trees. That's what they bought with their fortune.'

He thanked her and set off, leaving an extra coin for the information she'd given him. The place was easy enough to spot, the only building on the horizon, but first he paused to glance at their old house. Perhaps the woman had been right and it had been pretty enough once, but neglect had very quickly eroded its beauty. Now the garden was overgrown, an unkempt tangle, slates hung loose on the roof, windows and door gone, salvaged by the other villagers.

A few minutes later, as he rode down the driveway, he could see that the house the Gibtons had moved to was neither new nor especially grand. It looked like the home of a moderately prosperous squire. But it had pleasing, even proportions, and was built of ruddy brick with neatly mullioned windows. The grounds were carefully tended, and it was certainly several steps up from where they'd lived before. He glanced back over his shoulder. The cottage stood in the far distance, its outline faintly visible through a thin copse. How far they'd come, but what a small distance. How long before they had it pulled down, he wondered, and rewrote their history?

A breathless young serving girl dashed out to meet him, bobbing a quick curtsey even as her eyes took in his old clothes.

'I'd like to speak to Lord Gibton,' Nottingham announced. She ducked her head swiftly and ran back in the house. He tied the horse's reins to a tree and waited.

He'd met people with titles before. At first he'd been nervous, unsure how to address them, how to act around them. Some had quickly put him at ease, pleasant fellows with easy, open manners. Most, however, took their superiority for granted, as if the world had been created solely for their ease.

Baron Gibton was going to be one of the latter, the Constable thought as the man came down the steps. He was a scrawny man, hardly any meat on his bones, with a deeply lined, care-worn face under a glossy auburn peruke. He was dressed in a suit of deep burgundy velvet, the tails of his draped canary waistcoat hanging close to his knees, his stock and hose an un-blemished white. In London he'd have fitted in perfectly; out here, surrounded by countryside, he just looked affected and ridiculous.

'The girl says you want to see me,' he said briskly, eyes appraising Nottingham's appear-ance. 'Who are you, anyway?'

'I'm the Constable of Leeds, my Lord.' Not-tingham didn't bow or look down deferentially at the ground. 'I'm here about your daughter.'

Gibton stared for a few moments and then pursed his mouth, showing sharp teeth behind thin lips.

'Come in. I don't want everyone knowing my business.'

He turned quickly on his heel and strode inside.

The withdrawing room smelt heavily of wax polish. It was sparsely furnished with just a few pieces artfully placed, and looked strangely incomplete. The upholstered settle appeared recently purchased, its fabric still bright and unworn. A portrait of the baron and his wife, the paint barely dry, hung over the fireplace. Gibton sat down without offering any refreshment or comfort.

'A Constable doesn't come with good news,' he said gravely.

'No, your Lordship,' he admitted. 'Do you want your wife here?'

The man waved his hand dismissively. 'I'll tell her everything myself later. Is Sarah dead?'

'I'm sorry, she is.'

Lord Gibton looked into the empty hearth, not showing any emotion, and the Constable was astonished and baffled by the man's attitude. It wasn't the way a father should act. If it had been Emily he'd have railed and needed to know every detail.

'I believed she must be when her husband came here two days ago.' His voice was low and even. 'A girl like Sarah doesn't simply vanish.'

'She was found on Saturday,' Nottingham began to explain. 'We didn't know who she was.'

Gibton waved away his words. 'I don't want to know,' he said. 'Not now.' His hands rubbed over his knees, a gesture without thought, just something to do.

'Yes, my Lord,' the Constable agreed reluctantly, amazed at the man's lack of interest. 'There's one thing I have to tell you, though.'

'What's that?' Gibton didn't even turn his head.

'She'd been murdered.'

'I'd surmised that much, Mister ... Nottingham, was that it?' There was flintiness in his voice. 'You'd hardly ride out here for a simple death.'

'When she left to come here, her maid was with her. That's what her husband said.'

'Yes. Anne had been her maid for years. Sarah never went anywhere without her.'

'No one's seen the maid.'

Gibton looked up at him, engaged and curious for the first time. 'Are you implying Anne might have had something to do with this?'

'I'm not implying anything. I'm just trying to establish facts, my Lord.'

He considered that and nodded finally.

'Where did Anne come from?' Nottingham asked.

Gibton sighed. 'She was a village girl, the same as the girl we have now. Tell me, did you stop in the village, Constable?'

'Yes,' Nottingham admitted. 'I needed directions here.'

'And what did they tell you? That we were above ourselves?' He didn't wait for an answer. 'My family used to own all this land. All of it. Then my sot of a great-grandfather gambled almost all of it away. There was a small amount left, enough to live but not in any kind of comfort or style. Still, my wife insisted that Sarah should have a maid. A girl needs that. None of

52

them around here liked it. And they think even worse of us now we've inherited a little money.'

The Constable made no response. He didn't like this man, apparently so unconcerned about the killing of his daughter but taken over and eaten through with money and position. He wanted to be away from here, out in the clean air. He'd done what he needed to do and broken the news. He'd be back, he knew that, but only once he knew what questions to ask. Quietly he took his leave of the baron and let the horse make its own slow way back into Leeds as he thought.

Everything felt wrong in the Gibtons' house. He didn't know what to make of it, but there was a darkness, a chill there that disturbed him.

Six

Sedgwick eased himself slowly down on the bed and sighed with exhaustion.

'That feels better.'

Lizzie grinned at the pained look on his face and the way he stretched out his long legs.

'I thought you'd said you'd been sitting down all day.'

'Aye, on a bloody cart.' He shifted position carefully. 'My arse feels like someone's spent the last few hours kicking it. I don't suppose we have any ale, do we?'

'Aye, I bought some today, fresh brewed from old Mrs Simpson.'

'Would you be a love and pour me some?'

She raised her eyebrows. 'What did your last slave die of, then?' she asked, but a smile played gently across her face as she moved towards his mug.

As she passed it over, he took her hand. 'I do love you, you know,' he told her.

'You'd better,' she answered, eyes twinkling. 'That's your baby I'm carrying inside me.'

He drank deep, almost emptying the mug, then asked, 'So when...?'

'When's it due, you mean?'

'Yes.'

'Late February or early March, close as I can tell. But don't you be telling anyone yet, John Sedgwick. There's still a long way to go.'

'I know,' he agreed, standing up gingerly to take her in his arms. The truth was that he was eager to tell everyone, to let them all share his joy. Lizzie was right though, he knew that. He sounded out the months in his head. She was barely two months gone, and there was too much that could happen before the baby arrived.

The door crashed wide and James bustled in, running straight for his father and grasping him firmly round the legs. He'd become a solid little lad with a strong grip and a ready smile. At four he kept growing out of the clothes the deputy scrounged for him, and the knees of his breeches were always ripped from playing; Lizzie seemed to spend most evenings working with a needle and thread.

'And what have you been doing?'

'Me and Mark and Andrew went down to the bridge and we threw sticks.' The words came out in a breathless, eager stream, almost tumbling over each other. 'And we ran over to watch them come out the other side.'

'Did you? Who won?'

'Mark, because he had the best sticks, he said.'

'Maybe you'll win next time.' Sedgwick's face turned serious. 'You watch yourself on the bridge, though. I've told you before. The carts and horses always go too fast there.' He waited until the boy gave him a grin then tousled his thick hair. 'Now go on, your mam's got something for you to eat.'

And she'd become the lad's mother, he thought as he watched Lizzie cut bread and cheese and pour a cracked cup of small beer for James. More of one than Annie, his wife, had ever been. She wiped away his tears, cleaned his grazes and cuts, and loved him fiercely.

He felt lucky she'd come along, and he still wasn't completely sure what she saw in him. At first, once she'd moved in, he'd been scared, fearful of how fragile things could be, that she'd just up and leave. After the first three months he began to understand that she was here to stay, that they'd made a family of sorts, one where there was love and joy. Now he couldn't think of coming home to not find her here, welcoming, funny, warm. And the idea of being a father again, of her giving birth to his child, sent a surge of pleasure through him.

'What are you smiling at, John?' she asked.

'I'm just happy.'

She looked at him tenderly. 'I am too, love.'

Nottingham arrived at the jail early. He threw out the pair of grumbling drunks who'd been brought in the night before, then went to summon a baker to the Petty Sessions for selling adulterated bread.

A few faint, high clouds trailed across the towering sky as he ambled back down Kirkgate from the bakery on Lands Lane. It was going to be another hot day. He ran a finger under his

56

collar to loosen it from his skin, the flesh already damp against his fingers.

Sedgwick was standing by the desk, his face locked in thought, a small, secret smile on his lips.

'What did you make of Mr Godlove?'

The deputy turned as the Constable spoke. 'Morning, boss. I thought you said he was a farmer?'

Nottingham settled in his chair and took off his stock. 'That's what he told me.'

'He's a bit more than that. Owns most of Horsforth, most like. Big, grand house, more servants than you can count. I don't think he's one of those out in the fields at first light breaking his back.' He paused, considering what he'd just said, then added, 'Still, give him his due. He doesn't have any side to him.'

'Did he have much to say?'

The deputy rubbed a hand down his face. 'Not a lot that was useful. He wanted us to open the coffin so he could have a last look at her. Took me a while to persuade him that it wasn't a good idea. She's going to be buried properly tomorrow. The local curate came while I was there and couldn't do enough to help him.'

'What about his marriage?'

Sedgwick blew out a long breath. 'I really think he loved her.' He paused to frame his answer. 'He was genuinely devastated, boss. Couldn't sit still, kept pacing around the room while I talked to him.'

'Did you talk to any of the servants?'

57

'Aye, while he was with the curate. According to them, his wife had been shy at first. About the only person she'd really talk to was the maid she'd brought with her. They thought she felt she was too good for them since she had a title. Most of them had come around a little but they still weren't too sure of her. She didn't talk a lot, evidently. A couple of odd things, though.'

'Oh?'

'She and her maid would go off for the day once a week. Not always the same day, mind. The maid would never tell the other servants what they did. They'd leave after breakfast and come back late afternoon.'

'That's strange,' Nottingham said. 'No one has any idea at all?'

'Rumours and thoughts, you know what it's like. Nothing with any substance. The other thing is, though, the washerwoman there reckoned that Mrs Godlove might be carrying a baby.'

The Constable sat straight. 'Go on,' he said.

'No breech clouts last month, she told me.'

'And Godlove didn't say anything about it?'

'Not a word. I don't think his wife had told him.'

Now that was interesting, the Constable thought. He was glad he'd sent Sedgwick; the man had a knack for charming out information.

'So we have more questions, but we're not any further along.'

'Nothing to help us. What about the gentry?'

Nottingham recounted the visit to Lord Gibton, then added, 'There's something not right about it all.'

'What do you mean, boss?'

'When I arrived he knew it must be bad news, but he never pressed me for any details. What would you do if someone came and told you James was dead?'

'I'd want to know everything,' Sedgwick replied.

'Exactly. All he did was turn quiet. Said he knew she must have been murdered or I would not have ridden out there, and that was it. About the only time he spoke much was explaining how the family had lost their money and why his daughter had needed a maid. It was as if he had to justify everything about his life, never mind that his daughter was in the ground. It was just ... cold. It's not human.'

'How much did you tell him?'

'Not much at all. He never bothered to ask where she'd been found or how she'd died. I'll tell you, John, I don't know what to make of it. I've never seen anything like it. And something else – on my way I stopped in the village there, and the woman at the alehouse thought Godlove had paid them so he could marry Sarah.'

'What?' The deputy looked at him incredulously.

'I know it sounds ridiculous, it should be the other way round – the girl brings a dowry. But after meeting Gibton I can almost believe it, especially since the baron took such pains to tell me he'd inherited the money.'

'So what do you mean? They sold her to the highest bidder?'

'I don't know.' He shook his head. 'I'm sure the rich and titled have their own term for it. Godlove must have been what, thirty years older than her?'

'Something like that, aye.'

'She was a pretty girl. Why would she look twice at him, let alone marry him? There was nothing Sarah could bring to a marriage, the Gibtons didn't have money.'

'Except a title,' Sedgwick offered.

'Exactly. For some people having a wife with "The Honourable" in front of her name could be worth paying for. And who knows what their children would be?' He paused to consider that, then pursed his lips. 'Something that bothers me is what's happened to the maid? Gibton insisted she was devoted to Sarah.'

'That's what the servants said at Godlove's, too. No one had a bad word to say about her, but no one seemed to really know her. She hadn't gone out of her way to make friends.'

'She's from Roundhay, and the alewife didn't say anyone had seen her, so she must still be missing. We've had no more reports of bodies.'

'Do you think she's involved?'

The Constable shook his head. 'I doubt it.'

'So what do we do now?'

'For a start, we need to find the maid,' Nottingham said. 'Do we even know her surname?'

'Taylor.'

'We have to try and find her. She's the one

who was closest to Sarah Godlove. She might well be the key to all this.' He marked the item on one finger. 'We also need to know where Sarah went every week. That's a mystery and it might well be important.' He pushed a second finger back, then a third. 'And we should try and find out the truth about this marriage.'

'How?' Sedgwick asked.

'We ask questions. It's the only thing we can do. You go out to Roundhay and talk to the maid's family. Who knows, they might have had word from her—'

'If she's still alive.'

The Constable acknowledged the words. He knew full well she could easily be as dead as her mistress, the body hidden away somewhere.

'—or she might have told them things.' He sighed. 'Any information is better than we have right now. Anything you can find at all. Ask round the village. Sarah grew up there, people will have known her. You know what to do. Take the knife with you, too. See if anyone recognizes it.'

'Yes, boss.' He stood up and stretched, grabbing the weapon from the drawer.

'Do you want to ride up there?'

Sedgwick made a face. 'After being in that cart yesterday, I'll walk.'

The problem, Nottingham decided, was that he was dealing with so many unknowns. The people were just names, he didn't understand their lives. Neither Godlove nor the Gibtons had any association with Leeds, and Leeds was what was familiar to him, what he understood in his heart and his soul. Outside the city he was just another stranger. What he needed was someone who might know something about these folk, someone to guide him a little.

He retied his stock and set off down Briggate. Carters filled the road, cursing their horses and each other, while a farmer tried to drive a few cattle between the wagons, heading to sell them to the butchers in the Shambles.

A short way up from the bridge he stopped by a house, its shutters spread wide and the sashes raised. Glancing through the window he could see the printing press, its brass gleaming, and beyond it a man at a desk. His head was lowered, the quill in his hand scratching rapidly at a piece of paper. The Constable opened the door and walked in.

'Mr Nottingham.' The man stood, extending a hand whose skin was discoloured by dark stains. James Lister was small and round, all beaming eyes and bulging belly, with an open, jovial face. He'd only taken over the Leeds *Mercury* in January after the terrible winter had claimed the life of his employer, John Hirst. But in his life he'd forgotten more about Leeds and the area around it than most people had ever known. Where the merchants dealt in cloth, fact and rumour were his stock-in-trade. 'What can I do for you?'

The room smelt of ink, a deep, exotic scent that seemed to permeate the walls and the floor.

Bundles of paper were stacked in a corner, ready for the next edition, and stained wooden boxes of type lined the wall. The Constable had been here before, and the mechanics of making a newspaper always amazed him.

'I'm hoping you might have some information.'

Lister raised his bushy eyebrows and smiled slyly. 'And here I thought you were the one who knew everything, Constable. Sit down.' He gestured at the extra seat beside the desk.

'You heard about the body found at Kirkstall Abbey on Saturday?' Nottingham began.

'Of course.'

'And you know who she was?'

'Not yet. Do you know?' Lister asked eagerly, reaching for his quill.

'Her name was Sarah Godlove. Her maiden name was Gibton.'

Lister sat back and let out a long breath. 'I remember when they married last year. I wrote something about it, I'm sure. I couldn't have ignored that.'

'What do you know about Godlove and Baron Gibton?'

The man rubbed his chin. 'Where do you want me to start? Godlove's a rich man. His family owned a little land for generations. They did quite well as farmers, but it was his father who really made the difference.'

'What do you mean?' the Constable asked him.

Lister smiled widely. 'He started buying up

small farms that weren't doing well. Judicious purchases, too. He must have been a clever man. By the time anyone realized what he was doing, he must have owned most of the area between Horsforth and Bradford.'

'What about the present Mr Godlove?'

'He's not the man his father was; at least, that's what everyone says,' Lister reported gleefully. 'He runs everything smoothly enough, but there's no fire about him. His ambition, or so I was told,' he confided, 'is to be part of the gentry. He wanted to be rich and respectable.'

'And the marriage brought him that?'

'In name, at least.' He held up a warning finger, relishing the chance to gossip. 'The Gibtons aren't exactly the front rank of nobility.'

'He's a baron.'

'Ah, but a baron is very low on the scale, Mr Nottingham,' Lister said dismissively. 'Even a viscount is higher, and they're almost three a penny. But the Gibtons committed a cardinal sin in the eyes of the gentry – they lost most of their money.'

'The great-grandfather lost it. At least, that's what Gibton told me.'

Lister raised his eyebrows. 'Very candid of him. It's true enough, though. From what I've heard, the man should never have been let out anywhere at all. He'd wager on anything and everything and usually lose. Of course, he was drunk most of the time, which probably accounts for it. I suppose the family's cursed him ever since. There they were, couldn't even afford to live with the best society and all because of him. There was a little money, of course, they were hardly on the parish, but it wasn't the luxury they'd once enjoyed.'

'And now they seem to have money again.'

'I was getting to that. Patience, Constable, please,' he teased. He held out his hands, palms up, and raised the right one. 'So here we have a man with plenty of money who truly wants to be part of the aristocracy. He's not going to manage that himself, so he needs to marry into it. The only trouble is that, apart from his wealth, there's not much about him. You've met him?'

'Yes,' Nottingham said.

'He's not a man who leaves a lasting impression, is he? Let's be kind and leave it at that.' Lister winked playfully and raised the other palm. 'On the other hand there's a family with a title that's desperate – and I do mean desperate – for money. They have one real asset, which is a pretty daughter of marriageable age, and they've been preparing her since she was a baby. If they'd had more girls they'd probably have been rubbing their hands in glee. The only thing missing is a dowry. That means no one with a title is ever going to come near her, and they know it.'

Slowly he brought his hands together. 'A perfect match, at least for Godlove and the baron.'

'So he paid for her?'

'Yes, he did. A bride price, if you like, although no one's going to call it that, of course. It's far too crude a term, but it's what it amounts to. Young Sarah was sold off like good stock – good breeding stock. Godlove is suddenly part of the nobility, even if it's just by association, and the Gibtons have real money for the first time in God knows how long.'

'What about Sarah?'

'She certainly wouldn't want for anything with Godlove, of course. An easy life, although a dull one, I'm sure, stuck out in Horsforth with the sheep for your best friends. Not that anyone would have consulted her, of course.' He shrugged. 'You know how these things work. She's just an asset, a piece of property to be traded.'

'Her parents have done well out of it.'

'My understanding is that it was all Lady Gibton's work. She drove a bargain that would impress a horse trader. Did you meet her?'

'Not yet.'

'Count yourself lucky.' He shivered theatrically. 'Awful doesn't even begin to describe her. Just make sure you're never around when she loses her temper. I saw it happen once at an assembly. Everyone was getting as far away from her as possible. The serving girls were in tears. It was very ugly.' He paused. 'Is any of this useful?'

'Everything's useful at the moment,' the Constable answered with a small smile. 'It's all far outside my circle. And outside the city. I'm impressed you know so much.'

Lister bowed his head. 'You never know when something will come in useful,' he explained. 'It must be the same for you.'

'More or less,' Nottingham agreed. 'Still, if you ever want a change of employment, I can use someone who gathers this much information.'

The man patted his paunch contentedly. 'Not for me. I like the quiet life. All I have to worry about is people threatening legal actions against me.' He cocked his head. 'Are you really looking for someone?'

'I am.' This murder had shown him how tightly they were stretched.

'I should send my oldest boy down to see you, then.'

'You don't want him here?'

'I'd love to have him here,' Lister complained. 'He could take it all over in time. But it doesn't interest him.'

'What does?'

'I don't know,' he admitted sadly. 'I'm not sure he does, come to that.'

'Working for me means long hours. The pay is poor, too.'

Lister chuckled. 'The money's poor for everything in Leeds, unless you're in cloth.' His face turned serious. 'He's a good lad, Mr Nottingham. Reads and writes well, a good thinker, does what he's told – unless it's me telling him, of course,' he added ruefully.

'How old is he?'

'Almost eighteen. He was an apprentice last year, but only lasted three months.' He frowned. 'That was good money poured away for nothing. Then I tried him here and he didn't care for it. His mother doesn't know what to do with him and neither do I.'

'Send him to see me if he's interested,' the Constable said. He couldn't be any worse than some of the people who'd come hoping for the job.

'And just imagine,' Lister added, eyes twinkling, 'he'd have access to all his father's gossip.'

Nottingham laughed and stood up. 'Tell him to come to the jail.'

'I'll be printing something about Sarah Godlove's killing. Murder most cruel.'

The Constable turned and stared. 'Murder's never anything else, Mr Lister.'

Seven

Sedgwick never felt comfortable away from the city. Born and raised in Leeds, the quiet of the countryside was eerie to him. It took an hour of steady striding out to reach Roundhay village, a collection of ten cottages where the road made a turn. At least the Taylors wouldn't be hard to find.

A woman was working in the garden of the first house, down on her hands and knees, sleeves rolled up high as she pulled scrubby weeds away from carrot tops. To the side he could see mounds for the potatoes, and peas strung against the wall. She hadn't heard him approach, and jerked her head up sharply as he coughed.

'Morning,' he said with an easy smile.

'Morning,' she replied warily, wiping her hands on her apron. She looked to be in her late forties, hair tucked tidily beneath a cap. The heat had put a shine on her skin and he waited as she wiped her forearm across her forehead.

'You'll have a good crop this year,' Sedgwick said affably.

'Hope so. The more we grow, the less we buy.' The woman stared at him, then asked, 'Can I do owt for you?'

'I'm looking for the Taylors.'

She stood, pushing herself up with strong arms then smoothing down the dress. Her knuckles were red from work, and he saw that two of the fingers on her right hand were swollen and misshapen.

'I'm Catherine Taylor,' she told him, walking to the drystone wall that separated them. 'What do you need?' There was deep suspicion in her voice.

'I'm John Sedgwick. I'm the deputy Constable of Leeds.'

'Oh aye, and what brings you out here to see me, then? My husband's out in the fields over yon.' She tilted her head to the west. 'Her from the alehouse said a Constable had been out round here, too.'

'It's about your daughter. Anne.'

'Our Annie?' Taylor looked confused, then smiled. 'Nay, love, but you've got that wrong. She's been with Sarah Godlove – Gibton as was – for nigh on ten year now.'

'I know,' he said, watching as the edges of fear began to show in her face. 'Can we talk away from the road?'

After a moment's hesitation, she agreed. 'Aye, come on in. I've a fresh stoup of ale if you're thirsty.'

'I could do with that,' Sedgwick admitted. 'It's a long walk out here when it's warm.'

He followed her into the house. There was a stool and two wooden chairs on the flagstones,

70

an old, discoloured rug made from scraps of fabric between them, in front of the empty hearth. A table sat up against a wall, its wooden top scrubbed, a bowl of berries sitting on top under the window.

She brought him a wooden mug and he took a drink, feeling the liquid lubricate his dry throat.

'It's good, is that,' he said, taking another gulp.

Catherine Taylor sat down and gestured to the other seat. 'Now, what's all this about our Annie, then?'

'It's also about Mrs Godlove,' he began, emptying the cup and placing it on the floor.

'She married that rich man from Horsforth way. Wanted to keep Annie with her. And her parents got all that money not long before, too.'

He could tell she was talking just to delay the news. She urgently wanted to hear it and yet it terrified her.

'Sarah Godlove's dead,' he told her. 'Someone murdered her last Saturday.'

'What?' Her hand came up to her mouth.

'She was coming over to Roundhay, but she never arrived. She had Anne with her, but no one's seen your daughter since.'

'Annie?' She didn't understand. 'Annie?'

'Has she been here lately, Mrs Taylor? Have you seen her?'

The woman shook her head dumbly, in shock.

'I'm sorry,' Sedgwick said. 'We don't know where she is and we need to find her. She must know what happened to her mistress.'

71

'She's been with that Sarah since she was fourteen. She loves her. You're not saying she killed her?'

'No.' Sedgwick smiled kindly. 'Nothing like that.'

'Do you think she's dead?' Catherine asked bluntly.

'We don't know,' was the best he could offer her. And it was true, he thought. They really did have no idea at all. 'I was hoping she'd come here.'

'No.' There was emptiness in her eyes.

'When did you see her last?'

'A month ago, mebbe? Aye, four week ago last Saturday. She stayed over and we went to church together.'

'The servants at Godlove's told me that Sarah and your daughter would go off one day each week. Do you know where they went?'

'No,' she said. 'No. She doesn't say much about what they do, or her duties or owt like that.' She stopped herself suddenly, as if suddenly realizing all those days could now be past, a sorrowful, vanished history. 'Please, tell me, do you think Annie's dead?'

'I really don't know,' he answered her honestly. 'But if she comes here, we need to talk to her.'

'She's never been in any trouble, never done owt wrong.' Catherine Taylor was rubbing her hands together as if they were cold. 'She's a good lass, mister.'

'I'm sure she is. Look, there could be plenty of

good reasons no one's seen her,' Sedgwick tried to reassure her. 'Don't go thinking the worst yet.'

She looked at him, snatching at the hope, brittle as life, in his words.

'Does she have any friends in the village? Anyone apart from you and your husband she sees when she comes home?'

The matter-of-fact question seemed to give her strength.

'Aye, there's Maggie Blenkinsop. Well, Maggie Archer as was. She's the same age as our Annie and they were allus together when they were lasses.'

'Where does she live?'

'Right across the road. She'll be there because I know her babby's been ill. Can't do much when that happens.'

Sedgwick stood up, thanking her for the ale.

'Try not to worry,' he said, although he knew the words were pointless. He'd planted the thought and it would grow like a weed. 'One last thing.' He produced the knife that had murdered Sarah. 'Have you ever seen this?'

'No,' she answered after staring hard at it. 'Is that...?'

'Yes.'

He was at the door when she spoke again.

'Tell me summat, mister.'

He halted and turned back, stooping so his head didn't catch the lintel.

'When you told them about Sarah, did his Lordship and his wife ask about our Annie?'

'I wasn't the one who told them. But from what I heard they didn't even ask that much about their daughter.'

Outside, the sunlight seemed too bright and he blinked his eyes to adjust. All he'd managed to learn was that Anne hadn't come back here, and the price of that knowledge was her parents in torment.

He crossed the road and knocked on the door of the small cottage. It looked uncared-for, un-loved. There were vegetables in the garden but the weeds had taken proper hold, a few slates were missing from the roof, and the old lime-wash was heavily stained. From inside he could hear a baby howling and another young voice shouting loudly.

The woman looked harassed, old before her time. She had a baby in her arms and a girl of about three pulling at her ragged dress. There were dark half-moons like bruises under her eyes and her hand swatted half-heartedly at the girl.

'You're Maggie Blenkinsop?' he asked.

'Aye. Who're you, then? And how do you know my name?'

'I'm John Sedgwick,' he introduced himself. 'I'm the deputy Constable of Leeds. Mrs Taylor over the way told me who you were.'

'Oh aye?' She cocked her head slightly. 'And what do you want with me?' She shifted the child on her arm. 'Stop it,' she said to the girl who was pulling at the material once more. 'I'll not tell you again.'

'It's about Anne Taylor. Her mother says you're friends.'

Her face relaxed into a smile. 'Aye. She went for a maid and I stayed here and got meself wed. Sometimes I'm not sure which of us made the better bargain.' She turned serious again. 'So why's the Constable of Leeds out here about her? What's wrong?'

'She's missing,' he explained, watching the surprise spread on her face.

'Missing?' She spoke the word as if it was new to her. 'Annie?'

'No one's seen her since Thursday. She and her mistress left home then to come over here.'

'But...' she began and then stopped, her face empty, not knowing what to say.

'Her mistress was murdered.'

'Sarah?' Involuntarily, Maggie grasped the baby tighter and it began to cry. Tenderly, without even thinking, she rubbed the back of its head until the child settled.

'We're looking for Anne. We don't know what's happened to her.'

'She hasn't been here.'

'I know.' Sedgwick smiled kindly. 'Do you know anywhere she might go if she was afraid?'

The woman thought and then shook her head. The little girl had wandered away inside the house. She hoisted the baby, stroking it softly and whispering at it.

'If Annie was in trouble she'd come here,' she said finally. 'This is where her kin is, and her friends. We'd look after her.'

75

'If she does come back, we need to talk to her. It's important.'

'Who killed Sarah? Do you know?' she asked in wonder. 'Why would anyone do that to her?'

'We don't know,' he said. 'That's why we need Anne. We're hoping she can help us.'

'What did her mam say?'

'I think she's scared,' Sedgwick confided. 'She's terrified Anne's dead.'

'I'll get these two settled and go over.' She paused. 'What do you think?' she asked, gazing directly at him and daring him to lie. 'Honest now, is she dead?'

'I really don't know,' he told her, 'and that's the truth. Did she ever tell you that Sarah used to go off one day a week?'

'No. She doesn't talk much about what she does. Never has. But I don't think she likes it over there. When it was just her and Sarah, that was good. But all those other servants, she feels out of place, like they resent her.'

'Has she told you that?'

'Not in so many words. But little things, you know.'

'What about her mistress? Was she happy there?'

'I don't think so, not really. I remember back at the start of spring, she came over for a few days up at that grand house they have now. I'd been out to find some wood for the fire. I could hear them having a real shouting match, her and her parents. They were telling her she had to go back and she was crying and screaming that she

76

wouldn't.'

'But she went back in the end?'

'Aye.' She sighed and started to rock the baby gently, without thinking, letting the motion send it off into sleep. 'I asked Anne about it the next time I saw her. She just said it was nowt.' Maggie raised her head defiantly and stared at the deputy. 'You've come here and brought trouble. Annie's all they have left. There were three lads but they all died when they were little.'

'I'm just trying to find some answers, love, that's all.'

'I know.' She sighed. 'It's not your fault. I'd better go over to Catherine. She'll be needing someone.'

He started to walk away.

'If you find Annie, come and tell me, please. Whether it's good or bad.'

'I will. I promise.'

Eight

'Right, let's take stock of what we really know and the things we just think.'

The Constable had been next door to the White Swan and bought a fresh jug of ale. For once, Michael the landlord was happy. In this weather people were drinking more and his profits were up. In a rare, grand gesture he'd waved away payment. Now Nottingham and the deputy were seated in the jail in the shank of the afternoon, slaking their thirst and assessing the facts.

Sedgwick poured a mug.

'We don't know much at all.'

'We know Sarah Godlove was murdered and that Anne Taylor has disappeared,' Nottingham began. 'We know they left Horsforth on Thursday and that Sarah's body was found on Saturday.' He paused to take a drink. 'We know Sarah and Anne used to vanish one day a week, but not where. We know she'd been married to Godlove for about a year.'

'And that's all we know for certain.'

'True,' the Constable agreed, brushing the fringe off his face. 'But if you add in some of the other things we get a better picture. You heard that Sarah didn't want to go back to her husband, and we know she went to see her parents regularly. Also that she might have been pregnant. What do you think that means?'

Sedgwick considered. 'Could be lots of things.'

'Such as?' Nottingham prompted him.

'Maybe she just didn't like being around Godlove any more than she had to be.'

'That would make sense if she really had been sold to him. He seemed to love her but that doesn't mean it was returned.'

'I suppose the visits could be to a man. That would be reason enough to keep them quiet.'

The Constable pursed his lips. There was sense in that too. 'Which gives us someone else to find, and a possible suspect.'

'What about the husband, boss? Do you think he could be guilty?'

'No,' Nottingham answered firmly. He recalled the way Godlove had been at the jail. 'No, he was shocked when I told him.' He tilted his head, silently asking for Sedgwick's opinion.

'I agree. And the servants all seemed to think he doted on her.'

'Anne?'

'I suppose it's possible,' the deputy conceded, 'but why? She'd been Sarah's maid for ten years. Why would she do something now? What does she get from it?'

'My guess is that she's lying dead somewhere.'

'Probably,' Sedgwick agreed with a sigh.

Inside he'd always believed so but hadn't been able to bring himself to say it to the two women and dash all their hopes.

'So what do we look at next?'

The conversation was interrupted as the door opened and a young man walked in. They stared at him expectantly.

'I'm looking for Mr Nottingham,' he said.

The Constable stood up and smiled. 'I'm Richard Nottingham.'

'I'm Robert Lister. My father said I should come and see you.'

'Of course.' The son of the *Mercury* publisher. He was quite tall and well built, much like his father must have been before he ran to fat, with bushy hair falling past his collar and tied back with a blue ribbon. His gaze was clear and steady, and there was just the faintest trace of old spots on his cheeks. He'd dragged out his good suit for this, the Constable suspected, and given it a thorough brushing.

'I'll be off,' Sedgwick said.

'Go home,' Nottingham told him. 'You've walked enough today.'

'Still better than that bloody cart,' the deputy replied with a broad grin as he closed the door.

'Sit down, Mr Lister.'

The lad sat, glancing around before giving his attention to Nottingham.

'So you want to become a Constable's man?'

'I don't know,' Lister replied candidly. 'My father came home for his dinner and said you'd been talking.'

'Did he say what about?'

'No, he didn't.'

The Constable smiled. 'So why did you decide to come and see me?'

'I'm looking for work.'

'Your father knows people,' Nottingham suggested. 'There must be plenty willing to take you on.'

'He'd like me to work for him, but I don't want to.' The lad looked up sharply at the Constable, his eyes bright and thoughtful. 'He told you that, didn't he?'

'He did. But it doesn't explain why you're here.'

Lister breathed deep and gathered his thoughts.

'I want work I'll enjoy. Have you seen all the clerks and the shopkeepers? They look old before their time. I don't want to be that way.'

Nottingham smiled. 'A young man's thoughts.'

'Maybe,' Lister conceded, then grinned impishly. 'But that's how it should be, isn't it? I'm still a young man.'

Nottingham laughed. He'd immediately warmed to Robert Lister. The lad seemed straightforward, not full of himself. Whether he'd do well in this job was a different matter, though.

'I'll warn you right now, it's hard work. The hours are long and the pay is low. It's dirty, and it can be dangerous.' He paused, waiting for a reaction. Lister nodded slowly. 'How are you in a fight?'

'A fight?' His face sharpened in surprise. 'I don't know,' he answered after thinking. 'I had a few at school, I suppose, but nothing since then.'

'It's part of what we do. People get drunk and start a brawl. We have to stop it.'

'And put them in the cells?'

'Yes.'

'They're through there?' Lister gestured at the thick wooden door.

'The cells and the mortuary. If there's a suspicious death the body ends up here. Have you ever seen a corpse, Mr Lister?'

'Only my grandfather,' the lad admitted.

'It's not the same thing, believe me.'

'No, I don't imagine it is.'

'So why should I employ you, Mr Lister?' the Constable asked, leaning back in his chair with his arms crossed, watching the lad gather his thoughts.

'I'm willing to do what you need me to do,' he began. 'I'm not afraid of hard work or long hours. If other people survive on the pay, I can, too. I learn quickly. I can read and write; my teachers said I had a good hand.'

'As long as I can read it, that's all that matters,' Nottingham told him.

The lad dipped his head slightly in understanding. 'If you tell me to do something, I'll do it. And if I don't do it right the first time, the next time I will.'

The Constable pursed his lips. On the surface

everything about Lister was wrong for this job. He didn't know what it was to be poor. He'd lived a sheltered life, away from turmoil and crime. He'd have none of the instincts that men who scrabbled for pennies every day developed as part of their nature.

For all that, he had a feeling about the lad. He couldn't put it into words, but it was something he hadn't experienced with any of the others he'd talked to. There was a spark about him, he was smart. He could learn – if he really wanted to. And that was the question. How serious was Lister about all this?

'If I take you on you won't be able to talk to your father about your work. If I find anything in the *Mercury* you'll be gone.'

Lister nodded. 'I understand that. So does he.'

Nottingham waited, trying to gauge if his decision was the right one. Finally he said, 'Be here at six tomorrow morning. I'll try you out for a month.'

Lister stood up, beaming broadly, the expression the image of his father.

'Thank you, Mr Nottingham.' He extended his hand and the Constable shook it. 'I'll do my best for you.'

'You'll be working with Mr Sedgwick – he's the man who left when you came in. He's my deputy. Watch him, learn from him. He's very good at his job.'

'I will, I promise.'

'Do you go by Robert or Rob?'

Lister smiled. 'I don't mind, whatever you

prefer. My father calls me Robert.'

'Then we'll call you Rob.'

'Yes, sir.'

'A word of advice to you.'

Lister cocked his head.

'Wear some older clothes. Don't worry if your breeches are mended or there are holes in your hose. You won't stay clean in this job. Boots if you have them, too.'

'I'll do that, sir.'

'And Rob?'

'Yes, sir?'

'In private you can call me boss. Sir is for when there are others around.'

Lister smiled. 'Yes, boss.'

Alone, Nottingham wondered at what he'd just done. Everything in his reason shouted out against it. He gazed out of the window, barely paying attention to the people who passed or the yelling of carters as they navigated the street with their loads.

The deputy wouldn't thank him; he was the one who'd have the hard job of turning him into a Constable's man. It would be like teaching a baby to walk, with all the tentative steps and the falls, picking him up, brushing away the tears and pushing him back on to his feet.

But inside, he knew with an iron certainty that Rob Lister was the right person. It was the same feeling he'd experienced with Josh, and with Sedgwick himself. And he was going to follow that instinct.

He sighed.

So where did they go next with Sarah Godlove's murder? That was what he had wondered
before Lister had arrived. In truth he had no
idea. There seemed to be no path forward at
present.

They knew a little more now, but so much of
it was speculation, and none of it any real use.
Somewhere, though, he was certain there was a
key to unlock this, and it was probably in those
mysterious weekly outings.

She was meeting someone, he had a feeling
about that. People didn't go off so regularly for
any other reason. Who that someone might be
was another matter altogether. Anne Taylor
would know, but her disappearance was con-
venient for keeping the truth hidden. They had
to assume she was dead, too; if the girl had still
been alive she'd have run to find people and
places where she felt safe.

He was sure as he could be that Anne hadn't
murdered her mistress; there could be no reason
for it. And he didn't see Godlove as the killer.
The man was a genuine grieving widower. Beyond those names there was no one to suspect.

Nottingham was astonished that the mayor
hadn't demanded an arrest, or at least a report
every day. But there would be a terse note
requesting his presence before the week was out
and they were no further along.

He ran a hand through his hair and walked out
into the late afternoon sun. The heat clung to the
ground, pressing down like a pall, thick and
stifling. Men were wiping their necks and brows

with their kerchiefs, and the women looked warm and flustered as they shopped for late bargains, scurrying between patches of shade like insects.

At Timble Bridge he sat on the bank, deep in the shadow of a willow tree. Sheepscar Beck ran by his feet, the sound of the water over the rocks almost like music. After ten minutes he stood, dusted off his breeches and finished the short journey home up Marsh Lane.

'Richard? Is that you?' Mary came through from the kitchen, wiping her hands on a piece of cloth. Strands of hair had stuck to the sweat on her face. She looked at him with concern. 'You're back early. Is anything wrong?'

'No.' He smiled gently and embraced her. 'There was just nothing more I could do today.'

She pulled back, holding him at arm's length, not believing his words. After so many years she knew full well that he was married to his work as much as he was to her. And there was always work to be done.

'Nothing more to do?' she asked, her voice suspicious. 'I think that's the first time in twenty years I've heard that from you. What's the real reason?'

'I needed to get away,' he admitted.

She tucked her head against his shoulder, reaching up to stroke the stubble of his cheek. 'Is it going badly?'

'It's this business in Kirkstall,' he explained. 'We just don't know enough and we can't seem to find out more.' He sighed. 'The real problem is that none of the people live in Leeds. They're all out in the country. I don't know them, I don't understand their lives. I don't even know what questions to ask.'

'You'll find your answers,' she assured him.

He wanted to believe her, but he couldn't be so sure. He hadn't solved every crime put before him. He hadn't even caught every killer. Those were the ones he remembered, the ones that gnawed and burrowed into his mind. He dreaded that this killing might join that list.

'Come on,' he said, the idea coming to him from nowhere. 'Let's go up Cavalier Hill.'

'Richard!' she complained. 'I've got my old dress on. I don't want to go out looking like this.'

She was wearing her old brown muslin, darned and mended over the years, the sleeves pushed up over her elbows.

'You'll look just like a Constable's wife,' he told her. 'Is that such a bad thing?'

'Let me change into the mantua. It'll only take me a minute.'

He surrendered with good grace, even though one minute quickly turned to five. When she came down the stairs her hair was under a cap, the blue dress adjusted just so, and the smile on her face made the wait worthwhile.

It was only a short walk, following a path across a few fields over Steander. At one time these had all been farming strips, so he'd been told, where people planted the crops to feed themselves. Now sheep grazed here, snuffling

87

softly as they cropped at the grass. An empty tenter frame on the grass stood waiting for cloth to be tied and stretched.

At the base of the hill Nottingham took Mary's hand, feeling her grip tighten as the slope steepened. He slowed his pace, relishing the fresh air and the small, cool breeze blowing from the west.

By the time they reached the crown Mary was ready to stop and catch her breath. She sat in the long grass while he stood and gazed down at Leeds. By the river, looking so close he could almost reach out his hand to touch them, stood the dye houses, the smoke from their chimneys hazing in the clear sky. Closer, in a meadow, a group of men were beating a fleece pulled over some wood, the rhythmic sound of their work the only noise on the air.

He could easily pick out the landmarks – St Peter's, the New Church, the spire of St John's, the bright brick of the Red Hall. Across the valley on the far hills lay Armley and Farnley Wood, with Holbeck nestling south of the Aire.

Every year the city was growing, pushing out in every direction. The merchants were building their grand houses past Town End, and on the other side of the river dwellings were crowding into the secret places where he'd played as a young boy.

But it was all Leeds and he loved every inch of it. For his first eight years he'd lived a privileged life here, the child of a rich man, until his father had discovered his wife had a lover and thrown her and his son from the house. After that he'd grown up quickly, surviving, stealing, learning to live from one day to the next, his mother whoring and starving until there was nothing left of her.

Then the old Constable had taken him on. He'd seen something different, something good, in the feral boy that Nottingham had been then. And now he was the Constable of the city himself. He'd never lived anywhere else and never would.

Slowly he settled next to Mary. 'We used to come up here when we were courting,' she recalled. 'Do you remember that?'

'We did a lot of things when we were courting.' He grinned, eyes flashing, and she tapped him playfully on the arm.

'Sunday afternoons,' she continued. 'You'd call for me and if the weather was good we'd go for a walk.'

'Once your father trusted us to be alone together,' he reminded her.

'Well, he was right about that.' She blushed. 'He'd have beaten us both if he knew what we got up to. Sometimes I think it was a miracle that Rose wasn't conceived before we were wed.'

At the mention of the name the spell broke. Rose, whose death was still a large shadow on the horizon. He squeezed her hand lightly and she gave a brief, tight smile in return.

Names, he thought. What a strange, awful power they had. The nerve was still raw and painful to the touch.

They lingered for another half-hour, conversation muted and neutral, then ambled home. The sun was lower, still pleasantly warm on his face. The workmen had gone and the fields were quiet save for an occasional bleat. As they emerged on to the road he glanced ahead.

'Isn't that someone at our door?' he wondered.

'Emily,' Mary shouted. She gathered up her skirts and began to run.

Nine

By the time he reached them Mary had folded her daughter into a tight embrace. Emily was sobbing on to her mother's shoulders, the tears pouring. Her bag, bulging with all she owned, sat on the ground outside the house.

With a tiny shake of her head Mary indicated he should leave them. He unlocked the door, took in the bag and poured himself a mug of ale in the kitchen. Whatever had happened, it couldn't be good, that much was obvious. And just the day before the girl had seemed so happy...

His attention shifted as Mary led Emily in and sat her in the chair.

'Richard, can you bring her something to drink?'

He poured another mug of ale and took it in. Emily reached for it, her hand shaking slightly, eyes red and cheeks blotched as she looked up.

'Here you go, love.' He forced a smile. 'Long walk on a hot day.'

She drained the cup quickly and he took it from her. There was dust from the roads all over her dress, and hair spilled untidily from the bonnet. Mary knelt by her, a gentle hand on her shoulder, and asked, 'Now, what's this all about?'

Emily glanced from one parent to another, looking desperate and hunted.

'Mr Hartington's dismissed me for insolence,' she announced.

'Oh, pet,' Mary began, but Emily cut her off.

'It's not like that, mama,' she protested, tears spilling from her eyes again. 'This morning Mrs Hartington took the girls out. Mr Hartington came to my room and he...' She shook her head rather than say it. 'When I said no he told me to go, that I was insolent.'

Mary pulled her daughter close again, stroking her back as she cried, just the way she'd done when Emily was little. Over the girl's shoulder she looked up at her husband, raising her eyebrows.

Nottingham didn't move. Instead he breathed deeply, going over the words once more in his mind. The father in him was ready to dash up to Headingley and beat Hartington senseless, but he'd been part of the law for too long to do that. He had to cap the rage that was building inside him.

Tonight he'd talk to Emily, comfort her, and hear the full tale. Then he'd decide what to do. He knew it happened often enough, masters taking advantage of the female servants. If they wanted to keep their posts they had no choice but to agree.

He was proud of Emily for refusing. The girl snuffled and gazed up at him. 'You do believe me, papa?'

'Of course I do, love.' He smiled and took hold of her hand, cradling the thin fingers. 'You just get yourself settled. We'll look after you, you know that.'

She didn't want to eat, didn't want much of anything except to curl into herself. That was simply the way she was, and he knew it was better to let her be for now. He'd talk to her once she was in bed. For the moment she needed to feel safe.

Neither of them fussed around her; they treated her normally, as if nothing had happened, as if she'd never gone away. Finally, as the sky grew fully dark, Emily went off to her room.

He followed a few minutes later, a candle in his hand. At the door he looked in, seeing her under the cover and unable to forget that Rose had once shared the bed with her.

He placed the light on the table and eased himself down on to the old wooden chair.

'I'm sorry,' he told her.

Emily rolled over to face him. 'Why are you sorry, papa?'

'I'm sorry all this happened to you.'

She was silent for a long time. Then, 'Does it happen a lot? With men like that?'

'Sometimes.' He sighed. 'It always has, I suppose. Give some men money or power and they get to thinking they have rights just because a girl works for them.'

'He told me exactly what he wanted me to do.'

'Did he try and force you?'

93

'No,' she said.

'That's something,' Nottingham conceded softly. 'Many men don't take no for an answer.'

'But what am I going to do?' Her eyes were moist again. 'I loved the girls. And Mr Hartington said he'd never give me a reference. He was going to tell his wife I'd been insolent and he'd had to dismiss me.'

'You leave that to me, love.'

'I'm sorry, papa.'

'Don't be,' he said, reaching over and stroking her cheek. 'You've nothing to be sorry for. You go to sleep, it's been a long day.'

'What are you going to do?' Mary asked later, lying against him in the bed, her head on his chest.

'I'm going to talk to Hartington tomorrow.'

'Richard...' There was a quiet warning in her voice. He stroked her hair lightly.

'Don't worry. Everything will be fine, I promise.'

She kissed him.

The Constable was at the jail soon after dawn, hoping that Lister would be as good as his word and that his enthusiasm hadn't been a sham. He heard the clock at the Parish Church chime quarter to the hour and began to pace.

Just before the hour rang the door opened and Lister walked in.

'Good morning, boss,' he said with an eager smile. He'd listened to Nottingham's advice and dressed down. The suit had seen many better

94

days, the elbows shiny, the knees of the breeches worn, his shoes weary, unpolished and down on the heel.

'Very good, Rob,' the Constable approved. 'Ready for work?'

'I am, boss.' He said the title with pleasure.

'Make yourself comfortable, look around.' He offered the lad a mug of ale. 'You'll be spending enough time here, better know where things are.'

Sedgwick arrived five minutes later, his hair unkempt, yawning. Nottingham knew he'd already been busy, checking the night men and making the morning round.

'Morning, John. Everything quiet?'

'Mostly.' A frown crossed his face. 'One of the night men said a whore got cut last night.'

'There's nothing new in that, some customer thinks he deserves it for free.'

'This wasn't like that, boss. It was a pair of men who walked up to her. One grabbed her by the arm and the other used a blade on her cheek. Told her to leave Leeds.'

'Who's the girl?' Nottingham asked.

'She's new, only been here a fortnight or so.'

'Who's running her?'

'Someone called Hughes. He must be new too, I've never heard of him before.'

'So someone's warning him off through her.'

'Aye, probably. Most likely Amos Worthy.'

Worthy was the city's biggest procurer, a criminal who often supplied girls and loans to members of the Corporation and rich merchants;

in return, they made certain he was never convicted of anything. It was a situation the Constable hated. But it had become more complex when he'd learned that his mother had once been Worthy's lover, and that he'd looked after them during some of the bleak days when Nottingham's father had thrown them out. More recently, too, he'd helped find a killer who'd murdered one of the few men in Leeds the pimp respected. He was strange, with a code of honour that defied any easy definition.

The Constable thought for a minute. 'How many girls does Hughes have?'

'Four, that's what the lass said. Do you want to do anything about it?'

'I don't like it but let's wait and see what happens. If there's anything more we'll jump on it.'

'Yes, boss.'

Lister ambled out from the cells and the deputy raised his eyebrows.

'This is Rob Lister. Rob, this is Mr Sedgwick. He's going to teach you everything you need to know. Mind his lessons well.'

The men nodded at each other and the Constable noticed the wary look on the deputy's face.

'Take Rob out and show him the ropes,' Nottingham instructed. 'He's joining us. I think he'll catch on quick enough.'

'Yes, boss.'

'I'll be gone most of the morning. Go round the pawnbrokers and sellers again, see if any of those items the servants stole have turned up yet. If they haven't left Leeds I expect we'll be due to hear more about them soon.'

'Yes, boss.' He looked expectantly at Lister. 'Ready?'

Nottingham had taken the horse from the stable to go out to Headingley. He could have walked the distance easily enough, but riding would be quicker. More than that, he wouldn't look like such a poor man when he arrived.

He'd made inquiries into Hartington before allowing Emily to go and work for the family. Everything indicated a man of probity. He was in his thirties and married with two young daughters, well respected, a supporter of charities for the poor. There was some money in his family but he'd built on that quite astutely, buying and selling land in Leeds.

His house was new, up to the fashion with a plain front and plenty of windows, set behind a long sweep of lawn. It was understated, elegant, and expensive. The Constable dismounted, and waited until a stable boy appeared to lead the animal away.

'I'm here to see Mr Hartington,' he told the footman at the door.

'He's breakfasting, sir,' came the smooth, sure answer. Even in his best suit, no one would believe Nottingham to be a man of any wealth.

'Tell him that the Constable of Leeds would like to talk to him,' he said with quiet authority. 'It's important.'

He only had to spend five minutes in the withdrawing room before Hartington hurried in, a frown of annoyance on his face. He was a slight man, shorter than Nottingham, dressed with the casual ease of someone who could afford the best and wore it lightly. A full-bottom wig of glossy black brushed his shoulders, and his shoes buckles gleamed gold.

'Well?' he asked.

'You dismissed my daughter yesterday.'

'I did,' Hartington agreed, eyeing the Constable warily and keeping a discreet distance. 'I won't tolerate a servant talking back to me. I told her that when she first came here.'

'So saying no to rape is talking back in this house, is it?' Nottingham asked evenly, keeping deliberately expressionless.

Hartington's cheeks flushed with anger. 'What? She told you that?'

'She told me that and I believe her.' He could see the man's eyes shifting around the room, focusing on anything but his face.

'She's lying.'

The Constable said nothing at first then took a pace forward, close to Hartington. The man flinched.

'She's not. We both know that. Perhaps your wife would like to hear Emily's side of the story. After all, she and the children were gone when it happened, weren't they?'

'That's neither here nor there.'

'I think it is.' Nottingham moved one threatening step towards the door. 'The people you do business with in Leeds will be interested to know, too.'

'That would be slander, Mr Nottingham. It would be her word against mine.'

The Constable stopped and stared calmly at the man, his eyes cold, the anger an undercurrent in his voice.

'Not quite; I'd make damned sure it was my word, too, Mr Hartington. You'd better think about that. By the time anything came to court the damage would already be done. You'd better understand exactly what I mean. I'll make absolutely certain your reputation is ruined.' He sounded forceful and convincing, yet in truth he had no idea whether anyone would listen to him. He was just the Constable, not a gentleman of rank.

A weighted silence filled the room. Nottingham could see the worry on Hartington's face. He stayed silent a few more seconds, then said, 'You're going to write an excellent reference for Emily. The best you've ever written for anyone. Do that and we'll forget the matter entirely.'

There was the gamble, he thought, watching the other man closely. Hartington could still call his bluff and he had nothing more in his arsenal. He stared at the man, eyes never wavering, mouth set hard.

Finally, with a curt nod, Hartington caved in. 'I suppose it makes no difference to me if I recommend the girl or not.'

'I'll stay while you write it and take it home with me.'

'Stay here, then.' He stormed out of the room, slamming the door behind him. From elsewhere in the house Nottingham could hear the high prattle and laughter of girlish voices. He breathed deeply feeling his heart pounding hard.

The longclock ticked softly, the hands moving through a full quarter-hour before the footman appeared with the letter. The Constable read it quickly, nodded and took his leave. Outside he folded it carefully and put it in the deep pocket of his waistcoat. The horse was waiting, but it wasn't until he was back on the Otley road that he allowed himself the satisfaction of a smile. Hartington had done well in his humiliation; Emily would have no trouble finding another position. Nottingham might have another enemy now but it was just one more to add to the number.

'You see him over there? You've got to watch him, he'd have your purse as soon as look at you.'

'Which one?' Lister asked, staring at a gaggle of young men gathered around a shop window.

'The one on the edge with the fair hair.' Sedgwick pointed out a youth of about twelve dressed in cast-off clothes whose face radiated a pauper's innocence.

'He doesn't look dangerous.'

'That's why he's so good,' the deputy noted drily. They'd made a long circuit of the city and now they were walking back along Boar Lane, close to Holy Trinity church, the smell of horse dung rising strong from the piles on the road. Sedgwick had pointed out faces to the new man, named names, and taken him into the poor courts and yards the lad would have never seen otherwise.

He knew it had come as a shock to Lister to realize how little he really knew the place where he lived. But he'd need to know it, to know it deeply and know it fast if he was really going to be a Constable's man.

And, he had to admit, the lad had some potential. He'd listened hard and asked good questions. More than that, he'd quickly understood how little he knew and seemed eager to learn more.

In spite of the reservations he'd felt at first, Sedgwick found himself warming to Rob. He was outgoing and pleasant, taking things in quickly. There was education and a little money in his background, there was no hiding that, but he wore it without any of the usual airs and graces. They finished the walk by ducking along Currie Entry and then up Call Lane, past the Quaker Meeting House and back along Kirkgate to the jail.

'That's a start,' he announced as he opened the window to release the hot, stale air. 'Why don't you go next door and get us a fresh jug of ale from the White Swan.'

'I don't have any money,' Lister admitted hesitantly, and Sedgwick smiled.

'Tell him you're a Constable's man and you're bringing it here. He'll put it on the slate for us.'

101

He watched as Rob pushed himself up from the chair. 'One of the benefits of the job, lad. That and free food from some of the pie sellers. Play your cards right and one or two of the whores will give it away, too.'

The deputy sat back, frowning. It was impossible not to like Lister, with his ready, genuine smile, that sharp intelligence and eagerness. But he wasn't going to be won over quite so quickly. See if the boy had any staying power first and what he'd do when things became difficult. Until he'd proved himself, Sedgwick was going to remain a little wary.

The door opened.

'You're quick,' the deputy began, but it wasn't Lister who entered. Instead it was Joseph Croft, the old man who made his living cleaning the White Cloth Hall. He'd been one of Marlborough's men at the Battle of Blenheim back in '04, coming back proud but without an arm and surviving as a beggar until the merchants had eventually given him the charity of employment.

'Constable about?' he asked, his face anxious.

'Nay, Joe, it's just me this morning.'

'Tha'd better come then, Mr Sedgwick.' There was a raw edge to Croft's voice.

Sedgwick sat upright. 'What is it?'

The man said nothing, his skin ghostly pale.

Lister bustled back in with the jug, opened his mouth to speak, then looked at the others and closed it again.

'Right, Rob, we have work to do. Come on,

Joe, show us.'

The White Cloth Hall was just a short distance down Kirkgate, set back slightly from the street. The men walked silently, following as Croft led them down one of the wings, heels echoing on the cobbles. They went up the stairs to the store-rooms, each painted with the name of one of the local townships. Croft stopped at the one marked Kirkstall, and pointed.

'In there,' he said and stood back.

Sedgwick pulled the door open.

'Sweet God,' Lister whispered. 'It's Will Jackson.'

Ten

Lister was out in the corridor, bent over and retching up his breakfast. Sedgwick looked at the body swinging gently from the beam. One shoe had fallen off, lying on its side on the boards next to a dark stain of piss. A low stool had been kicked over.

'It's Jackson, right enough,' Croft said.

'Let's get him cut down,' the deputy sighed, pulling a knife from his coat and sliced the rope. 'You take the legs.' Between them they manoeuvred the corpse to the ground and Sedgwick cut the noose from the neck.

Another suicide, another sad tale, he thought. From the look of him he'd been no more than twenty-five, a neat, trim man.

'When did you find him?' Sedgwick asked.

'Right before I came for you,' Croft answered, his eyes firm on Jackson. 'I was getting everything ready for the cloth market.'

'When did you last look in here?' Sedgwick stood. Jackson had hung himself with a length of rope knotted over the beam. Nothing special, nothing unusual. He'd probably purchased it at the chandler's shop.

'After the market on Saturday.' Croft ran a

hand across his thin, grey hair. 'Allus make sure they never leave anything.'

'And what do you know about him?' Sedgwick gestured at the corpse.

Croft thought for a moment. 'Nothing, really. I'd seen him a few times, that's all. He was a cloth dresser, I think.' He shrugged his shoulders helplessly.

Rob came back into the room, his face a pale, terrible white, wiping awkwardly at his mouth with the back of his hand.

'Was he a friend of yours?' the deputy asked.

'In a way. Not a close one,' Lister replied. 'I'd see him out drinking sometimes and we'd talk.' He paused. 'I can't believe he'd do this.' He looked at Sedgwick with wide, uncomprehending eyes.

'Have the coroner see him, then I'll have a couple of the men bring him to the jail,' the deputy told Croft then turned to the younger man. 'Come on, Rob, we'd better get you out in the fresh air.'

The air was full of all the odours of the city but Lister gulped it in deeply, leaning against the smooth, finished stone of the building with his hands on his knees.

'The first one's always bad,' Sedgwick told him, watching the young man's face. He kept the sympathy out of his voice. 'You'll see a lot worse if you stay in the job.'

'Can you become used to something like that?'

'Not really. There are never any easy ones. But

105

you learn how to look at it.' He clapped the lad on the shoulder. 'Let's go back to the jail, you look like you need a drink.'

The Constable had returned and was sitting at his desk, scratching away at a piece of paper with the quill pen.

'How did he do?' he asked as the others returned.

'He's had a rough start,' the deputy answered as Lister filled a mug. 'Suicide at the Cloth Hall. A fellow called Will Jackson. Rob knew him.'

Nottingham raised his eyebrows.

Rob swilled the ale in his mouth and swallowed it. 'Like I told Mr Sedgwick, I didn't know him well, just in the beer shops and inns. He was a junior partner in one of the cloth dressers.'

'Do you know which one?' the Constable asked.

'No. I'm sorry,' Lister said.

'Never mind, we can find out easily enough. No doubt he killed himself?' he asked the deputy.

'Positive, boss.' Sedgwick poured himself a drink. 'The men are bringing him over here.'

'Right. We'd better get him in the ground as soon as possible in this weather. The church won't have anything to do with him if he's a suicide.' He turned to Rob. 'What about his family?'

'I remember his parents died during the last year of his apprenticeship. And I seem to recall something about sisters.' He looked embar-

106

rassed. 'I don't remember more than that.'

'Do you know where he lived?' Nottingham brushed the fringe off his forehead.

'Near the bottom of Briggate somewhere, I think.'

'Good. You two go and see what you can find and then go over to his work and talk to them. Then we can be finished with this.'

The Constable saw Lister grimace at the rough dismissal of the death.

'Rob,' he said gently, 'I'm sorry. But this is a suicide. We have plenty to keep us busy without that. You'll learn that.'

The lad nodded.

It only took a few minutes to obtain the man's address. They knocked on the door of a pleasant-looking house set fifty yards up from the river and the housekeeper reluctantly took them up to the rooms Jackson rented. His front window looked down on the street, the bedroom at the rear over the long, neat garden.

'He didn't leave a note at the Cloth Hall,' Sedgwick explained to Lister. 'See if there's anything here, anything to show why he killed himself. You look in here, I'll take the back.'

Jackson had money; he certainly hadn't lived hand to mouth. There were three suits, all of good cut, spare shirts and hose. The furniture was old but of good, lasting quality, the mattress of goose down, the sheets clean, expensive linen.

Why, the deputy wondered? Why would someone with all this, someone with a business, kill himself ? There was no sense to it. He kept looking but there was nothing to answer his question and he went into the living room.

'Have you looked at the desk yet?' he asked Lister.

'No.'

It was there, lying on top of a pile of papers. The last thing Jackson would have written. In flowing script on a clean sheet of paper, he'd penned, 'My sweet S is dead. There can be no more for me with her gone.'

The quill had been cleaned, the small knife for sharpening it lying next at the side, the inkwell carefully capped. A man's final actions.

'Rob,' Sedgwick asked, 'how well did you know Will?'

'Not well at all, I told you,' Lister answered distractedly. 'Why?'

'I think he might be connected to the murder we have.'

He left the lad to sort through the correspondence, trying to find anything he could – love letters, the names of relatives, more about Jackson's work. That was something he could do easily enough without anyone gazing over his shoulder. Sedgwick hurried back to the jail, the note carefully folded in his pocket.

Nottingham was still labouring over his reports, the remains of a mutton pie on the desk.

'I think you'd better have a look at this, boss.'

He waited as the Constable read and then the two men looked at each other.

'Sarah Godlove?'

108

'That's what I was wondering.'

Nottingham reached into the desk and found the note he'd discovered in the dead girl's dress. He placed it next to the brief lines Jackson had left. The writing matched.

'That would explain her being away one day each week, meeting him, I suppose.' He sat back, scraping a hand over his chin. 'Good work, John. I think we'd better find out all we can about Mr Jackson. Men have murdered their lovers before.'

Sedgwick nodded. 'Rob's going through his things.'

'What do you think of him?' Nottingham asked.

'He's got plenty to learn,' the deputy said cautiously.

'I know. But we all did when we started. I remember what you were like.'

'He's quick, I'll give him that. If he stays he might be all right. If.'

'I think he'd make a good deputy when you become Constable.'

Sedgwick smiled. 'If the Corporation lets it happen that way.'

'They'll listen to my recommendation,' the Constable said firmly. 'No promises, mind.' He waited until Sedgwick nodded his acknowledgement.

'Still, plenty of time before that happens, boss.'

'I bloody well hope so.'

Sedgwick turned to leave.

'John?' Nottingham held up the paper. 'Worth learning to read?'

Sedgwick grinned. 'Aye, boss.'

When he walked back into Jackson's rooms, the deputy saw that Lister had thrown his jacket over a chair and was poring over the papers from the desk, sorting them into four piles on the table.

'What do we have?' he asked.

'Those are nothing,' Rob answered, pointing at his handiwork. 'Just bills. Those are work – he was with Elias Tunstall, by the way – and those are family. Three sisters, one of them's in Leeds, married to a merchant.'

'And what about those?' Sedgwick gestured at a small collection.

'Those are his love letters.'

'All from the same girl?'

'The handwriting's the same in all of them and they're all signed S. No dates on any of them.'

'S is Sarah Godlove, the murdered girl. Jackson's writing matches a note she had hidden on her.'

'Well...' Lister began, then couldn't think of anything more to say.

'An interesting turn, isn't it?' the deputy said. 'You finish looking through these and we'll take them back to the jail.'

'John?' Lister asked soon after, looking up from one of the notes. 'Where did Sarah live?'

'Horsforth. Why?'

'Listen to this: *Can we meet in Burley or Kirkstall this time, my love? I won't have the time to*

110

come all the way into Leeds. He wishes us to go to a ball in Bradford that night so I must be back in good time. Both of those are on the way in from Horsforth. She was found at the abbey, wasn't she?'

'Aye,' Sedgwick agreed thoughtfully.

The Constable divided up the tasks. Lister would continue to search through the papers. Sedgwick would go to Tunstall's to break the news and see what he could discover. He himself would take word of Jackson's suicide to his sister.

The house on Vicar Lane was run down, as if the people inside had stopped caring about it some years before. The windows were dirty, the limewash old and worn, its colour faded from brilliant white almost to grey. Not the house of a successful merchant, he thought as he knocked on the door. But then not every merchant made his fortune; many lost everything.

'I'm Richard Nottingham, Constable of Leeds. I need to see Mrs Bradley,' he told the maid, a toothless old wraith who showed him through to the dusty withdrawing room, sketching a curtsey on her way out. He had to spend ten minutes waiting until Elizabeth Bradley entered, skirts rustling, her face freshly powdered and hair up. She looked to be in her middle thirties, careworn and harassed but putting on a good front.

'Maggie said you're the Constable?' she enquired, confusion on her face. Had she dressed up to receive him, he wondered?

111

'I am. I'm sorry, Mrs Bradley, but I have ill news for you.' There was never a way to break a death easily. Murder was difficult enough, but suicide was something impossible to understand.

'What do you mean?' she asked sharply. 'Has something happened to Henry?'

'No.' He looked at her. 'You'd better sit down,' he told her. 'It's your brother.'

'Will?'

'Yes.'

She looked up at him, uncomprehending. 'What is it? Is he in trouble?'

Nottingham paused.

'I'm afraid he's dead,' he said finally. 'He killed himself.'

'Will?' She spoke the word again. 'Will?'

'Yes.' He watched with concern as her eyes began to lose focus, and took her hand to steady her. 'Do you want me to get the maid?'

She shook her head slowly, squeezing her eyes firmly shut to stop any tears leaking out. Her fingers squeezed hard around his, the grip tight. She needed to control herself, he knew that, to let the shock pass. She let go of him, pulling a linen handkerchief from her sleeve and crushing it into a ball in her small fist.

'It's Will?' she asked. 'You're sure?'

'It is,' he told her in a gentle voice. 'I'm sorry.'

'But why ... why would he kill himself?'

'I don't know,' the Constable answered. 'We're trying to find out. Can you think of any reason?'

'No,' she said after a while, her voice full of bafflement. 'He said that the business was doing well. He was making money. He was going to invest in Henry's – my husband's – firm.' She put her hand to her mouth. 'Henry.'

'Mrs Bradley.'

She looked at Nottingham, her thoughts jerking back hard to the here and now.

'Were you and your brother close?'

'He always came to church with us on Sunday. We go to the new church, we have a family pew there.'

'What about your sisters?'

'Alice lives in York and Susan is in Pontefract. I'm the oldest.' Her eyes widened as another understanding reached her. 'I'll have to tell them, won't I?'

'Yes. I'm sorry.'

She dabbed quickly at a tear before it could run down her cheek.

'Did your brother have a girl, by any chance?'

'Will? A girl?' she asked in astonishment. 'You didn't know my brother, did you?'

'No.'

'Will didn't have time for courting. He was always working. I used to tease him about it, tell him he'd end up a rich old bachelor.' She smiled briefly at the fleeting memory. 'Why do you want to know?'

'Because it might give a reason. A cause.'

She shook her head. 'No, I don't think it can be that.'

He stood up. 'My condolences again,' he said

113

formally, and moved towards the door.

'Constable?' He heard her draw in a breath and knew what was coming. He'd expected her to ask. 'Is it possible that my brother's death wasn't a suicide? An accident, perhaps?'

He knew the reason for the question. No family wanted the shame of a suicide. It was a stain that never washed out, the quiet whispers behind hands and the pitying looks without words. But there was nothing he could offer her except a short movement of his head that committed him to nothing. By now the word had probably spread too far to be drawn back.

He strolled up Vicar Lane to the Head Row, then back down Briggate to stop at the Ship. The food was tasty, the meat fresh, not rancid and covered in spices, and Michael always carried good ale.

But he barely noticed what he ate or drank. Instead he was thinking about Elizabeth Bradley. She'd said little but revealed much. Will Jackson obviously kept his own life away from his family. If he'd been courting an available girl there'd have been no reason for that.

He'd also had money to invest in his brother-in-law's business, so the cloth finishing must have been making a profit. That seemed to rule out money as a possible reason behind his death.

Nottingham put the last of the mutton pie into his mouth, washing it down with the ale and made his way back to the jail.

Elias Tunstall had a shifty face, Sedgwick decided. With a sharp nose and a widow's peak to his greasy hair, he had the look of a rat, eyes constantly moving around as they walked through the business premises of Tunstall and Jackson, Cloth Finishers, on the Calls.

'Why?' he asked desperately when the deputy told him of the suicide. 'Why would he want to do that?'

'We don't know yet. That's what we want to find out. Is the business doing well?'

'It's doing grand,' Tunstall answered, puffing out his thin chest. 'We've got more work than we can handle.' He deflated again as the realization hit him. 'Don't know what we'll do now, mind.'

The voices in the nap shop stopped as soon as Tunstall entered and he glared around the men. Over in the corner the preemer boy, a lad of maybe twelve, was taking wood fibres out of the teasels used to raise the nap of the cloth. Two men worked side by side on the frame, pulling the combs over the wool.

'I want you working, not gabbing,' Tunstall said, heels clacking brightly on the floor as he led Sedgwick along.

In the next room the men laboured silently, working with scissors near as tall as themselves to crop the nap to an even length. Sleeves rolled up and kerchiefs tied at the neck, they moved carefully and precisely, faces drawn in deep concentration. One slip could ruin a length and it would come from their wages, the deputy knew.

Beyond that, in a long hall with windows and doors cast wide open to try and draw in some air, others worked the irons in the steamy, oppressive heat, pressing and bundling the cloth, ready to go back to the merchants and be sold.

'There's brass in this,' Tunstall explained, cuffing a boy who was struggling with a bucket of water, 'and we're making it.' He paused. 'For the moment, any road.'

'Did Mr Jackson seem upset about anything lately? Was he quiet?'

'Will?' Tunstall chuckled, baring his yellow teeth. 'As pleasant a soul as you could meet. Always ready to laugh with the workers, said it made them feel better, but I don't know that it's true.'

'Was he courting?' Sedgwick let the question slip casually. Tunstall shook his head emphatically.

'Always working, that lad. If he wasn't here he'd be off seeing customers. Did that one day every week. About the only time he wasn't busy was Sunday and he'd have crept in here then if he could.' He sighed. 'He was no more than a lad, too. What could have made him do summat like that?'

'We'll try to find out,' the deputy promised. 'Did he go out to customers the same day every week?'

'No, different days each week.' Tunstall answered without thinking. 'But he kept the orders coming and that was all that mattered. What

116

about his family?'

'The Constable's informing his sister.'

Tunstall wasn't going to say too much, but he might have more luck with the workers, Sedgwick thought. They were men who'd need a drink after working here. Catch a few of them in an alehouse, buy them a jug or two and their tongues would loosen. Men always saw more than the bosses imagined.

The afternoon was passing by, and the deputy decided he might as well wait rather than return to the jail. He slipped through the streets to Dyers Garth and lay back lazily on the riverbank. The swirl of the water was lulling and after a few minutes his thoughts started to drift. Come winter he'd be a father again, God willing. A new little bairn, a part of him. He'd loved James as a baby, and found real peace in holding him and watching him sleep. But he knew that the fear would be there, that something would happen, that Lizzie would die in childbed, that the newborn wouldn't survive. It happened all too often, not one dead but both, leaving only a vast emptiness the heart couldn't fill.

He breathed deep to clear his head, letting the sun bring back some contentment, and dozed until the bells of the Parish Church tolled six. Slowly he roused himself, brushing grass off his breeches, and wandered back to the Calls. The men came out laughing, loud in their brief freedom. Some went their way, but one group of five passed through Back Lane to Low Holland and the alehouse that had been made from a cottage there.

The deputy gave them five minutes, time enough to sit and wet their throats after a long day's labour. Then he entered, greeting Nettie behind her trestle and pointing to the twice-brewed that would fight the day's heat.

'I know you,' one of the men called to him. 'You were at our place earlier. Talking to t'boss.'

'Aye, I was.' Sedgwick lifted the mug, took a long, deep swallow and walked over to join them on the bench. 'I had some news for Mr Tunstall.'

'What was that, then?' another man asked. He had a face that seemed faintly familiar, but for the moment the deputy couldn't put a name to it. 'What's the Constable's man want at Tunstall's?'

'It was about Mr Jackson.' Suddenly he remembered the man's name – Caleb Rountree. He'd questioned him once about some stolen property, but they'd never been able to prove anything. 'Did you know him, Caleb?'

The others laughed that the law would recognize him and Rountree reddened, burying his face in his mug.

'What's happened to him?' an older man asked quietly.

'Dead,' Sedgwick told them, looking around the table. 'Killed himself.'

'What?' Rountree crashed his pot down on the wood, eyes wide in disbelief. 'Give over! What would he want to do summat like that for?'

'I don't know. Any of you know him?'

The older man struck a flint and lit his clay pipe, the sound of his drawing on the tobacco the only noise at the table. The others glanced at each other, unsure what to say.

'He were better than Tunstall,' the man said finally. 'No side on him for all he were the boss. He knew the jobs and he could do them himself if need be. Crop a good length, too.'

Sedgwick motioned for Nettie to bring a jug.

'He worked us hard enough, though,' Rountree complained.

'You know much about him?'

'What's to know?' asked Rountree sourly. 'They have their lives, we have ours. Not like we're going to mix, is it?'

'Never know,' the deputy said. 'You might have heard something. Rumours.'

'The wife saw him in town once,' the older man said idly. 'Middle of the day and he was with a lass.'

'On a work day?'

'Aye. She told me when I got home, that's how I remember.' He shrugged carelessly. 'Neither here nor there, I suppose.'

'How long ago was that?'

The man scratched thoughtfully at the thatch of curls on his head. 'Had to be before winter, I think. Couldn't tell you any better than that.'

No one else seemed to have anything to offer. Sedgwick stood, careful to leave the ale. 'If you think of anything else, come and find me,' he said. As he walked away Rountree was already greedily pouring for himself.

By evening Lister had gone carefully through all the letters, scribbling notes in his tiny, cramped writing. Finally he threw down the quill in frustration.

'Well?' Nottingham asked.

'There's nothing about any plans, just love notes and meetings.'

'Keep looking tomorrow. There might be something in there. How do you care for the job?'

'It's surprised me,' Rob replied thoughtfully. 'I like it.'

The Constable smiled grimly. 'A suicide isn't the best way to start, but you've done well. Go home and back at six tomorrow. And not a word to your father, please.'

'I won't say anything,' he promised.

Nottingham didn't dawdle on the way home, but strode out of the city, fingering the letter in his pocket. His boots clattered over Timble Bridge and up Marsh Lane, and the door opened on a rusted hinge with a soft creak more redolent of winter than bright summer.

Mary came quickly from the kitchen, her eyes expectant then glowing as he grinned.

'You did it?' she asked with a laugh.

'I did,' he told her with surprise and produced the paper from his pocket. 'She'll have no trouble finding another position with this. Where is she, anyway?'

'In her room. She's been there most of the day, poor love. Go and show it to her, Richard, it'll cheer her up.' She gave him a full, deep kiss and he drew her close, stroking the back of her neck until she pulled away. 'Go on, make her happy.'

He tapped on the door of Emily's room and entered. She was sitting on the bed, a book open in her lap although she wasn't reading. As she turned to him he could see the redness of old weeping in her eyes and the puffiness of her lips. He held out the letter.

'Take a look at that,' he said and waited as she unfolded it and skimmed the words once, then again, her mouth widening as she read.

'Papa.' The word was part question, part squeal of joy. She ran to him, arms wide, and hugged him. 'But how did you...?'

'Never you mind,' he said, happy to see her mood so suddenly lifted. 'Don't worry, Hartington won't say a word, and you should be able to find another position quite easily with a recommendation like that.'

'With something like this I could be governess to the king.' Her pleasure filled the room. 'Thank you, papa.'

He left her reading the paper again, feeling that perhaps today had been worthwhile.

'For my money Sarah Godlove came into Leeds every week and met Jackson,' the deputy said firmly. It was still early and the morning light shone with the promise of another warm day as the three of them sat in the jail. 'I know we don't have proof yet, but...'

Nottingham sat forward thoughtfully in his chair, elbows on the desk, fingers steepled under his chin.

'We can find that,' he said slowly, 'or as close to it as we're likely to get. You said Jackson was seen with a girl. They must have gone somewhere and they couldn't have been alone in his rooms. After all, they had her honour to protect.'

'Aye, that's true enough,' Sedgwick agreed.

'Go and talk to his landlady. If anyone visited him there you can wager she'll know and can probably give us a description.' He turned his eyes to Lister. 'We know Sarah liked to ride. Go and talk to the stables. If she was coming here she'd have wanted her horse somewhere safe.'

'Yes, boss.' Rob frowned. 'And if we find out that it is her, what do we do then?'

'Then we have a place to start digging. Think about it. She's married and seeing another man. That gives Samuel Godlove a reason to kill her if he knows about it. Or Jackson, for that matter.'

'What about the baby?' the deputy wondered.

'If she was carrying a baby,' Nottingham warned heavily. 'All we have is a servant's take for that. And if there is a baby it might easily be Jackson's.'

'What about Anne Taylor?'

'Who's she?' Lister asked.

'Sarah's maid. Vanished after his mistress died.'

'Do you think she might have done it?'

'No,' the Constable told him. 'She's dead, like as not. She hasn't been in touch with her family. Where else would she go?'

The others left, and Nottingham picked up the pile of love letters Sarah had sent Jackson. Her writing was rounded, girlish, large on the page.

My heart aches for you, she'd written. *How can I wait until we meet again? You're the blood in my veins, every thought in my head. The minutes pass like lifetimes, but my love for you grows with each one. S.*

He took up another page.

My love, today was so wonderful. I feel bless-ed by your love. I can taste you, smell you, but I'm saddened that I have days before I see you again. Life would be so perfect if we were always together. I love you. S.

On the third he read, *How I wish we could always be together so my joy could be complete. Without you there would be nothing to live for.*

Her eagerness, her passion, leapt out at him. They were the words of a girl, but he had no doubt about the depth of her feelings. She'd loved Jackson completely. And his love for her must have been as absolute as hers – why else would he have killed himself once he learned she was dead? He felt saddened and sickened by the sad waste of life.

He settled to finish his report, surprised but grateful that the mayor hadn't demanded an arrest yet. Still, he thought as he walked up Briggate towards the Moot Hall, by the end of the day they might know a great deal more.

On both sides of the street the traders were setting up for the Saturday market, their stalls spilling into the road. Men were shouting and boasting, servants flirting and gossiping, full of anticipation as they waited.

He heard someone chuckle and turned to find Thaddeus Harris at his shoulder, a broad smile showing off a set of broken, rotted teeth, watching as his apprentice finished setting up the stall.

'Seen Amos Worthy, Constable?'

'No,' he answered, surprised at the question. 'What's he done?'

'Thought he might have come in to see thee. Someone robbed him last night.'

Eleven

He left his report with a clerk at the Moot Hall and walked swiftly down Briggate. Anything involving Amos Worthy was grim news. Nottingham was more than ready to believe it had been his men who'd cut the whore as a warning; it was his style. But Worthy was also a man of strange honour, and he and Nottingham shared a tangled history that reached back through the decades.

The old, unpainted door on Swinegate was unlocked, the passage running straight through to the kitchen, and the Constable walked in without knocking. Worthy would be there in the tottering old addition to the already ancient house, enjoying the warmth of the fire in the hearth even in the midsummer heat.

In his sixties, the man had aged since the winter. His hair had thinned, his face was a little more gaunt, and he'd taken to walking with a silver-topped stick since he'd been stabbed in the thigh. He was a rich man but he still dressed in the same old dirty clothes every day, hoarding the money he made from his girls and all the rest, a man with his finger in many of the city's pies, some legal, most not.

125

Even now, older and looking a little smaller, he wasn't a man to be crossed. He had power and a violent temper. His justice was quick and his justice was bloody.

He had a pair of men in the room who stirred and pulled their blades as Nottingham entered, but the pimp waved them away.

'I thought you'd be here sooner or later, Constable,' he said. 'Little birds been singing, have they?'

'A few words,' Nottingham conceded, settling on a stool by the table and pouring a mug of small beer.

'Help yourself, why don't you, laddie?' he said wryly. 'Come to gloat?'

'Come to warn you,' the Constable corrected him. 'What happened, Amos?'

Worthy shook his head slightly. 'Save your breath, laddie. I'm going to find who did this.'

'And then?'

'Make them pay,' he answered matter-of-factly.

'Kill them, you mean.'

'Aye.' He reached across, tore off part of a loaf and began to eat, ignoring the crumbs that fell on to his old waistcoat, a patchwork of stains and dirt.

'No,' Nottingham said.

Worthy raised his eyebrows. 'No?'

'How much did she take?'

'Ten guineas.'

It was a sizeable sum, the Constable had to admit.

'If anyone dies, it's after a trial.'

The pimp snorted. 'That's if you catch them.'

Nottingham said nothing, but kept his gaze on the man. 'I hear you have some competition, too.'

'Oh aye? Who would that be, then?'

'Someone called Hughes. Arrived recently with his girls.'

'I've heard the name,' Worthy said absently. 'You know how it happens, Constable. They come and go.'

Forced out or dead, Nottingham thought.

'One of his lasses was cut the other night.'

'Shame,' the pimp said flatly, his eyes blank.

'I won't ask if it was your doing.'

There was no response.

'Whoever did it needs to hear what I'm saying, though,' the Constable continued. 'It stops here.'

Worthy raised his eyebrows.

'Oh aye?'

'And if you think Hughes is behind this theft, don't. There's been a service lay in the city. How did it happen?'

Worthy at least had the grace to lower his head. 'I took on a new lass last week after the last one left to get wed. There's a whole house upstairs needs looking after.'

'Was she called Nan?'

'Aye. Been around, has she?'

'I think there's two of them, her and a man. What did she look like?'

'Pretty enough,' he answered. 'Not too tall,

127

long dark hair, blue eyes, not filled out yet.'

'How old?'

'Fourteen, fifteen?' Worthy shrugged. 'I didn't ask. She had a reference.'

'And you never thought she'd be stupid enough to steal from you.'

The pimp turned, his face dark, his voice quiet and menacing. 'It'll be the last time she steals from anyone, Constable.' He spat on the floor. 'I have people out looking for her.'

'Call them off, Amos.'

'Why?' he asked. 'If she stands trial she'll hang for the ten guineas.'

'And your way's better? Find her and kill her?'

'Aye, laddie, it is. I can't do anything else. She's made a laughing stock of me.'

Nottingham understood. If Worthy didn't catch the girl and take his revenge, others would think he was losing his power and come after him. Hughes was already trying to push his way in, to challenge the man's power. His own men might start doubting his judgement and sharpening their knives. Worthy lived in a world that had no use for mercy or compassion. But understanding that didn't mean accepting it. The Constable took a drink.

'I told you, you're not the only one she's done this to. There are two of them, we've been looking for them.'

'Well, you haven't bloody found them yet, have you?' His voice was sharp as metal.

'We will.'

'Not before I do, laddie.'

'We'll see about that, Amos.' He stood up, brushed the fringe from his forehead and left.

Sedgwick was already back at the jail, putting a prisoner into one of the cells, the man shouting in drunken incoherence.

'This early?' Nottingham asked.

'Left over from last night, more like. He was wandering all over Boar Lane.' The deputy hung the key back on the hook. Ale was good, being drunk once in a while was fine, but he had no time for public stupidity.

'Did you find anything out at Jackson's?'

'A woman used to come to visit one day a week, right enough. Not always the same day.'

'Very good.' The Constable settled back in the chair.

'She visited with her maid, so the landlady thought everything was proper. Thought it was a relative who cared for him.'

'Even better. And what about a description?'

'The woman was young and blonde, tiny little thing according to the landlady. Seemed very respectable, always wore an expensive gown. The maid was just a little older, with dark hair. Got to be Sarah, boss.'

'Yes,' Nottingham admitted. 'But we have something else to think about.'

'Oh?' He pursed his lips, waiting.

'That girl from the servant lay. Her name was Nan, wasn't it?'

'Aye.'

'Well, Nan's either been very bold or very stupid. She stole ten guineas from Amos Worthy last night.'

Sedgwick's face broke into a grin and then laughter. 'Oh, that's lovely, boss. I could kiss her for that.'

'You'll not get a chance if Worthy finds her first,' the Constable told him seriously. 'Word's spread about it. He said he's going to kill her.'

'If he does we have him for murder.'

'And then someone new comes and takes his place, like this Hughes. If he doesn't find her then people will think he's lost his power and they'll be on him like wolves.' He sighed. 'He's the devil we know.'

'So what do we do?'

'We find her first,' Nottingham answered simply. 'That's our job. She and whoever's with her can't be from around here. They'd never have stolen from Worthy otherwise, that's just tempting trouble.'

'We haven't had any luck so far,' the deputy pointed out.

'Then we're going to have to work harder. I want you on it, John.'

'Why not Rob? It would be a good start for him.'

The Constable considered the idea, then said, 'No. You know what you're doing, and Worthy has his men out looking. It's going to be quite a while yet before Rob's ready to go up against them. I'll keep him with me on the murder. Use some of the night men if you need help. You know what to do if you have a problem with Worthy's men.' He paused, thinking. 'Try the inns first. If they have money the chances are they'll be spending it. A good room, drink, clothes.'

'Aye, boss.'

Lister returned soon after, horse dung from the road thick on his shoes, a satisfied smile on his face.

'Third place I tried,' he said.

'Definitely Sarah Godlove?' Nottingham asked.

'Yes.' The smile became a wide grin. 'She used the same stable every time, that one on Cripplegate, just off Boar Lane. The first time she was there the ostler asked her name and she didn't have the wit to give a false one.'

'Good work.' The lad knew what questions to ask and how to ask them, it seemed. 'Did he mention the maid?'

'Always with her, he said, but only one horse.'

'That sounds right enough. And from the description, the pair of them visited Jackson's lodgings every week.'

'So what now, boss?'

That, the Constable thought, was a good question. If Jackson and Sarah were lovers, Samuel Godlove became the obvious suspect for the killing. Yet he'd seemed innocent enough when he came to report his wife's disappearance, and distraught when he learned she was dead. So either he hadn't done it or he could have had a career on the stage.

'I think we'll go to Horsforth on Monday and talk to Mr Godlove again,' he decided. 'How are you on a horse?'

The early evening was heavy with the scents of wild flowers as they strolled up the bank of the Aire. Lizzie's arm was through his and they both kept an eye on James as he ducked and scuttled through the trees or ran too close to the water's edge.

Bees buzzed, a deliciously lazy, summer sound, and John Sedgwick felt fully content being here with his family. He glanced over at Lizzie, a soft smile on her face, one hand moving to rub at her belly, polishing the life growing in there.

'Tell me when you're ready to go back,' he said.

She looked at him happily. 'Not yet. This is lovely.'

They'd gone beyond the city and its bustle and buildings, past the upper tenters where the cloth lay stretched on the frames and out into the country. Across the river sheep were bleating as a shepherd walked towards them, crook extended to gather them in. But on this side they might have been the only people in the world.

'Is everything all right?' he asked her. 'With the babby, I mean.' He indicated with a dip of his head.

'John.' She stopped, pushed herself on to tiptoe and kissed him lightly on his pox-marked cheek. 'You can be a soft bugger at times.

Everything's fine. I'd tell you if it wasn't. Come on, I'll race you to that oak over there.' She picked up her skirts and started to run, looking over her shoulder and laughing, the cap tipping back on her head. He began to dash after her. He loved her, but he was damned if a woman was going to beat him at this.

She was breathless by the time her fingers touched the wood, ready to sit and rest in the shade. He took off his coat, folding it into a pillow for her then wandered off hand in hand with James to find flowers they could pick for her.

He needed this feeling of freedom and fresh air. The afternoon had been hours of frustration, full of hints that promised something but evaporated as he approached them. Someone had told him of a couple staying at the New King's Head and spending freely, but the landlord soon scotched that, and neither the Old King's Arms nor the Rose and Crown had lodgers who might be them. He'd talked to his touts, but all he'd received for his time was a series of shaken heads.

Whoever they were, the thieves at least had the sense to lie low. If they'd had any brains at all they'd be partway to London by now, he thought, watching as James snapped the stem of a pale gillyflower and added it to the posy in his pudgy hand.

'Do you think we have enough?'

'Not yet,' the boy told him firmly, moving back to the riverbank where the sun reached the plants, stopping to stare at the deep red of some wild roses.

'Don't touch those,' Sedgwick warned. 'They have thorns on the stems, see?'

'How do you pick them, then?' James asked.

'You don't. Just leave them like this. They look grand enough as they are, don't they?'

'I suppose so,' the boy agreed reluctantly before running on, his feet raising tiny plumes of dust on the track.

Lizzie was dozing when they returned, but James wasn't going to let her rest. He pushed gently against her shoulder until she stirred and opened her eyes, then he put the small bouquet in front of her face.

'We got these for you, mam,' he announced proudly. Her arms snaked out and pulled the boy down, kissing his forehead and making him giggle.

'They're beautiful,' she said, and glanced at Sedgwick. 'Thank you. And thanks to your dad, too.'

He knew she treasured the way James had taken to her as his mother, and that the flowers would end up pressed and kept somehow, a memory for the years to come.

'Ready to go home?' he asked. 'About time me laddo here was in bed.'

Twelve

A few clouds were drifting up over the horizon, offering the faint hope of a shower later in the day. The farmers would be happy, Nottingham thought. After so long without water they'd welcome rain on the crops before they wilted in the field.

He kept the horse trotting, Lister beside him on another animal. It was a comfortable pace, one that would see them there soon enough but without so many of the aches riding usually brought.

'The work hasn't been the easiest so far, Rob,' he said, glancing over his shoulder. The lad was still in his old suit, although he wore a pair of good leather riding boots, the Constable noticed, polished to a glow, and he sat in the saddle as if he'd done it all his life.

'I'm enjoying it,' he replied with enthusiasm. 'It's certainly not what I expected.'

Nottingham laughed. 'And what did you expect?'

'That I'd be spending all my time dealing with drunks and whores.'

'You'll have more than your share of those, don't worry,' the Constable advised. 'They take up enough of our time, but it's usually the night men who arrest them. Don't forget theft, too.'

'And murder?'

'Murder's rare, thank God.' Nottingham turned serious. 'When it does happen, it's usually lovers or a fight between drunks. Easy enough to solve.'

'Is it?'

'You'll learn, lad.'

They took the bridge over the Aire close to Kirkstall forge and began the long climb up the hill.

'Sarah was found at the abbey, wasn't she?'

'Yes.'

'It's not too far from Horsforth,' Lister speculated, and Nottingham agreed.

'I know, but that doesn't necessarily mean anything. Just remember that. You've got to keep an open mind. Most of this job is just watching and listening.'

'Doesn't it worry you, boss?'

'What?' he wondered.

'Talking to someone like Mr Godlove. He's one of the richest men around here, that's what my father says, anyway.'

The Constable smiled.

'It comes with the job. High-born, low-born, paupers and wealthy, it doesn't matter; any of them can be innocent or guilty. We talk to them all. And at bottom they're all just human.'

'And if they commit a crime?'

Nottingham looked at him. 'Then we arrest them. We're paid to take care of crime, whoever's responsible. Always remember that.'

Just as Sedgwick had described, Godlove owned a big house, probably once a manor and added to over the generations until it had sprawled out, becoming grand and imposing. It stood back from the road, down a long, landscaped drive, but it was apparent that this was a working farm, not a showpiece estate. The doors to the barns stood open and the cluck of chickens came from somewhere behind them.

The lawn before the house was carefully sculpted, sweeping down the slope to give a wide view over the river valley. The Constable paused, drinking it in with pleasure, and for a fleeting moment he envied Godlove the vista.

They dismounted and handed the horses over to a stable boy. Nottingham dusted off his coat and breeches before knocking on the heavy door.

'Does he know we're coming?' Lister asked.

'Never tell them that,' the Constable advised. 'You always want to catch people unprepared.'

A servant, looking with disdain at their old clothes, showed them through into a withdrawing room and loudly closed the door behind them.

'And now we wait,' Nottingham said wryly. 'You might as well make yourself comfortable. The rich always take their time.'

It took almost half an hour for Godlove to appear and then he bustled in as if he'd been dragged from important business. He wore a suit of brown kersey, worn and creased, along with stout shoes and holey stockings. With no waist-coat, he looked as though he'd thrown on the coat to see his visitors.

'Constable,' he said, eyes alight. His face had taken on the pinched look of a man pummelled down by life. 'I'm sorry, I came as fast as I could. I was out in the fields. You have news, I take it?'

'I'm afraid not, Mr Godlove. But I do have some more questions.'

The man's shoulders slumped. 'You've asked me questions, your deputy's asked me questions,' he said, an edge of desperation in his tone. 'Please, when are you going to start giving me some answers?'

'As soon as we have them, sir,' Nottingham replied evenly. 'It's taking us time to learn more things. The more we know, the better the chance of finding whoever murdered your wife.' He made it sound perfectly obvious and reasonable.

'Go on,' Godlove agreed with a weary sigh. 'I'm sorry, you're right. If it helps find Sarah's killer it's worthwhile.'

'Where did you meet your wife?'

The man looked up in surprise. 'At the Assembly Rooms in Leeds. Why?'

The Constable ignored the question. 'How long ago was that?'

Godlove had to think. 'Two years, two and a half, perhaps?' He paused. 'She was sixteen, so two and a half years.' As before, his gaze challenged the Constable to mention the difference in ages.

'I'm told that your wife and her maid went out one day every week.'

'Yes. It gave her a chance to get away from here for a few hours. She'd see friends, visit the sick among the tenants, go shopping.' He sighed. 'This is an isolated place, you can see that. I think she needed more of a social life than we had here.'

'Of course,' Nottingham agreed with a kind smile. 'Did the two of you go to the assemblies together?'

'Sometimes. Sarah was young. She had high spirits, she loved to dance.' Nottingham watched carefully and saw pain flicker across the man's eyes.

'Do you know a man called William Jackson, by any chance?'

'Jackson?' Godlove frowned. 'No, I don't. Why, does he have something to do with Sarah's death?'

'It was just a question,' the Constable assured him. 'There is something that's come up, though. About the time you announced your engagement, the Gibtons came into some money. I have to know, was that anything to do with you?'

Godlove dropped his head, then raised it again once he'd decided how to phrase his answer.

'Once Sarah's parents and I agreed to the betrothal, they felt that her new state required more money than they could provide. Theirs, too,' he added carefully. 'I have plenty of money, more than I'm ever going to spend, so I settled

139

some on them. That way they could live more according to their title.'

'Was that title important to you?' Nottingham asked.

'Sarah was important to me,' the man replied carefully. 'Who she was, not what she was.'

'But she was the Honourable Sarah Godlove, wasn't she? That can mean a great deal to a man.'

'It can, Constable. I'll admit that.'

'Did it to you?' Nottingham looked into the other man's eyes. 'I really do need the truth,' he said quietly.

'Yes, it did,' Godlove answered finally. 'Look at me. I'm wealthy. I have land. I give generously to charity. But the only way people like me can find that kind of respectability is by marrying it.'

'So Sarah Gibton was an attractive proposition? A title and parents who had very little.'

'At first. Once we were married I began to fall in love with her. I hoped that in time she might come to love me.' He smiled wanly. 'Hope and love can live a long time.'

'How was she with you?'

'A perfectly dutiful wife in every way,' he replied carefully. 'She had a great deal of freedom. I'm active on my estate, and I'm out all day.'

Nottingham nodded. He felt guilt at the questions he'd had to ask and what he'd forced the man to reveal.

'Thank you,' he said. 'We've taken up enough
140

of your time.'

'Constable,' Godlove said as a farewell, and left the room.

'What did you make of that?' Nottingham asked as the horses walked down the hill.

'I felt sorry for him,' Lister said.

'So did I.' He'd seen the awkwardness and embarrassment in Godlove's manner, the pain behind his admissions. 'Did you notice anything else?'

'He never asked about the maid.'

'Very good,' the Constable said. 'Not too surprising, though. It's the way of the world. The rich never see the poor unless they need them.'

'Why did you ask him about Will, boss? If he knew his wife had been seeing Jackson he wouldn't have admitted it.'

Nottingham shrugged. 'You never know, I've had stranger things happen.'

'And why the questions about how he met his wife?' Lister wanted to know.

'Because he wasn't expecting them. Catching people off guard is a good way to trip them up.'

'Do you think he killed her?'

'No,' the Constable answered eventually. 'I don't think he could have hurt her. And I don't think he knew about Will Jackson at all.'

'What about the baby? Mr Sedgwick mentioned that.'

'If there was a baby,' he cautioned. 'We don't know about that.'

'It would explain a lot, though,' Lister countered. 'Especially if the baby was Will's.'

Nottingham frowned. 'That's too many ifs for my liking. Something we haven't considered yet is the idea that Jackson might have murdered her and killed himself later.'

'Will wouldn't do something like that. He didn't have any violence in him at all.'

'Rob,' the Constable said gently but insistently, 'anyone can be violent in the right circumstances. The unlikeliest people commit murder if they're pushed hard enough. You want ifs – what if Sarah told Will she was going to stop seeing him and be faithful to her husband? If he loved her passionately enough that could make him kill her.'

'I suppose that's possible,' Lister admitted reluctantly.

'There, you see. When we get back to Leeds, go to the stable and find out the last time she was there. The same at Jackson's lodgings. If she was there when she was supposed to be on her way to Roundhay it could change things.'

'Yes, boss.'

The clouds were thickening behind them and the smell in the air had changed, the promise of rain growing stronger on the breeze.

'Come on,' Nottingham said, nudging the horse into a canter, 'we'll beat the shower back to town.'

The first large drops fell as he walked up Briggate towards the jail, leaving spots the size of pennies. Glancing to the west he could already see blue sky in the far distance. This shower

142

wouldn't last long, but as a respite from the heat it would be welcome. By the time he turned on to Kirkgate the rain was a heavy veil, rapidly soaking his coat and feeling luxuriantly fresh and cool against his face. He ducked through the door and rubbed a hand over his hair, pushing the wet fringe back from his forehead.

'Bit damp, boss?' Sedgwick laughed.

'Careful, John, or I'll send you out to buy us some ale.' He sat behind the desk. 'Any joy on the servants yet?'

'Nothing at all. You said Worthy's men were out looking for them?'

'That's what he told me.'

'It's strange,' the deputy said worriedly. 'No one I've talked to has mentioned them.'

Nottingham pursed his lips in concentration.

'He's got to have men out, he can't ignore this.'

'So they're looking in different places. That's what worries me.'

The Constable rubbed his chin. It meant that they had some information of their own, something the law didn't know.

'Do you have any ideas?' he asked.

'I've been asking, but no one's saying anything. Maybe his men have been putting the fear of God in everyone. He must really want that lass.'

'He does, and if he gets her first she'll be a corpse by the time we see her. The same for anyone with her. Amos needs this to keep his reputation. And he needs to find her quickly.'

'Maybe they've already gone,' Sedgwick offered hopefully.

'For their sake, I hope so, but I doubt it. Come on, John, anyone who'd steal from Amos Worthy can't be too smart. They'll still be here somewhere. Somebody knows something.' He glanced out of the window. The shower had moved east, leaving the air clear and clean, the sky pristine. 'Just keep looking. Give them money if you have to. I need to go and see the mayor.'

The Moot Hall bustled with the busyness of any working day. Clerks scurried along corridors while aldermen in their finery stood and chatted, comparing clothes and profits. He caught the eye of Grady, the mayor's man of all work, who gestured him through.

Kenion was in his chair. He looked up from a lengthy document and waved the Constable to a chair. Minutes passed in the muted tick of the longclock before he finished the last page.

'Right, that's that. What do you want, Nottingham?'

'I was wondering what you'd heard from the Gibtons about their daughter's murder.' There had been no summons, no demand for action, and it troubled him.

'Three notes so far, and probably another one today.' The mayor ran a hand over his pink jowls. 'The last time they threatened to go to the Lord Lieutenant.'

'What have you told them?' He was intrigued.

Normally the mayor would have been ranting for an arrest. This hatred must run deep, he thought.

'That you're doing everything you can and hope to have an arrest soon,' he said with aching weariness, as if he'd repeated the lines far too often. 'Does that sum it up?'

'As much as it can,' the Constable agreed.

'I told them that if they want to go to the Lord Lieutenant, they can, but it won't make a bit of difference.' He sat back again and folded his arms, glancing up from under bushy eyebrows. 'Do you want to know why I haven't been roasting you? That's why you're here, isn't it?'

'It is,' he admitted.

'I don't like their ways. High-handed as they come. If they lived in Leeds it might be a different matter. And,' he added, 'two more months and I'll be done with all this. Come September John Douglas will be sitting here, and good luck to him. I've had enough of it. I'll be glad to get back to business.'

'What about Godlove? Have you heard from him?'

'He wrote that he wanted to be informed of all the progress, and that he was sure we'd find her killers. Sounded like a man lost in grief to me. Anything else?'

'That's everything.'

The Constable rose to leave.

'Nottingham,' the mayor said. 'Find whoever did it.'

Without mistake, it was an order.

145

Thirteen

Lister was waiting when he returned to the jail. The lad looked thoughtful, as if he was trying to work out an answer to a vexing question.

Nottingham poured himself a mug of ale and asked, 'What did you find?'

'She was here on the Thursday, right enough. Stabled her horse about ten, as far as the ostler remembers. Will's landlady let her and her maid in a little later and they stayed for two hours.'

'I don't suppose she happened to hear any conversation?'

Rob shook his head. 'Not for want of trying, though, from the look of her.'

'Did she see Sarah when she left?'

'Just heard the door. And Will went out soon after. Sarah collected the horse and left early afternoon.'

'Good, that's one more piece.' He smiled at Lister's look of confusion. 'Do you ever play puzzles?'

'I did when I was young.'

'Sometimes a crime is like a puzzle and you need to discover the answer bit by bit until you reach the answer. This one's going to be like that. You knew Jackson. Do you know who his close friends were?'

'Some of them.'

'I want you to talk to them, see if they knew he had a girl. We also need to find out where he was after Sarah left and the day after that. Go to his business, too, see if he was there and working.'

'Yes, boss.'

'When you get down to it, most of what we do is asking questions,' the Constable explained. 'When we've done that we sift through the answers and hope for important information.'

'Wheat and chaff,' Rob said. 'I'll do my best, boss.'

'Good lad.'

Alone again, he tried to make sense of things. He was glad that the mayor was obstructing the Gibtons. When progress was so slow it made his life easier. Still, however difficult it was, they were crawling forward, inch by inch. It was just as he'd told Lister; there'd be no quick solution to this.

And then was the problem of the false servants. He knew that there was a good chance Worthy could discover them first using threats and violence to find information. If he did find them and kill them, proving he was behind it would be a difficult matter. Nottingham knew all too well just how cunning the pimp could be. When it came to his own survival, the man had no scruples. He'd cover his trail and even sacrifice one of his men if it would keep him out of prison and away from the noose.

147

What else could they do? Sedgwick knew his job, he'd do all he could to find the thieves. Still, the Constable had a few sources that were purely his own; perhaps it was time to talk to them.

Hercules lived in a tiny outbuilding tucked at the back of the yard of the Rose and Crown. No one knew if he'd been born with that name; few had ever asked. His room had an earth floor and a small pallet of ancient straw covered in blankets once used for horses. Age had stooped him into a figure dressed in patched rags, looking more like a scare-the-crow than a man. In return for his lodging and the scraps of food left by customers, he swept out the inn and cleaned the stables. He was the man no one noticed, an invisible heartbeat, but someone who heard everything. Sometimes, in exchange for a few coins he'd never spend, he gave Nottingham information.

He was exactly where the Constable expected to find him, in one of the stalls, brushing the coat of a horse to a soft shine. Hercules had little love for most people, but he was content around horses, whispering tenderly to them in a voice wracked and ruined by the years, and they responded to his gentle care. He heard Nottingham approach and pointed him to a corner as he continued working.

'You've heard Amos Worthy was robbed?'

Hercules nodded, his mouth close to the nag's ear, words coming out as quiet as breaths.

'He's looking for the girl who did it. So am I.'

148

The man turned. He had a face that had aged without grace, carrying all the deep wrinkles of life, his beard thick and white, reaching down on to his chest, his eyes a deep, penetrating blue.

'I heard them talking,' he said. 'Her and her man. They were here after it.'

'Did they stay here?'

'Saved their brass. A few drinks and they were off.'

'Do you know where?'

'No. Never said that I heard.'

'What did they look like?'

'Young 'uns, the pair of them.' He searched his memory for a moment. 'She had dark hair, I know that. Skinny as a twig, too. A clever face. She was in charge.'

'And him?'

'Dark hair, too. Not tall, but he was broad. Scars on his hands like he'd done a lot of fighting. He was older than her, mebbe twenty.' He stopped. 'Brother and sister, mebbe? They had that look about them, that and the way they talked.'

'So how did you know who they were?'

Hercules took something from the pocket of his filthy, disintegrating coat and fed it to the grateful horse.

'She were boasting about it, wan't she? Said how easy it had been to fool the old man. Lower her bodice a bit, show some leg.'

'So they didn't know who he was?'

'No.'

'Anything else useful?' Nottingham asked.

'He called her Nan and she called him Tom. And they didn't sound like they were from Leeds.'

'Where, then?'

'Yorkshire, don't know where. That's all.'

The Constable left a couple of coins on the floor of the stall and walked away, leaving the man and the horse peacefully together.

Brother and sister, he thought. It made sense; at least they'd trust each other. And if they weren't from Leeds they probably wouldn't have known who Worthy was. They might not even know he was pursuing them or what to expect if he found them.

Rob Lister found Henry Hill lounging in Garraway's coffee house on the Head Row. From the scatter of pages on the table, he'd been leafing through the latest edition of the *Mercury*.

The son of a country landowner, Hill had never worked. Instead, he spent his time at the house the family owned in the city, an old, rambling place near the bottom of Kirkgate, and he gambled, drank and whored as the mood took him. He was charming and funny, but for all his louche manner and London-cut clothes, he kept a clear eye and keen intelligence. He'd known Will Jackson as well as anyone.

'Hello, Henry.' Lister sat on the bench opposite him.

'Rob.' Hill greeted him with his usual lazy smile. 'People are saying you've become a working man.'

'I have.'

'And for the Constable?'

'Yes.'

Hill sat back and raised his eyebrows. 'That's hardly something I'd have expected from you.'

Rob grinned. 'Not enough cachet, you mean?'

'Too much work, more like.'

The pair of them laughed and Hill signalled for two dishes of coffee. One day, Lister thought, Henry might do something. He had abilities, if he ever chose to use them; he was an incisive writer and had a sharp mathematical mind. But if it happened it would be in his own time; the man was in no hurry, enjoying his freedom and his surfeit of money.

'That was terrible about Will,' he said.

Hill shook his head. 'I can't believe he did that. I've been trying to make sense of it.' He looked up at Rob. 'Do you know why?'

'A woman,' Lister told him.

'Are you sure?' Hill asked in surprise. 'It must have been a great deal more serious than he ever showed, then.'

'You knew about her?'

Hill pursed his lips. 'Not really. You know what Will could be like, he played his cards close and never said too much. He did drop a few hints when he was in his cups, though.'

'Oh?'

He drank and wiped the corners of his mouth fastidiously with a cloth napkin before looking curiously at Rob. 'I have the strange feeling this conversation isn't just social.'

'It's not,' Lister admitted easily and lifted the dish to taste the steaming, bitter coffee.

Hill seemed amused. 'Well, I never imagined I'd be talking to a Constable's man. Why are you interested in Will, anyway? It hardly seems to be anything to do with the law if he killed himself.'

Rob tried to make his words light. Whatever he said wouldn't be convincing. 'Loose ends, if you like. What did he tell you about the girl?'

'Oh, next to nothing, really.' He waved his hand idly in the air. 'Is she married? I thought she must be since he'd say so little about her.'

Lister didn't respond and finally Hill gave up with a small, gracious bow.

'He told me they were lovers. But the last time he was drunk he was talking about how things might change in the future.'

'Change?' Rob asked sharply.

'I don't know, he was very secretive about it. He didn't say any more than that.'

'When was this?'

Hill thought. 'The Wednesday before he killed himself?' he wondered. 'Yes, it must have been. I ran into him on my way home from the cock-fight at the Talbot and we went on to the White Swan.'

'And you didn't see him after that?'

'No. I went up to visit dear papa for a few days to keep in his good graces.' He sighed. 'I'll miss him, you know. Will was a good friend to me over the years.'

'I know,' Rob agreed quietly.

152

'Come out with me sometime soon,' Hill suggested with a wan smile. 'When you find some better clothes and you're not asking questions.'

'I will,' Lister promised.

He strolled down to the Calls with a faint feeling of satisfaction, ignoring the thick, rancid smells of ordure from the tannery. Talking to Henry was the first thing he'd handled himself and he believed it had gone well. He'd asked his questions and he'd learned a little more about Will.

He was certain he could enjoy this work. So far he'd done so much more than he could ever have imagined in his life. He was seeing a Leeds he'd never known, never even guessed at, as if someone had drawn a whole new city over the one that was familiar to him. But however gruesome it might be, all this was giving him the sense of being alive. It made him think and that was more than any job in the past had done.

Far more than that, he liked the Constable, and John, too. They weren't cowed by wealth or title, and that was something to admire. He believed he could learn from them. His father might imagine he'd leave after a week, as he'd done in so many other situations, but he was sure he'd stay a great deal longer if he could satisfy the boss.

At the cloth finishers he noted that the name of Jackson on the sign had already been crudely painted out. He didn't have to wait long for Tunstall to appear, looking anxious and harassed.

'I wish you people would stop coming here,'

153

he complained. 'First it was that what's his name, the tall one, and now you. It's bad for business when people see the law arriving.'

'We're just trying to find out about Mr Jackson,' Lister said mildly.

'He killed himself, that's what happened. You know that.' He threw his arms in the air in exasperation.

'You've taken him off the sign fast enough.'

Tunstall fixed him with a fierce gaze. 'Well, wouldn't you? Who wants to deal with a firm where one of the owners killed himself ? Who wants to be reminded of that? Our orders are already down. The sooner he's forgotten the better, if you ask me.'

He pushed his hands into his coat pockets defiantly, rocking on the heels of an expensive pair of buckled shoes. There was money here, Rob thought and smiled pleasantly at him.

'Then it's best we find out everything as soon as we can, isn't it?'

Tunstall sneered. 'Go on, then. But I hope it's the last time.'

'The week before Mr Jackson killed himself, was he here all week?'

'Most if it, aye.'

'When?' Lister asked. 'Do you remember?'

'I know he was here on the Monday because we had to sort out some problems with one of the pressing irons and that put us behind. Tuesday, let me see ... aye, we had to keep on those lazy sods in there to finish an order. Wednesday we were looking over the accounts and talking

154

about whether we needed a bigger place.'

'Business was good, then?'

Tunstall gave a bitter laugh. 'Business was bloody wonderful until he went and killed hisself. This week I can hardly get any bugger to talk to me.'

'What about the rest of that week?' Rob prompted.

'He was gone Thursday, I remember that. Said he had people to see.' He paused and thought. 'He popped in after dinner. Checked a couple of things and left again.'

'What was he looking for?'

Tunstall shrugged. 'No idea. He was only here a minute or two. He looked poorly, and he didn't come in Friday, either, I remember now. Sent a message that he wasn't well.'

'And when he came back?'

'He was fine. Whatever he'd had, he was over it, working hard like he allus did. First I knew of anything wrong was when someone said he was dead at the Cloth Hall, and I didn't believe it.'

'No signs at all?'

'Nothing.'

'Then I'll leave you,' Lister said.

'Just make sure you don't come back. I've a business to try and run here.'

He found Sedgwick and the Constable in the White Swan. There was a plate of bread and cheese between them and a mug of ale on the table.

'Sit down and help yourself,' Nottingham told

him. 'What did you find out?'

As they ate and drank Lister passed on what he'd learned. The Constable studied him thoughtfully.

'So now we know that Jackson had the time to kill Sarah. But if they were lovers, why would he want to do that?' He glanced at the others. 'Any ideas?'

'What if she'd told him it was over?' Sedgwick suggested. 'That could do it.'

'Go on.'

'Well, if she was pregnant, maybe she was going to be faithful to her husband and she broke things off.'

'But Will told his friend that things might change,' Lister pointed out.

'He didn't say what kind of change, though, did he?' the deputy countered.

'No, true, but...'

'What it means is that we need to look more deeply into the idea that he murdered her,' Nottingham interrupted firmly. 'Right now we have two people with the time to do it, him and Samuel Godlove, and I really don't believe Godlove was behind it.'

'So what do we do?' Lister wondered.

'Dig,' Sedgwick told him.

'He's right,' Nottingham agreed. 'Rob, I need you to go through Jackson's papers again. I'll go to his lodgings and see if there's anything more. And I'll see if he has any knives that match the murder weapon.'

'Yes, boss.'

'But,' the Constable warned, 'we need to be careful. Keep your mind open. Just because Jackson seems the likeliest killer, it doesn't mean he did it. We need to keep looking for others, too.'

'And try to find the maid,' the deputy added, but Nottingham sighed.

'She's dead somewhere, John. She knew too much. She probably saw too much. No one would kill Sarah and leave Anne alive.'

Lister slid out of the bench. 'I'll go and make a start.'

After he'd gone the Constable turned to Sedgwick. 'What do you think of Rob?'

'He could be good,' the deputy said warily. 'It's early days yet.'

'True,' Nottingham agreed. 'But I have the sense he'll be here a while.'

Sedgwick raised his eyebrows slightly. 'Maybe. His family has money, why would he keep doing this?'

'Because he seems to like it.'

'I'll wait and see.'

The Constable stared at him. 'Give him a chance, John. He's not after your job.'

'Maybe he'll want yours in time, though,' the deputy said.

Nottingham smiled slowly. 'I've told you, you're the one I'd always recommend.'

'But you don't make the decision, boss.'

'No,' he agreed with a nod. 'I've always said, they'll listen to what I say. Don't worry about it. There's no need, not for a long time yet.'

Fourteen

Nottingham walked down to Jackson's lodgings. He needed to see the place himself, to gain a sense of the man and try to understand him. He wandered between the two rooms, standing at the window and looking down on the people moving along Briggate, taking in the smells and atmosphere of Jackson's life, everything overlaid with the staleness of a life ended and closed.

He'd probably inherited the furniture from his parents, the Constable thought, running his fingertips lightly across the dust on the dark wood. It was old, battered here and there, but serviceable enough for a young man who didn't spend much time at home.

The rooms were clean and uncluttered. He took the remainder of the dead man's papers from the desk and folded them into the large pocket of his coat. In the bedroom he pawed through Jackson's clothes, hunting for notes and scraps.

The man owned three suits, plus the one he'd been wearing when he died. That was an extravagance for most men, and from the feel of them, he hadn't spared money on the cloth. Two were made from fine worsted, fashionably cut with deep cuffs on the sleeves, the breeches intended to be tight and flattering. There were five waistcoats, two of brocade in colourful patterns, the others more sober, for business most like. One pair of shoes with silver buckles and a pair of boots, lovingly cleaned to a high shine. A drawer held clean linen, and he ran his hand under the clothes for any pieces of paper that might be hidden.

He found a knife, but it was nothing like the one that had killed Sarah. Other than clothes and papers, the two rooms held little that gave any sign of who Jackson really was. This was a place where he existed, not where he lived. And there was certainly nothing of Sarah. No keepsakes, no love tokens, no memories. After half an hour he gave up.

At the jail he passed everything to Lister.

'Go through it all,' he instructed. 'Business as well as personal. I know Tunstall said everything was fine, but let's check. You never know what you'll find.'

'Yes, boss.' He raised his head from the papers.

'It's slow, but it has to be done, Rob.'

'I don't mind,' he answered with a smile. 'It sounds strange, but I'm enjoying it.'

He needed to know more about Jackson, Nottingham thought as he walked down to the river and out along Low Holland. Just up the bank the cloth was being stretched out in the sun. A mild breeze came off the water, a gentle coolness that felt pleasant on the hot afternoon.

He knew the building he wanted, although he'd never been inside it before. Tom Williamson had just moved into his new warehouse down by the Aire the month before. Built for him, it offered more space than the tumbledown place in the yard behind his old, cramped house on Briggate, and made loading cloth on to the barges much easier.

The Constable pushed open the door and entered. Already everything had the unmistakable smell of cloth. The office, its battered desks looking out of place in this new setting, stood to one side, empty as all the men worked together to store the lengths the merchant had purchased at the afternoon's coloured cloth market.

Williamson himself was supervising, stripped to his breeches and shirt, sleeves pushed up to show pale, scrawny arms. Nottingham waited, watching as the men worked in concert with pulleys and brute strength to put the cloth away on the shelves. The high windows, glass still clear and clean, were open to pull in fresh air, but everyone was sweating and cursing.

He waited quietly until they'd finished and Williamson walked towards him, towelling off his face and neck with an old scrap of linen. He was in his middle thirties, a slight man, full of energy, drive, and the kind of honesty all too rare in a merchant. He smiled as he noticed the Constable leaning against a wall.

'Richard,' he said pleasantly. 'What do you think of it?'

'Impressive,' he answered truthfully. The large new place, its stonework bright, was an indication of the ambition Williamson had as a merchant, and of the fortunes of the wool trade in Leeds. Across the city, business was growing fast, with orders coming in constantly, and all because of the quality. No one in the country could match it. Profits were good and going to become even better. Tom Williamson had grown up in the business, his father a merchant, his own apprenticeship served in the city and abroad, and he'd taken over the firm when his father had died two years before. Now it was on the cusp of being one of the largest in Leeds.

The merchant poured himself a mug of ale and drank quickly before offering one to Nottingham.

'It's a big investment,' Williamson said with pride. 'But give it two or three years and it'll be paying for itself. Come on, let's go outside, I need some air after all that.'

Nottingham followed him and they sat together on the riverbank.

'So what brings you here, Richard? You're not one for social calls.'

'Will Jackson.'

The merchant frowned. 'I heard. That was terrible,' he said with a long sigh.

'Did you know him?'

Williamson took another drink. 'Not especially well. We'd say good day when we met, that type of thing. But from what everyone said, he was up and coming, making a name for himself.'

'Did you do business with him?'

'I've used Tunstall's a couple of times, mostly when there were orders I had to fill quickly.' He wiped the sweat from the back of his neck. 'You know how it is, you develop a relationship with companies. There's a cloth finisher we've used for years. They're fine, so I don't have any reason to change.'

'What do you know about Tunstall's?'

Williamson eyed him curiously. 'Trying to find the reason he killed himself?'

'More or less,' Nottingham answered evasively. In part, at least, it was the truth. The merchant considered his answer.

'As far as I know, they're going well. Jackson really built the business up. He came to see me a few times, trying for my custom. I imagine Elias is worried now.'

'So I've heard.'

A suicide left a long, stained shadow, one that people were eager to avoid. Trade at Tunstall's would suffer as long as people remembered what Jackson had done.

'It's not like you to investigate suicides, Richard, even if they're in a place like that. Is there something more?'

'Possibly,' was as far as he'd go in response. Tom was a friend, one of the few merchants who didn't look down on him or his office. But something stopped him saying more and he wasn't sure why. Perhaps he felt too unsure about everything at the moment, still trying to tie down the tenuous connections between people's lives.

'I don't envy you your job,' Williamson said, shaking his head.

Nottingham laughed. 'Why's that?'

'All you see is misery. People hurt, robbed, even dead.'

'But we catch the people who did it. That rights a wrong. Surely that's a good thing?'

'It's what you have to go through to do it. It makes my life seem very straightforward.'

'For what it's worth, I couldn't be a merchant.'

Nottingham stood up, leaving his own history unspoken. His father had been a merchant, one who'd sold his business and moved away after throwing out his family. All he'd left his son was his surname.

'Be glad you're not,' Williamson told him. 'It's a brutal business, Richard.'

The Constable grinned. 'Just not as brutal as mine.'

With a wave he headed back to the city. He felt frustrated. The more he learned, the less he seemed to know or understand about this case. As he walked he pried the pieces apart in his mind and tried to slowly reassemble them to see if they made any more sense.

They had a girl who'd been murdered, one who'd been married for just a year to a man much older than her. She might have been pregnant. She had a lover she saw weekly who had killed himself after she'd died. She'd gone to

163

visit her parents and taken her maid, but never arrived. The maid was missing.

Her husband had paid her parents handsomely to have her in marriage, but he'd fallen in love with her.

That was what they knew. He was certain that she hadn't been the victim of a robbery on the highway. If that had happened she'd just have been left by the road. They wouldn't have used an expensive knife and left it in her body. So it was someone who knew her.

He needed more. He needed the small pieces that would connect these items and let him see the real picture. As it was, the fragments he possessed couldn't even tell him how large that picture might be. Until he had more information, something solid, he'd be like a dog chasing its tail and becoming more and more frustrated. Someone had wanted Sarah Godlove dead. If he could only understand why, he might be able to find out who.

The Constable was still trying to make sense of everything as he entered the jail.

'Boss?' Lister said, shaking Nottingham into the present. 'I think I've got something here.'

'What's that?' He sat down, hopeful for anything that might move them along.

'I've been going through Will's business letters. From the look of them he was trying to sell his share of Tunstall's.'

'What?' He stopped. 'Are you sure?'

'I'm positive.' He picked up the letters and riffled through them. 'From what I can see, it

164

started about three weeks ago. He wrote to a few people who might be interested. Said he was looking to leave Leeds.'

The Constable's heart started beating a little faster. 'Did he say why at all?'

'Not that I've found,' Rob replied. 'He had two people who were interested, one from Bradford, another from Wakefield. Quite seriously, too, from the look of the letters. But it all stopped about three days before he killed himself.'

'Which would be when news of Sarah's death would have started to spread,' Nottingham mused.

'They could have been running off together.'

'It's possible,' he allowed guardedly. 'How much was he asking for his share of Tunstall's?'

'Enough to live on quite well for a while.'

The Constable sat down, brushing the fringe off his forehead.

'Go back over all the letters from Sarah, see if there's anything to indicate them leaving together.'

'I didn't see anything before—' Rob started, but Nottingham held up his hand.

'We didn't know what to look for before. There might be something in there that makes sense in the light of this. Have you found anything else?'

'That's all.' Lister started to knead his neck. 'What's it like outside?' he asked with a weary grin that made the Constable laugh.

'Don't worry. You'll be back out there soon enough, and then you'll be wishing you were

165

back here with some papers.'

'If you say so, boss.' Rob smiled.

'Just make sure you go through everything today. Tell me in the morning if there's anything more.'

'Yes, boss.'

Past Timble Bridge he looked into the distance, watching the small specks of men working in the fields, and the sheep grazing contentedly on the grass. This murder was weighing hard on him. Every scrap, every pace ahead had to be hard won, it seemed.

He wanted to put it all behind him when he stepped through his doorway, but he knew it was never as simple as turning a key in a lock. Whatever he did, it would nag quietly at the back of his mind. It was simply his way. He loved his job, too much perhaps.

Emily was sitting in the chair. She'd been reading, but looked up with a warm smile when he entered. Her eyes were bright and her skin clear, all the traces of her misery now history. In a way he envied her her youth, being able to put things behind her so quickly.

'I went to see Mrs Rains at the Dame School today,' she told him.

'Was she surprised to see you?'

'Yes,' Emily answered with a little laugh. Mrs Rains had recommended her for the post as Hartington's governess.

He settled down across from her. 'What did she have to say?'

'Well,' she began, and from the way she lowered her head, the colour rising in her face, he could tell that she was eager with good news, that it needed to burst out of her. 'She asked if I'd like to teach there with her.'

'Really?' he asked and she nodded emphatically, biting her lip, her grin wide. 'Oh, love, that's wonderful.' He reached across, squeezed her hand and kissed her flushed cheek. 'What did your mother say?'

'She said she thought it was the best news she'd heard in a long time. She's gone into town to buy some cloth to make me a new dress for work.'

Nottingham laughed, infected by her joy. 'So when do you start?' he asked.

'Next week,' she answered excitedly. 'She wants me to begin on Monday. It's going to be so lovely, papa. I can live here, and the school's become quite busy now, I'll be doing a lot of teaching on my own, too. That's why I'm reading now.' She indicated the small pile of books next to her. 'I have to be ready.'

'You'll do very well,' he assured her. 'I have faith in you – and so does your mother.'

'Thank you, papa.' Her smile was wide enough to light up any room. 'And thank you for persuading Mr Hartington to write his recommendation. I don't know how you managed to do that...'

He stood up and ruffled her hair.

'Don't you worry about how. You've got a position that'll suit you well. Just make sure you work at it.'

'I will, papa,' she promised with pleasure.

In the kitchen he found cheese under a cloth, bread and ale and he'd just returned to the sitting room when Mary arrived home with two lengths of cloth under her arm.

'Oh, Richard,' she said, 'I'm sorry I'm late. I had to go and buy these.' She glanced at their daughter, eyes twinkling. 'Did Emily tell you?'

'She did, and it's glorious news.'

'If she's going to be teaching she needs a new dress and petticoat, so I thought I'd sew one.' She gave Emily the plain cotton. 'You can make the petticoat,' she told her. 'It'll be good practice for you. I'll do the dress.'

'Yes, mama,' the girl replied with no real enthusiasm. Mary rolled her eyes and vanished into the kitchen. Nottingham followed her. Dust motes hung in the sunlight through the window.

'I haven't had a chance to cook anything today,' she explained.

'This is fine,' he told her, holding up his plate. 'What do you think about our daughter, the teacher?'

'I think she'll probably be self-important and insufferable for a while,' Mary answered with a sardonic smile. 'But it'll be good for her. And she'll be here with us.'

'You've missed having her here, haven't you?' He reached across and stroked the back of her hand.

'I liked it with just the two of us,' she said with a low, thoughtful sigh. 'But somehow it feels

168

more complete with her here again.'

'She'll go in time, you know. She'll meet someone and be wed.'

Mary looked up at him, her eyes wide. He knew she was thinking of Rose, married and so soon dead.

'That's for the future, Richard. She has plenty of time for that.'

He took a mouthful of cheese and drank from the mug.

'We could take a walk later if you like,' he suggested. 'Just the two of us. Emily has her reading to keep her busy.'

'And I'll have my sewing if I'm going to finish her dress by next week. I need to measure her, cut out the fabric.' She sighed and closed her eyes for a moment. 'I can't, Richard, I'm sorry. I'm going to be up until all hours every night.'

'It's fine,' he told her softly and dropped a gentle kiss on her forehead.

His coat hung on the hook and he delved in the pocket for the folded and crumpled copy of the *Mercury* before sitting down. As usual there was little in it he wanted to know. Reports copied from the London papers that had circulated a week or two before, a short item each on Sarah Godlove and Will Jackson that offered nothing new. There were marriages in Mirfield, and someone was offering Dr Daffy's pills, proven to be efficacious for gout and too many other things to count. He dropped the newspaper on the floor and closed his eyes.

169

The banging on the door woke him. He started up, blinking and disorientated for a second. He was alone in the room. Somewhere upstairs he could hear Mary and Emily talking. Light was still coming through the window, but lower now – he must have slept a couple of hours.

'Wait,' he shouted in a thick voice, shaking his head to clear it. He lifted the latch. Sedgwick was waiting outside. This wouldn't be good news, he could see from the deep frown on the deputy's face.

'Someone found a body, boss. I think it might be Sarah's maid.'

Fifteen

He took his coat from the hook and pulled it on as they walked quickly into the city.

'Where was the body?'

'In some woods out along the river, going towards Kirkstall.'

'Who found it?'

'Someone out snaring coneys,' the deputy said. 'It's private land,' he added pointedly.

'I don't care if it's the King's bloody court,' Nottingham said, 'not if there's a corpse. Is someone bringing it in?'

'Aye, I've got two of the men on it.'

'Have you seen her?'

'Yes,' Sedgwick answered, his face sombre, the pock marks on his cheeks standing out in the dying light.

'How bad is it?'

'Bad, boss.' He grimaced. 'Been there a while and the animals have been at it.'

'So what made you think it was Anne Taylor?'

They were heading up Kirkgate at a crisp pace. As they passed the Parish Church the Constable cast a glace at the churchyard; even in the twilight his eyes immediately picked out Rose's grave.

'Well, it's a girl, I can tell that much, and what's left of her hair is dark. Slender.'

'Was she clothed?'

'Not much of it left, but she had been. I don't think we'll ever be able to find out what killed her. I told the coroner. The men will bring her in after he's seen her.'

They settled in the jail to await the body.

'We need to see if there's any way to identify her and tell the family,' Nottingham said. 'They'll want to bury her.'

Sedgwick slipped next door for a mug of ale and the Constable pushed at his cheeks with his palms, rubbing away the last of the sleep. If the corpse was Anne it would simply confirm what he suspected. But it didn't help them find the killer.

He was still sitting with his thoughts about it when the door opened and two of the night men struggled in with a bundle on a willow hurdle, covered with a wretched, stained old blanket. They knew what to do, and carried it through to the cell the city kept as a morgue. On their way out he gave them a few coins for ale; if the remains were as far gone as the deputy had said, they'd need a drink.

He went through and pulled off the cover. But after a single glance he had to turn away, breathing slowly and shallowly to keep down the bile rising in his chest. Sedgwick hadn't said enough. This was far beyond bad.

Nottingham took a kerchief from his breeches pocket and tied it around his face, trying vainly to keep the stench of death away. The putrefaction was so strong it made his eyes water and he had to keep stopping to wipe them with his sleeve.

The corpse had been a young woman, he could make out that much, but God only knew what she'd looked like. Her eyes were gone, pecked away, the skin all over her body chewed by beasts. One arm had been gnawed off, the teeth marks still sharp on the bone, maggots and flies crowding around the thick dried blood of the stump.

He did what he could to try and find anything recognisable in the decomposed flesh, stopping often to clear his mouth with a swig of ale, carefully examining what was left of the body. With what little remained there was no possibility of discovering what had killed her; John had been right on that. He did manage to find a birthmark, a small patch of darker skin on the skin around her hip, but nothing more. It might be enough to identify her.

He came out shaking his head and downed a deep cup, not tasting the beer but feeling it swill through his mouth, cleansing it.

'Better get her out of here as soon as possible,' he said, sitting down gratefully. 'Find someone to take her tonight. And have the undertaker put her in a coffin with the lid nailed down.'

'Right, boss.'

'This man who found her, what did he have to say for himself?'

'He hadn't been around there for a couple of

173

weeks, or so he claimed. He'd gone down to set up some snares, found her and sent word into town. When I got there he was shaking and pale. Couldn't tell me much, just what he'd found. You think it's the maid?'

'Probably,' Nottingham admitted. 'There's not been any other reports of missing girls. Was she well off the path?'

'Aye, in among some trees. She'd been covered with branches before the animals got to her. I looked around but I couldn't see anything else.'

'Probably nothing else to find,' the Constable said in an empty voice. 'There is something more, though. When Rob looked through Jackson's letters it looked as if he was going to sell his share in the company and leave Leeds.'

'So the pair of them would go together?'

'In the end it makes sense, doesn't it?' The Constable poured himself another mug of ale. The taste of death had gone from his mouth now and he could finally savour the drink. 'If they went off to London or somewhere no one would know them. They could live as man and wife.'

'What about Anne?'

'Most likely she'd have gone with them. Think about all the questions if she went back to her family.'

Sedgwick stretched in the chair and yawned. 'All of which makes Godlove the most likely to kill her.'

'I know.' Nottingham ran a hand through his hair. 'But I can't see it. If he did, the man's a fine

174

actor. Why, John? That's what I really can't understand. Why would anyone want Sarah dead? The way I see it, we only have Godlove, or Jackson if she'd decided to stay with her husband. Am I wrong? Have I missed something?'

'We'll just have to keep digging, boss.' He yawned again, covering his mouth with his hand.

'I'll go up to Roundhay tomorrow and talk to the servant's parents.'

'I'll go if you want, boss. I've met them.'

The Constable shook his head. 'No, it's only right they hear it from me. You go home.'

'I will.' The deputy stood. 'One thing I should tell you.'

'I hope it's good news,' Nottingham said wearily.

'It is.' He smiled proudly. 'Our Lizzie's going to have a baby. I'm going to be a father again.'

The Constable laughed. 'John, that's wonderful.' He stood and extended his hand. 'How is she?'

'As good as ever. She didn't want me to tell anyone, but...' He shrugged helplessly.

'I know,' Nottingham said, 'I felt the same, wanting to tell everyone. Still, at least it explains the gormless smile you've had for a few days. Make sure she looks after herself.'

'I will, boss.'

Sedgwick made a circuit of the city, checking on all the night men before he went home. By the time he finally reached the room it was full dark,

175

the stars generous in the sky. Enough of the moonlight came through gaps in the shutters that he could see his way. After undressing he knelt, stroking James's hair as the boy slept on, unaware. A brother or sister soon enough, he thought, then crossed his fingers. Too much could go wrong. God forbid he'd lose Lizzie or the baby.

She was asleep when he climbed into the bed, her body warm enough that he had to roll away from her to stay cool. If anything the heat had increased since night had fallen and he pushed the threadbare sheet down to let the air at his body.

Once the baby arrived he'd want more time at home, a chance to be with Lizzie, to see the little ones grow. He'd need to have Lister trained by then, assuming the lad stayed – he hoped that he would. Rob was learning quickly, applying himself and doing whatever they asked.

He reached over to lightly touch Lizzie's back where it curved out to her hips. Her skin was soft, and she stirred slightly as his fingertips rested on her.

'John,' she mumbled finally, 'don't.'

With a quiet smile he fell into sleep.

The three of them were sitting in the jail at six. The air had grown heavier, and simply walking into town Nottingham had felt the sweat rolling down his back, leaving his linen shirt sticking to his skin.

'Did you find anything else, Rob?'

176

'Nothing, boss.'

'No matter. We know a little more than we did. Did Mr Sedgwick tell you what happened last night?'

'Yes.' Rob blanched. 'He did.'

'I'm going up to Roundhay this morning to try and find out if the body is Anne Taylor,' Nottingham confided. 'You two work on these missing thieves, we need to find them quickly. I don't even know what else we can do on the Godlove murder at the moment.'

By the time he reached Roundhay village he was soaked from the heat and the horse was lathered with perspiration, eager to drink at the stone trough by the road. He let it have its fill then tied it and made his way to the first cottage. The door was open, and the smell of pottage cooking on the fire made him hungry.

He knocked and waited until the woman came bustling through. She halted when she saw him and he noticed the expression in her eyes change to one of bright fear.

'You've come about Anne, haven't you?' she asked.

'I'm sorry, I have. I'm Richard Nottingham, the Constable of Leeds. Is your husband here, too?'

'He's over in t' fields.'

'Is there someone you can send to fetch him?' he asked soberly. He wanted both of them, to give comfort to each other if nothing more.

'Wait,' she ordered and walked to the cottage across the road. After a few words she returned.

177

'He'll be here soon.' Awkwardly, hesitantly, she said, 'You'd better come in and have a stoup of ale. It's not at its best, I was going to brew some more today.'

They were words just to fill the space, he knew that, to ward off the ghosts that drifted in the silence, but the drink was welcome as they sat in the shade of the room. Finally a short, stocky man arrived, rubbing at his hands with a dirty kerchief. His arms were well muscled from years of labour in the fields.

'What is it, love? They said you needed me quick.'

She glanced at Nottingham. 'This man here's come out from Leeds about Annie. He's the Constable.'

'Oh aye?' Taylor turned and Nottingham could see the anguish in his eyes, the prayer for good news that wasn't going to come.

He stood up. 'I'm sorry to have to ask,' he said quietly, 'but does Anne have a birthmark?'

'She does,' her mother said firmly, fingers reaching out to grip her husband's hand.

'Where?'

'About here,' she answered, pointing at her hip.

'What does it look like?'

For a moment the woman seemed confused. 'Not like anything, really. Just darker, I suppose.'

'I'm very sorry.'

Taylor gathered his wife close, never taking his eyes off the Constable. She was huddled

178

against him, her arms tight around his back, releasing the tears that had been building since the deputy's visit. The man's face remained stony.

'Where did you find her?' he asked.

'In some woods, just outside the city.'

'How long had she been there?'

'A while,' Nottingham admitted.

The man gave a short nod.

'I'll arrange to have her brought out here so you can bury her properly,' the Constable offered. 'I'm sorry.'

'Thank you.'

The man kept his wife tight against him. Nottingham stood. He had nothing more to say that they'd want to hear. Quietly he made his farewell and left them. Outside the heat wrapped around him like a blanket as he climbed back on the horse.

Should he go and see Gibton while he was out here?

'Thank you for coming out yourself.' Taylor was standing there, a man who moved silently, for all his bulk. 'And for not saying she'd been killed.'

'It was the least I could do.' He looked at Taylor. 'I lost a daughter myself earlier this year.'

'The wife really believed she was still alive.'

'I'm sorry,' he repeated.

'Never a word of concern from them, of course.' He inclined his head towards the distance, but there was no need; the Constable

179

knew exactly who he meant.

'To be fair, they've lost a daughter of their own,' Nottingham said.

'Aye, I know that.' He coughed and spat on the ground. 'And I went round to say how sorry we were when I heard. Him there didn't even say he was grateful, never mind that our Annie had been Sarah's maid for years.'

'Grief can do that.' He was surprised to hear himself defending the Gibtons.

'Mebbe,' Taylor conceded with a frown. 'But then her comes out and starts shrieking at me, saying it must have been our lass who led Sarah astray.'

'Led her astray?'

'Aye.' He stared up at Nottingham and shook his head in bitter exasperation. 'Exactly what she said. Made no sense but she's always been a shrew. Mad, some folk reckon.'

'What about this money they got last year?' He could see that the man needed to talk, to do anything to take his mind off his loss.

Taylor spat again. 'No secret that the man paid for the lass's hand. Annie told me that herself. Didn't tell her mother much, mind, but we'd talk sometimes when she visited.'

'And what about Sarah, how did she feel?'

'Not too happy, from what Annie said. Seems she had a young man before, and she didn't want to give him up.'

'What did her parents say?'

Taylor stroked the horse's head between the eyes and didn't answer for a few moments.

Then, 'Told her to grow up, that they'd arranged a damn good marriage for her.'

'How serious was all this romance?'

'Strong, I reckon.' Taylor moved, setting himself in the shade on the other side of the animal. 'She'd been seeing him a little while. Loved him, Annie told me. He was just unsuitable for what her parents wanted for her marriage.'

'Not rich enough, you mean?'

'Aye, summat like that.' He gave a cold smile.

'Do you know if Sarah gave him up after she was wed?'

'Annie never said she was still seeing him.'

Nottingham brushed the fringe off his forehead. The hair was damp and stuck to his skin. He debated telling Taylor what he knew. If Anne had confided anything in him, it might help.

'From what we've been able to find out, Sarah was still seeing him regularly. They were planning to leave together.'

The man raised his eyebrows. 'Well, I'm glad love meant more to her than money, any road,' he said.

'Did your daughter give you any indication?'

'Not really.' He scratched his head. 'Last time she was here she did say Sarah might be with child.'

Nottingham's eyes widened. 'She told you instead of her mother?'

Taylor smiled wistfully. 'She loved her mam well enough, but like I said, I was the one she talked to. Allus was that way.' He sighed. 'You think the child might be this other man's?'

181

'It could be,' Nottingham agreed guardedly. If she was pregnant by Jackson, then this would be the perfect time to leave and set up somewhere new. They'd arrive as a couple with some money and a baby on the way. Who'd think twice about that?

Taylor looked thoughtful. 'And what about Annie? Were they going to take her?' he asked.

'I don't know,' the Constable answered truthfully. The man had been forthright, and he deserved honesty in return. 'If I had to guess, I'd say yes. She'd been privy to all Sarah's plans, after all. She'd always gone with her mistress when she met her lover. They trusted her. So, for what it's worth, I think Anne would have gone with them.'

'You think our Annie and Sarah were killed because of all this?'

'I don't know why they were killed,' Nottingham told him with a weary shake of his head. 'I'm trying to find out. And that's why anything I can learn is useful.'

'When you find out, will you come and tell us?' Taylor asked. 'Just so we know why Annie had to die.'

'I will,' Nottingham promised. He pushed his heels against the horse's flanks and the animal moved off. Perhaps it was time to see the Gibtons again, after all.

He rode along the drive to the house with his thoughts rolling and tumbling. A gardener was working, scything part of the lawn, arms moving in long, limber arcs. Even though high clouds remained teasingly in the sky, the heat was still gathering and Nottingham wiped the sweat from the back of his neck.

When he dismounted no one hurried out to greet him. He tethered the horse and walked slowly to the door, raised the polished brass of the knocker, warm to his touch, and let it fall against the wood.

It took a minute until he heard footsteps pattering inside and the serving girl opened the door, face flushed with running.

'I'm sorry, sir,' she said with a small curtsey. She was close to Emily's age, hair gathered loosely under a cap, her eyes full of worry and work in a friendly, good-hearted face.

'Is Lord Gibton in?' he asked. 'I'm Richard Nottingham, Constable of Leeds. I've been here before.'

'I remember, sir,' she replied. 'Lord and Lady Gibton are gone for the day.'

'Ah well. I wanted to tell them how things were moving in the hunt for their daughter's killer.'

'I'm sorry, sir,' the girl repeated. 'They'll be back this evening, I think.'

'How long have you worked here?'

'Me, sir?' The girl looked astonished at the question. 'About a year, I think.'

'Do they keep you busy?'

Her eyes flicked around quickly, making sure no one was in earshot. 'They do, sir. There aren't enough of us to do all the work,' she said quietly.

He nodded sympathetically. 'What's your name?' he asked.

'Alice, sir.'

'Did you see Mrs Godlove when she was here?'

'Yes, sir, course I did, lots of times. She came to visit regular, about every month, her and Anne.' She hesitated. 'Do you know what happened to Anne?'

'That's why I was out in the village. We found her body. I'm sorry.'

Alice looked down for a moment. When she raised her head again only willpower was keeping her features composed.

'You know they were supposed to visit when she was murdered?'

'I heard that. But I wasn't here.'

'Oh?' It was Nottingham's turn to appear surprised.

'He give us all time off, me, the cook, the footman and the gardener. There's only the four of us work here, sir. The place needs lots more but the master won't pay to have more people. Three days, he give us. We all have family local, he said we could go and see them.'

'So you never saw if Sarah and Anne arrived?'

'No, sir, but she wasn't expected, anyway. We all went on Thursday morning, and we come back Saturday night, like they told us.'

Now that, he thought, was very strange. He'd never heard of anyone giving all the servants time off together.

184

'Every single one of you went?' he asked, and she nodded. 'Why would he do that?'

'It was the mistress, sir.' She lowered her voice to a whisper. 'She takes the black dog sometimes and gets right bad. The master said she didn't want anyone but him around. He was even willing to pay us for the time, which isn't like him, if you know what I mean. That's how serious it was. But we hadn't to say anything about it. He doesn't want people to know how she gets. Then he said if we weren't back on time not to bother returning. Same if we ever breathed a word of it.'

'And did you all show up?'

'Yes, sir.' She gave a hard, frustrated smile. 'No choice, really, there are no jobs 'less you go into Leeds and I don't like it there.'

'Has he ever done this before?' Nottingham asked, still astonished.

'No, sir.' Alice blushed slightly. 'But, God forgive me for saying so, they're an odd pair.'

'How do you mean?'

'We all try to keep out of her Ladyship's way. She has an evil temper on her. She comes out with language you don't hear in an alehouse, sir, and she'll even let fly at the master with her tongue.' She stopped abruptly, realizing she might have said too much.

'Don't worry,' the Constable assured her, 'I won't say a word.'

'Thank you, sir.'

'How was Lady Gibton when you got back?'

'Still in her bed. But come Sunday she was up

and off to church, right as you like. Please, sir,' she begged, her eyes desperate, 'promise you won't say anything?'

'I promise,' he assured her. 'I'll come back and see Lord Gibton another time. Best we both forget I was here today, don't you think?'

Alice smiled gratefully. 'Yes, sir. Thank you.'

Sixteen

He decided to take the long road back to Leeds. For a short journey that had seemed so straightforward when he set out, he was returning with much to consider. The old Roman road petered out where it crossed the bigger Newcastle road and he turned, letting the horse take its time as he rode towards Chapel Allerton. There was a tavern there that he knew, a place he'd visited often when there were hangings up on Chapeltown Moor. They'd have water for the animal and something good to slake his own thirst.

So Sarah had had a lover before she was wed, and he was as certain as he needed to be that it had been Will Jackson. And it hadn't ended after her marriage. He understood why she'd played things so close and her maid had said nothing. Secrets always spread like a wild fire once they were out; a word, a whisper was all it took.

What really puzzled him, though, was what he'd learnt at the Gibton house. However strange the man was, he'd never heard of behaviour like that before. From all the tales, he hoped he'd never meet her Ladyship, but things must have been bad if he'd sent the servants away for a few days. The timing, too, was especially interesting.

It was no surprise, perhaps, that Lord Gibton hadn't mentioned it during their interview. More secrets to keep quiet. A family with plenty of those, it seemed.

At the inn he settled the horse at the trough and bought a mug of ale, deliciously cold, with just enough edge of bitterness to satisfy him. Two farmers were talking quietly in another corner of the room, but otherwise he had the place to himself.

The more he thought, the more he wondered at the curious coincidence of Lady Gibton's dark mood happening just when her daughter was due to visit. He didn't care for coincidences. He mulled it over, slowly and deliberately examining the idea, until eventually he was willing to concede that coincidence was all this might be. Sarah's visit to her parents was a surprise. Godlove had told him that right at the start. So they wouldn't have known she was coming.

The more he discovered about the family, the more it disturbed him. There was an ugly strain of madness in them. But there was more than that. He knew the gentry had their own ways, but to blatantly sell their daughter the way they had, that was cold, calculating, and beyond his understanding. At times a life with no social position to worry about was much easier.

He gulped down the remainder of the ale, and left. Time to reflect had only brought more confusion. While he'd been inside, clouds had thickened in the west until they were bearing down dark and thick from the Pennines and promising another storm to clean out the day.

Riding back down to Leeds the city was spread out before him, the spires of the churches standing out, with the sharp, warm colour of Red House visible on the Head Row. He felt a languor spreading through him, and for all the world he could have sprawled out and slept for an hour under a tree.

But he wasn't going to have the chance. It was still only late morning and there was plenty to do before he could rest. He returned the horse and walked back to the jail, his joints aching from the ride. He was getting older, no doubt of it. In his forties now, he was still fit and fair, but the pains and rheums came more easily and lingered longer. The hair that had once been so blond and handsome, his pride when he was younger, was paler now, with streaks of silver to mark the time. At least, he thought vainly, he hadn't gone bald the way so many did. There were a few small mercies.

The jail was empty save for one man in a cell. The deputy had left a note; the man was a pickpocket he'd caught in the act. Sedgwick and Lister were trying to find the missing servants. If Worthy reached them first they'd face the task of hunting for evidence against the pimp; that, he knew, would be close to impossible. None would peach on him. The vulnerable would keep quiet out of fear, the rich to seek favour.

He tried to write a report, but after two lines he put down the quill; he simply couldn't settle to it. It was the weather; it made his skin prickle and concentration was impossible. He pulled on the coat and left, ambling down Briggate and letting his feet take him where they would.

By the time he paid real attention he was already south of the river and walking out along Meadow Lane. In the last few years it had begun to turn into a grand avenue; a few merchants had built their homes over here, looking haughtily over the river, the courts and yards of the poor hidden away in the spaces behind the clean, proud frontages and deep, lush gardens. In the distance lay the Quaker Meeting house and burial place, a small, simple structure of plain stone.

Nottingham knew a few Quakers, all of them honest, sober men. He didn't understand their faith but he admired them for it. The last traces of his own belief had died in February with his older daughter. He still attended church, but the words he heard there had become nothing more than a familiar form that had lost all its meaning. Mary felt the same, he knew. How could anyone offer his soul to a God who'd rip his family apart for no reason?

He began to retrace his steps and had just reached Leeds Bridge when the first thunder came, its echo reverberating like doom along the valley. As if in answer, the first large drops of rain arrived, followed by the swift, startling crackle of lightning. The Constable stopped and raised his head, letting the water land on his face.

While others ran for shelter he stayed still, the coolness washing his skin, the comfort of the rain reaching his heart. He could feel the downpour soaking through his coat, but it didn't matter. Already the air seemed fresher, the sultriness vanishing.

By the time he reached the jail the heavy shower had passed, the air clear, dust damped down on the streets. The sun was out again but the overbearing heat had broken. Lister and the deputy were already there, deep in discussion over a mug of ale.

'Get caught in it again, did you, boss?' Sedgwick asked with a grin.

'Stayed out in it,' he replied, pushing a hand through his hair. 'It felt good after a morning in the saddle. Now, anything more on these thieves?'

'They're not staying at any of the inns,' Lister told him. 'But,' he added, 'a couple who could well be them have been seen drinking at a couple of alehouses and in the gin shop down on Call Lane.'

'When did someone last think they saw them?'

'Night before last,' the deputy answered. 'So it looks as if they're still here. They've probably found a room in one of the courts.'

Nottingham rubbed his chin against the back of his hand, feeling the rasp of stubble against his skin.

'Then it's only a matter of time until Worthy finds them. He's put the word out and there'll be plenty eager to get into his good graces with a quiet word. This pair must be stupid. Either that or they still don't know he's looking. Or they're planning something else here.' He thought for a minute. 'Is there any pattern to the places this couple might have been?'

'Mostly down towards the river, the Calls, Call Lane, up by Currie Entry. All this side of Briggate, though.'

'Right. John, take some of the men and start asking in the courts down there. Find the old women who sleep with their eyes open, they know everything that's going on. See if you can track these two down. I want them before Worthy can get his hands on them.'

'Yes, boss.'

'What about me?' Lister asked.

'I've got something else for you, Rob. I need to find out more about Baron Gibton's wife. Do you know anyone in those social circles?'

'Not really,' he said doubtfully. 'But I suppose my father would. Do you want me to ask him?'

'Yes, as long as you tell him that none of this can appear in the *Mercury*.'

'I will,' Rob agreed readily. 'What do you want me to ask these people?'

'I've been hearing some interesting things.' He recounted what he'd been told that morning. 'I want to find out just how mad she really is. I've never heard of anyone dismissing the servants for a few days before.'

'And if anyone's reluctant to say?'

Nottingham cocked an eyebrow. 'That says a

lot in itself, don't you think?'

'I suppose so,' Rob agreed.

'There's as much in what people don't say as in the words that come out of their mouths,' the Constable advised him. 'Remember that. I told you that listening well is a big part of what we do. Listening for what they don't say is just as important.'

'Yes, boss.' Lister grinned. 'Can you tell me something?'

'Go on.'

'Why do you want me doing this? I could have been out with Mr Sedgwick, helping to chase down those thieves.'

Nottingham smiled and patted him on the shoulder. 'Because you're more useful to me this way. Being your father's son will get you in to see the type of people who know the Gibtons, and they'll be more likely to talk to you than to me. Does that make sense?'

Lister nodded, doubt still in his eyes.

'Look, we all have our strengths,' the Constable explained. 'We just need to make the most of them. John can get more out of those women in the courts in five minutes than I could in a month. You'll be better at this. It makes sense to do what we do best.'

Rob knew where he'd find his father. The man spent far more time at the *Mercury* office than he did in his own home. He was at his desk, scratching away quickly with his quill, hair unkempt, the cuffs of his old, mended shirt black from ink. He never so much as glanced up when the door opened.

Lister flopped down in a chair and waited. He wouldn't receive any attention until his father had his thought written down satisfactorily. Finally the older man lifted his head. He started to smile then switched to a look of concern.

'Don't worry, they haven't got rid of me yet,' Rob grinned. 'I'm here on business.'

'Well, I'm pleased to hear that,' James Lister said with relief. 'You've bounced from job to job so much—'

'I plan on staying with this one, father. It's interesting. The Constable and Mr Sedgwick have a great deal to teach me.'

The older man raised his eyebrows. 'If you want to know about crime, I suppose they do,' he said archly. 'Now why has Mr Nottingham sent you here?'

'He wants me to talk to some people who know Lady Gibton, to see if she's as mad as she seems. And that's not for the paper,' he added quickly.

His father pursed his lips in distaste. 'Of all people, Robert, you should know I can keep a confidence as well as anyone.'

'When it suits you,' Rob laughed.

The older man shook his head in a sly grin. 'You know Matthew Simpson, don't you?'

'You know I do.' The pair were often in the inns together.

'Talk to his parents. They've dined with the Gibtons quite a few times and they might be able to tell you a few things. And if you catch Lucy Simpson on her own and charm her a bit she'll give you all the gossip you can stand.'

'That's a start,' Rob said. 'Is there anyone else?'

James Lister sat back, steepling his fingers over his ample belly.

'Try old Mrs Mapperly, if you can get any sense out of her,' he said finally. 'She lives out past Town End in one of those small cottages. If I remember rightly she knew Catherine Gibton's family; I can't recall their name just now.'

Rob stood. 'Thank you.'

'So you really do like this work?' his father asked doubtfully.

'I do. It's not like anything else. I think I've learned more about Leeds in the last few days than I ever knew before.'

'Just be careful,' his father warned. 'There are things worth knowing and things best left alone.'

'Don't worry, father, I'll be fine.'

The Simpsons lived on Kirkgate, between the jail and the church, just three doors from where Ralph Thoresby had kept his museum, empty now since his death but still famous in Leeds.

Matthew was off attending to his work as a lawyer, but his mother was happy to entertain one of his friends. Lucy Simpson was a smiling, guileless woman, one who didn't have enough to occupy her time, Lister guessed. She dressed smartly in all the fashions fresh from London, doing everything she could to hide her age, pulling her stays a little tighter each year, attending all the assemblies and concerts, and dining in the houses of friends all across the area.

'Catherine Gibton?' she said in surprise. 'Why would you want to know about her?'

'You know I work for the Constable now?' he asked her confidentially, and when she nodded he continued. 'It has to be secret. That's all I can tell you.' He knew her well enough to be certain she'd take the bait and he was right. In less that half an hour he'd learned everything he might want to know about Lady Gibton, although he was certain much of it was wild gossip, slander and outright lies.

But it was enough to establish that Catherine Gibton was a woman of delicate nerves, given to deep, dark moods and violent outbursts. She took every slight, real or imagined, to heart and never let any of them fall away.

She could lock herself away for days at a time when the black dog came, refusing food and raging loud and long into the night. If Lucy Simpson was to be believed, she'd become even worse in recent years; her madness could strike with little warning. It had reached the point where the baron and his wife attended fewer and fewer affairs. The title meant that the invitations still arrived, but so often they were refused.

It was a curious portrait Matthew's mother had painted, Rob thought as he walked up Briggate, the afternoon sun pleasingly warm on his back. The woman sounded like a terrible creature, shrill, fearsome and impossible to please, and in a strange way he felt sorry for the husband who had to live with it all.

He crossed the Head Row and passed St John's church, strolling out into Town End. This was where many of the merchants had chosen to build their large new houses, the brash statements of wealth that showed they could afford the cleaner air outside the city. The grammar school stood apart from everything in a field, and the whole area was a curious mix of country and town.

Virginia Mapperly's cottage was definitely part of the country. Old and run down, it must have stood there for generations, he decided, tucked away beyond the grandeur of the new mansions. He knocked politely on the door and waited, pulling down on his coat and waistcoat and checking that his stock was well tied. A good impression could count for a great deal.

The woman who eventually answered stood straight-backed, dressed in a silk gown that was long out of fashion but beautifully kept. Her right hand, mottled with the brown spots of age, rested on a polished stick and she regarded him with a long, inquisitive gaze.

'I don't know you,' she said in a firm voice.

'No, ma'am,' he agreed. 'I'm Robert, James Lister's son. He suggested I come to you.'

'I see,' she replied slowly, and he felt she was assessing him. Her hair was carefully brushed, powder on her face; she was elegant, looking as if she might be about to leave for an important

197

engagement. Finally she gave a sharp nod and said, 'Don't dawdle on the doorstep then, young man, you'd better come in.'

She still sat the way her governess must have taught her, rigid and upright on the polished wooden chair, her back rod straight. Across from her, taking the low stool she offered, he felt like a child.

'I knew your grandmother well,' she told him. 'She died before your time, I think?'

'Yes.'

'A wonderful woman, and hard pressed to keep that hellion who's your father in check,' she told him with a secretive smile. 'Did you know he was always in trouble? The masters at school would beat him, then his father would beat him because the masters had been forced to.'

Lister laughed. It was hard to imagine his father that way, rebellious and rabble-rousing.

'He said you knew Lady Gibton when she was young.'

'So that's why you're here.' She looked at him again, more curiously this time. 'And why do you want to know about her, I wonder?'

'I work for the Constable,' he explained, watching her eyebrows rise in surprise. 'We do need to know about her, and I'll keep all your confidences, but I must also ask that you don't say anything to anyone else.'

'And how did you come to work for Mr Nottingham, young man?' she asked.

'He was looking for someone, and I needed a

job.' He began to shrug then stopped, remaining on his best behaviour.

'His father was a merchant here, you know.'

'Really?' He didn't know that. This was a day for revelations, he thought.

'It's old business now,' she said dismissively. 'If he wants to tell you, I'm sure he will. Or you can always ask your father.'

'I'll do that.'

She looked at him, studying him closely, then seemed to come to a decision.

'So, Catherine Hall. That was her maiden name,' she explained. 'What do you want to know about her?'

'Anything you can tell me.'

'Well, Master Lister, pour me a glass from that decanter and I'll tell you what I know. It's not a great deal, I warn you.'

He took her some of the deep-red wine, watched as she sipped and set the crystal down delicately on a table. Her furniture, like everything in the room, was carefully chosen, and none of it cheap. She was a woman who'd had some money, he guessed, and who chose to keep the standards she'd always known even if her income was much lower now.

'She was the prettiest child I ever saw,' Mrs Mapperly began, smiling briefly at the memory. 'And very well behaved when she was little. Her father was a butcher, you know. He had a shop on the Shambles and did well for himself.'

'Is the family still there?'

She put a finger to her lips and continued.

199

'Everything was fine until Catherine was seven. Was it seven or eight? I forget after all this time. Anyway, she was outside her family's shop on Briggate and a cart toppled as it went by. She was trapped underneath. They managed to get her out and she seemed well enough, just bad bruises and scrapes, that kind of thing.' She paused to take another sip of the wine and stared into the liquid for a long time before picking up the tale. 'My guess is that she hit her head and something happened to her mind, though. After that this lovely girl developed an evil temper. She'd been so placid before, a kind, sweet thing to match her looks, but when she drew into her mood she started screaming and howling if anyone tried to stop her doing things. God knows her father tried to beat some sense into her, but that didn't work.' She took another small drink, swirling the glass lightly and watching the light refract off the wine. 'Her temper improved as she grew older, but she'd still fly into rages and break things. I think people forgave her because she'd turned into such a beautiful girl. People will tolerate a lot in beauty, it seems,' she said reflectively. 'All the young men wanted to marry her, but they weren't good enough for her mother. After all, the family had made a little money in trade, and with Catherine's face she thought she could aim high. Have you met Lord Gibton?'

'No, ma'am,' Rob replied.

'He was a charming young man back then. I suppose he had to be since the family had lost most of its wealth. Anyway, he believed he was getting a prize in Catherine, and her mother did everything but throw the girl at him so she'd have a title. I suspect the pair of them have spent all the years since then regretting it.'

'What do you mean?'

'He was so smitten with her looks that he never saw what was beneath them, and she discovered he wasn't being modest and that the Gibton family fortunes really were as badly off as he claimed. I suppose she must have inherited something when her parents died, but most of it went to her older brother.'

'Does he still live in Leeds?'

'No. He moved on as soon as he could. I can't blame him, really. He worked hard, never gave any trouble, and saw his sister receive all the attention. He was always going to be in her shadow here. He finished his apprentice as a butcher then went to set up shop in Sheffield.'

'How did you know the Halls, Mrs Mapperly?' Lister asked.

She finished the glass of wine and set it down.

'We were neighbours. My husband was a butcher, too. So I saw Catherine grow up. There were plenty of nights she'd keep us awake as she shouted and screamed. Poor girl,' she said with real sympathy.

'When did you last see her?'

'Oh, not for many years now.' She let out a long, slow breath. 'I suppose it would be not long after her daughter was born. She brought the baby to visit her parents, not that she came too often, mind you, once she was living out in Roundhay. I remember thinking that I felt sorry for the little girl, having to grow up with a mother like that.'

'You know her daughter died?' Rob asked.

She nodded and he could see the start of tears in the corners of her eyes.

'I read it in your father's newspaper.'

He sensed that he was losing her to the memories of years ago, when she had a husband and a life in the city. She hardly seemed to notice when he rose to his feet.

'Thank you,' he said as he rose, bowing briefly as he left.

Seventeen

The man's body had been heavily battered. Nottingham stared grimly at it on the slab in the cell they used as a morgue. He'd been young, the shape of his body and the thickness of his hair showed that, but his face had been so heavily pummclld, the bones all broken and the flesh swollen, that it was impossible to make out any features. He turned away. They'd found the corpse after a boy in threadbare breeches and a torn shirt had dashed into the jail, his features white with shock, eyes full of fear and excitement, and led them down to see his discovery in the woods by Sheepscar Beck.

Whoever he was, the man had put up an almighty struggle, his knuckles ripe and bloody, but he'd been overwhelmed. And then very carefully and coldly beaten to death. The Constable had examined him closely but hadn't found any deep cuts and there were no signs of stab wounds.

'What do you think?' he asked Sedgwick.

'It could be.' As soon as they'd seen the body they'd both wondered if this was Tom, the brother of the false servant Nan. It was exactly the kind of punishment Worthy would dole out for what the girl had done. 'He'd be about the right age, anyway. And killing him this way would fit. It would send a lesson.'

Gently, Nottingham pulled the sheet over the man. There was nothing more to see and no clues in the pockets, just a few small coins and a well-used handkerchief. The clothes gave nothing away, cheap and anonymous, once good perhaps, but he'd likely bought them from a stall at third or fourth hand. He could have been anyone from anywhere.

'But if this is Tom it still leaves the girl,' the deputy said.

'I know,' the Constable agreed slowly. 'And if Amos has her she'll get much worse than this.'

'What can we do about it?'

He ran a hand through his hair in frustration. Inside, he was sure this was the lad called Tom, and that the pimp's men had killed him. Worthy would have taken part; he wasn't a man to leave the satisfaction of revenge to someone else.

'I don't even know how we can prove who this is,' he said angrily, 'let alone who's responsible.'

'That's what he wants, isn't it?' Sedgwick said. 'Everyone knows, but there's no one can say or tie it to him. He's shown no one can cross him but we can't touch him. It's clever, you have to give him that.'

'And it's his reminder that he can flout the law.' Nottingham's eyes were dark with fury. 'I don't care what that boy had done, he didn't deserve to die like that.' He took a deep breath and reached for his coat. 'I'm going to see Amos.'

'Boss—' Sedgwick began, but the Constable had already left.

He pushed his way through the door and back into the kitchen. Worthy was standing there, leaning against the table and catching the sun through the dirty window. For once the fire wasn't lit, but the summer heat trapped in the room left it unpleasantly warm.

There were no guards lounging by the back door or against the wall. Worthy was eating in silence, bread and cheese on his plate, a full cup of ale before him. He turned slowly and smiled as the Constable entered.

'I wondered how long it would be before you showed your face,' he said. 'Do you want something to drink? Stop that thirst?'

'You know why I'm here.'

'Of course I do, laddie. You think I had something to do with the body you have in the jail.'

'I know you did, Amos.'

Worthy's eyes shone. 'If you're so certain, you'd better prove it, Mr Nottingham.' He held up his hands, turning them to show both sides, the skin unbroken. 'Does that look like I've been fighting?'

'So for once you had someone else do the work for you.'

'You want be careful, laddie.' His voice turned colder and more serious. 'Words like that could seem like slander.'

'How did you know someone had died if you weren't involved?'

'Little birds are always telling me things.' He broke off some of the bread and began to chew, letting crumbs spill carelessly down over his long waistcoat.

'They told you fast.'

'No point in knowing if you're not the first. It's old news by the time some other bugger has it.'

'What about the girl?' the Constable asked. 'What have you done with her?'

Worthy put down the bread and stared straight at him.

'I'll spell this out to you so you don't go making any mistakes. I don't have the girl. But I'll bloody well find her. And if you think I have summat to do with whoever you have on that slab, go ahead and prove it. I'll lay odds you can't do it, though. You want a wager on it?'

Nottingham didn't react, holding the older man's gaze for a long time.

'Get out,' the procurer said finally. 'I want to eat.'

The sky was just taking on its evening colours when Sedgwick arrived home. He closed the door with a long, exhausted sigh.

'Papa!' James ran to him, clutching at his legs and gazing up with large blue eyes, silently demanding to be picked up. The deputy grabbed him round the waist, tossing him lightly into the air and catching him as the boy squealed with joy. He nuzzled his nose against James's face, smelling the warm innocence of his hair then turning a circle with his son in his outstretched arms.

'You be careful,' Lizzie laughed. 'He had summat to eat a little while back. If he's sick you're going to be the one cleaning it up.'

'He'll be fine, won't you?' He pulled the lad close and kissed him then let him slide back down his body to the floor. Lizzie came over, holding him and feeling the weariness in his bones.

'Bad day?' she asked.

'Aye,' he answered, thinking again of the bloody, misshapen face on the slab and wanting to leave it all behind. 'But I'm home now.'

'Come on, get your coat off,' she told him, pulling lightly at the sleeves. 'You're settling in for the evening. There's some food on the table. You want some ale?'

He nodded and she filled his mug. The first long sip tasted good, the second even better. He sat down, moving his head around to try and ease the tension of work out of his neck.

'One of those days when you wonder why you do it?' Lizzie asked.

'Aye,' he said, taking her hand, and pulling her down so she sat on his lap with a happy squeal.

'I'm getting heavier, you know,' she told him and patted her belly. 'And I'll be bigger fast enough.'

'You'll be lovely.'

With a smile she punched him playfully on the

207

shoulder. 'You say that now, John Sedgwick. But when I'm waddling round big as one of them houses at Town End you'll think different.'

'I'll love you if you're as big as the bloody Moot Hall,' he laughed along with her and buried his face in her hair. He relished his work but he knew that this was what really kept him going, the prospect of coming home to these two. Here he could be a different person, or at least a different shade of the same person, gentler and kinder.

She stroked his hair as they sat, combing through it absently with her fingers, watching James as he played. Gradually he could feel himself relax, enjoying the closeness of this woman who wanted to be with him.

'We'll have to get a larger room,' she said.

'What?' he asked absently.

'Drifting off?' she asked with a sly sparkle in her eye. 'I was saying we'll need a bigger room when the baby's born.'

'We could start looking sooner, if you like.'

'I'd love to have a real home sometime,' she sighed. 'Nothing fancy, just more than one room.'

'Better dream on or find yourself a rich man, then. It won't happen on my wages.'

'One day when you're Constable.'

'If that ever happens, what with this new lad,' he said with a sigh. 'His father publishes the *Mercury*, so he'll know people.'

'Mr Nottingham said he'd speak up for you, didn't he?' Lizzie asked.

'Yes.'

'Then go ahead and trust him. Look at you, John Sedgwick, you're worried about someone who hasn't even been in the job five minutes.'

'I know,' he admitted sheepishly.

'You trust Mr Nottingham, don't you?'

'Of course I do.'

'He'll do what he said, you know that. And maybe you'll get me that house after all.'

'Well, there's a house with the job.' He grinned. 'Just don't go holding your breath, though. The boss has a few years in him yet.'

'I know,' she said. 'I'm just wishing. And you look like you're dead on your feet.'

'I'm fine for the moment,' he told her and glanced out of the window. 'It's not even properly dark yet.'

'I was thinking we could put James to bed and have an early night. You know.'

'I suppose I could stay awake for that. Just.'

'You'd better,' she warned him with a smile. 'Fall asleep in the middle and you'll wake up missing some bits.'

He woke midway through the night, a sudden idea springing into his brain. Even as his eyes opened it began to fade and he struggled to keep it there. Slowly he untangled his arm from around Lizzie, and moved silently across the room, digging a scrap of paper and a pencil from his coat.

As he pulled the sheet back over himself she stirred against him, her breathing becoming soft snores for a few moments before subsiding. He smiled, feeling loved and satisfied.

The morning seemed a little cooler, the air easier to breathe as the deputy walked to work. He could hear the bright chatter of servants through the open windows and the rattle of pots on stoves as they started to make breakfasts.

He'd had some bread and a few sips of ale, enough to set him up for now. He was never hungry first thing, but ravenous by dinner when he usually had a pie from one of the shops or street sellers.

The Constable was already at the jail, his coat draped over the chair and sleeves rolled up to show the hair on his arms bleached pale by the sun.

'There was a set-to overnight, boss. That's what Morris the night man told me,' Sedgwick said with a frown and Nottingham looked up, setting the quill aside.

'Nothing new there, John. It can't have been that bad, there's no one in the cells.'

'Bad enough.' He sat down across from the Constable. 'Seems like some of Worthy's men were going at it with some others.'

Nottingham sat upright, attentive. 'How many in all?'

'About eight or so. Morris wasn't sure.'

'And who were these other men?'

'He didn't know, but my guess is they belonged to Hughes.'

'Revenge for the whore who was cut.'

'Aye. And it lets Worthy know Hughes won't be leaving, too.'

'How many were hurt?'

'I don't know. Morris was on his own so he stayed out of the way.'

'Best thing,' Nottingham agreed with an approving nod.

'He did think one or two looked in bad shape.'

The Constable pinched the bridge of his nose, hoping to stop the throbbing he could feel building in his head.

'He beats someone to death and now this. Amos must be feeling pressed if he needs to push hard.'

'What did he say yesterday, boss?'

'Just what you'd expect. He knew all about it, of course, and challenged me to prove he had anything to do with it.'

'So what now?'

The Constable sighed. 'The good news is that he claims he doesn't have Nan.'

'Do you believe him?'

'Yes,' he replied slowly. 'If he knew where she was he wouldn't have said a word.' He sat and steepled his hands under his chin. 'I think it's time to go and meet Mr Hughes. Find out where he lives and we'll pay him a visit.'

'Yes, boss.'

Sedgwick slipped out, returning in less than ten minutes with a broad grin.

'House on the Calls. When do you want to go and see him?'

Nottingham gave a dark smile, stood up and

put on his coat.

'No time like the present, John. Let's see what our newest citizen is like.'

They walked down Kirkgate, then down Call Lane, taking their time, for all the world like two friends out enjoying the morning. Only the determined looks on their faces gave them away.

'How do you want to do this, boss?'

'I think we'll just make the acquaintance of Mr Hughes and remind him that we have law in Leeds. See if that's enough for him.'

Sedgwick pounded on the thin door with the flat of his hand, rattling it in its old, ill-fitting frame. The house was a cheap dwelling place, mortar slowly crumbling between the brickwork, the chimney pot sitting askew on the roof. They waited a minute and the deputy knocked again, banging until he heard the key turn inside.

'What do you want?'

The man was young and shirtless, showing off a stocky physique with well-muscled arms. His face was sallow, with a recent cut above his right eye and a deep bruise flowering around his left. His head was shaved smooth, glistening in the sunlight.

Nottingham glanced at the man's knuckles, cut and swollen, and knew without doubt he'd been part of the battle.

'Well?' the man asked, rubbing at his eyes, his voice still thick with sleep.

'You're Mr Hughes?' the Constable asked.

The man put his hands on his hips and smiled

212

comfortably. 'I am. Who wants to know?'

'I'm the Constable of Leeds. I want a word with you.'

'Oh aye?' Hughes raised his eyebrows.

'Inside,' Nottingham told him firmly. He locked eyes with the man, holding his gaze until Hughes moved aside.

The parlour was a jumble, with clothes and rubbish idly scattered across the floor. The sound of voices came from upstairs, men and women both, and footsteps clattered on the boards over their heads.

'What do you want, Constable?' Hughes asked. He picked up a dirty mug from the floor and took a swig from it.

'In a fight, were you?' Sedgwick asked.

'Mebbe.' He looked from one of them to the other.

'Where are you from, Mr Hughes?' the Constable wondered.

'Why? Does it matter?' His tone had become sullen.

Nottingham smiled graciously. 'Just taking an interest. From the sound of you it's not anywhere around Leeds.'

'Doncaster,' Hughes conceded.

'How many of you are there?'

'Eight. Four girls and the rest of us.'

'One of your lasses was hurt recently,' the deputy said.

'Someone cut her, aye.'

'That's a crime. Why didn't you report it?'

Hughes shrugged.

213

'So you're running four whores, Mr Hughes?'

'Am I?'

'You are.' The Constable's voice turned hard. 'Your girl wouldn't have been out and there wouldn't have been a fight last night if you weren't.'

'Old man Worthy paying you, is he?' Hughes sneered.

'Only the city pays me, Mr Hughes. You'd do very well to remember that.'

Hughes looked doubtful, uncertain whether to believe what he was hearing.

'And if I have some girls?'

'It's against the law,' Nottingham began, 'but men are always going to pay for girls. As long as there's no trouble we pay it no mind.'

'I didn't start any trouble.'

'But you kept it going last night,' Sedgwick told him. 'We don't play fear or favour here.'

'It stops, Mr Hughes,' the Constable ordered. 'And I'll be telling Amos Worthy the same.'

'The old bugger's past it, anyway,' Hughes said, 'letting himself be taken in by a servant girl.'

Nottingham said nothing, allowing the silence in the room to build.

'You know the rules now.'

'And if I don't obey them?'

'Then you'll pay the consequences,' the Constable said simply, 'and by Christ, you'll wish you'd listened. Good day, Mr Hughes.' He turned on his heel and left, followed by the deputy.

Outside, the pair walked in silence for a while.

214

'You think he'll listen?' Sedgwick asked finally.

Nottingham shook his head. 'No. He thinks with his pizzle and his fists, that one. He's not going to listen to reason. Have some of the men keep an eye on him. He's going to be trouble.'

'What about Worthy?'

'I'll talk to him again. Keep looking for Nan.'

'If we find her first Worthy's going to look weak.'

'That's for him to deal with. He got one of them, and I'll be damned if he gets the pair.'

They walked into the empty jail and Sedgwick looked around.

'Did Rob come back this morning?'

'He did. I sent him back to Jackson's rooms to see if there's anything more he can find. He's probably still there. He did turn up some interesting stuff about Lady Gibton. Seems she really does have a touch of insanity. That backs up what her husband said to me.' He paused. 'I don't know who killed Sarah Godlove, but every bit of this seems to stink of money and power,' he said with distaste.

'You'll find that anywhere,' the deputy commented.

'Very likely,' Nottingham agreed. 'But it's dirty stuff, wherever it happens. And it's not in Leeds. I'd never heard of any of these people before this happened.'

'Godlove didn't seem too bad.'

'Maybe not,' he answered. 'But I'm going to have to look at him again. The more this goes

215

on, the more things seem to point towards him. If he knew about his wife and Will Jackson he certainly had a reason to kill her, in his own mind at least.'

'I thought you'd decided he was innocent.'

The Constable sighed in frustration. 'I know, that's what I thought. It's what I still feel. But the more I look at it, I just don't know where else to turn.' He ran a hand through his hair. 'We shouldn't have to take all this on. It's not as if Leeds doesn't have crime without looking outside the city.'

'I wish we could arrest that bugger Worthy.'

'So do I,' Nottingham agreed, his eyes flickering towards the morgue. 'If we did he'd be out in an hour, though. There's no evidence. And even if we had something, his friends among the aldermen would have him gone soon enough.'

'Nothing we can do?'

'No,' the Constable said vehemently. 'Sod all.'

'I had a thought about Jackson.' He reached into his pocket and found the paper, squinting to make out his sleepy scrawl. 'What if his business partner knew he was going to sell out his share of the business?'

Nottingham stopped moving the papers on his desk and looked at the deputy with curiosity.

'What do you mean?'

'Well, Tunstall wouldn't be happy if he found out, would he? He'd be getting a new partner, no say in the matter.'

'Go on.'

'It could be reason enough to commit murder.'

'The only problem is that Jackson killed himself.'

'But what if he didn't?'

The Constable thought, then answered slowly.

'I just don't see it, John. Either way Tunstall would end up with a new partner. And the note indicates Jackson was a suicide. It was in his own writing. Do you think Tunstall's that clever?'

'Aye, maybe you're right,' Sedgwick conceded sadly. 'It came to me while I was sleeping.'

'Never ignore your hunches,' Nottingham advised. 'They'll be right often enough.'

'Just not in this case.'

'No, John. Sorry.' He smiled. 'So what are we going to do about Nan? If Worthy really was telling me the truth then she's still out there.'

'After what happened to her brother, or whatever he was, she'll have run as far from here as she can.'

'I hope so. But if she hasn't, we still need to find her. If we don't, Worthy's men will and we'll be looking at another corpse.'

'All the inns and alehouses must be sick of us asking about her by now.'

'At least they'll notice her if she walks in,' Nottingham said. 'Get the men out on a sweep of them again. And the places where she might sell what she's stolen. She still needs to eat and drink.'

'Yes, boss.' He stood and prepared to leave.

'How's Lizzie?'

'Strong as an ox.'

The Constable smiled. 'Then let's pray she remains free of any trouble.'

'Aye, true enough.' Sedgwick held up a pair of crossed fingers. He was smiling but inside he was wishing fervently that all would go well. To lose her would break him and devastate James. The boy had only just become used to a loving mother. He could learn to share her with someone else, but not to be without her entirely.

He'd never had to do so much riding when looking into a crime before. It wasn't something he relished. Still, it could have been worse. The weather was set fair, the sun pleasant and not too hot, a faint breeze like whispers beyond hearing. If he really had to ride to out Godlove's estate, this was a day for doing it.

The horse took the hill at a slow, easy pace that suited the Constable. He didn't know what he could ask Godlove that he hadn't already asked, or if there was anything that might trip him up. But at least by talking to the man he was doing something, trying to press matters forward.

As he rode along the long drive he could see workers out in the field, but no activity in the yard. At the stable a boy took his mount but told him that the master had left early for an appointment in Bradford.

So much for this journey, Nottingham thought wryly, and went to the kitchen in search of something to drink while the horse was watered and brushed. With the oven going the room was sweltering, the door wide open to try and release some of the heat, the cook red-faced and sweaty.

'Mr Godlove's gone, they said.'

'Aye, away at the crack of dawn to Bradford. Didn't even take time to eat owt first.' She wiped her brow with a forearm and eyed him carefully. 'I've seen you here before. Summat to do with the mistress,' she said suspiciously.

'I'm the Constable of Leeds,' he told her, keeping close to the fresh air by the door.

'Wasted your time coming out here today, then. I suppose you want some ale.'

'I'd love some,' he said with a grateful smile.

She gestured at the table. 'It's on there, help yourself. Have you found out who killed her, then?'

'No,' he admitted, pouring a tall mug and taking a long, welcome drink. 'Not yet.'

'The master's been all inside himself and upside down since it happened. He doted on that lass, you know.'

'What was she like?'

The cook crossed her arms, the pink flesh on her upper arms jiggling.

'Not going to say ill of the dead,' was all she offered.

'Do you remember the day she left?'

'Easier to remember the times she was here,' the woman snorted. 'Off out every week, then to see those parents of hers, sometimes out with the master. Couldn't keep track of her. Didn't think much of it when she left. Until she didn't come back, of course,' she added hastily.

He took another sip. They brewed well here,

with a rich, deep taste. Better than he'd had in many inns.

'Was Mr Godlove here that day?'

She shook her head. 'After the mistress left he decided to go off to Bradford. Don't blame him, really. Saddled up his horse about an hour after she went, saw him through the window there. Stayed away overnight, and all. Dinner I made would have gone to nought if I hadn't ended up giving it to the men. Not that they minded, of course.'

'When did he come back on Friday?' Nottingham tried to make the question one of friendly interest, a simple way of making conversation. She stopped for a moment, casting her mind back.

'Late,' she answered finally. 'Gone dark, I remember that, because the stable lad had to get up to look after his horse.'

He drained the mug and decided not to press the cook further. She'd probably been here for years, with a strong sense of loyalty to Godlove. Better to let it rest. But it was interesting news and worth storing for later.

'Do you know when he'll be back today?'

She laughed. 'He doesn't tell me, love. He'll be here when he's here. But he didn't say not to cook, so he'll probably come back this afternoon.'

'Could you tell him I was here looking for him and I'll come back tomorrow?'

'Aye, I'll do that. You're the Constable, you said?'

'That's right.'

She nodded sagely. 'Important job, is it?' she asked.

'I suppose so. The title's worth more than the pay.'

She looked him up and down. 'Aye, love, I can tell.'

He was still smiling as he rode back down the hill. She'd put him in his place right enough. He glanced at his old coat, shiny at the elbows and collar, his white stock discoloured to ivory, the brilliant yellow of his long waistcoat faded with age. It was a tatterdemalion appearance, he understood that. It might be all well and good in the city, where people recognized his face and knew his position, but out here it just marked him as a poor man.

Still, the things she'd told him had been revealing. Sarah Godlove hadn't managed to win the affection of the servants, it seemed, and she apparently hadn't cared too much for being stuck on Godlove's estate.

But it was the man's absence when his wife vanished that was the most disturbing point. It meant that he could have killed her; he had the time and the chance. And if he knew about Jackson, he had a reason. Things seemed to be starting to point to Godlove and that worried him. He'd been so convinced of the man's innocence, that he was a sincere, grieving widower. Was he losing his instinct? Or was the man really that good an actor? If so, he was even fooling his servants. Whichever it was, it gave the Constable pause. He prided himself on being able to pick out a falsehood quite easily. If he couldn't he was worthless at his job.

He'd be back out to talk to Mr Godlove, and this time he'd be very much on his guard. He'd bring John along, too, and see what he thought. The problem was that they couldn't arrest someone of that rank without very good cause, and finding evidence to convict might be nigh on impossible.

As he made his way slowly along the road back into Leeds, turning by Kirkstall Forge, the ruined tower of the abbey looming out to the west, Nottingham was forced to admit that it was quite possible he'd never know for certain who'd killed Sarah Godlove, or even the real reason why.

He hated failure. He hated to see a life taken and not being able to find the person responsible. It didn't happen often. As he'd told Rob, most murders were simple to solve. But a few had eluded him and he remembered every single one of them, the faces, the dates, the way he'd been unable to bring them justice. He didn't want to add this one to the list.

At the ostler's he dismounted, thighs aching, knowing he'd have to do it again the next day. Still, at least he now had real questions to ask Godlove, and he'd need solid, believable answers.

The others were at the jail, the deputy wearing his frustration on his face and Lister sitting back thoughtfully, cradling a mug of ale in his hands,

breadcrumbs scattered loosely across his waistcoat.

'Doesn't look like either of you has had a good
morning,' Nottingham said, perching on the
corner of the desk. 'John, I want you to come
out to Horsforth with me tomorrow.'

'Riding?'

'Best way, unless you really prefer Shanks's
mare. Godlove wasn't home. But the cook said
he left the same day as Sarah. Went to Bradford
and didn't come back until late the following
day.'

'Still think he's not guilty, boss?'

The Constable shrugged. 'That's why I want
you there when I talk to him. You can tell me
what you think.'

'I will.'

'What about you, Rob? You're lost in thought.'

'I've been going over Will's papers again,
boss. I can't find anything else in his rooms.'

'And?'

'Nothing,' he said with a long sigh. 'There's
just nothing there that can help.'

'So we're stuck,' Nottingham said. 'Still, it
was worth a try.' He was about to say more
when the door was pushed open hard. A young
boy, maybe eight years old, wearing just a shirt
and torn breeches, his feet bare, looked up at
them with wide, terrified eyes.

'Please sir, you've got to come now,' he said
breathlessly. 'Some men are attacking a lady.'

Nottingham looked at the other two and reached into a desk drawer, taking out three heavy

223

cudgels.

'Ever used one?' he asked Lister.

'No.'

'Sounds like you'll get some practice,' the deputy told him.

Moving at a run past the surprised people on the street, they followed the boy into the thicket of courts that ran off Lands Lane. The lad disappeared into the entrance of one, a space hardly wide enough to pass through in single file, to a yard where the broken-down houses stood around a small, bare patch of ground that hardly ever saw the sun.

'In there. I heard them.' The lad pointed at a building with its front door missing. Nottingham could hear grunts and shouts coming from inside. He turned and gestured at the others, took a deep breath and charged through the door with a shout, the other two close behind.

The two men trying to kick down the door turned together. They were both large, with battered, worn faces and thick hands, but they were unarmed, knowing their size and power could intimidate most people.

The Constable didn't even need to think. He brought the cudgel down on one man's forearm, hearing the hard wood break bone and the loud, agonized cry that followed. Sedgwick was already attacking the other man, then Lister started, flailing at the skull of the first. Nottingham moved aside to give them room.

It had only been the work of seconds, barely a skirmish, but he still found himself panting hard from it, energy and excitement jangling through his body. Sedgwick's man was laid out on the dirty floorboards, while the other held his arm carefully, blood flowing freely from the wounds on his head.

'Wake that one up,' the Constable ordered, 'and take them to the jail. See what you can get out of them.'

The deputy used his boot to rouse the unconscious man. He stirred slowly, moving gradually to his knees then vomiting loudly.

'Get him out of here before he does that again,' the Constable ordered. 'The smell here's bad enough as it is.'

There was no resistance in them. As hard men they had nothing to offer beyond their size. They were brutal enough against someone weak, but crumpled if anyone showed them some fight.

Once they'd gone and silence had returned to the stairwell, he knocked on the door. Two of the panels had been smashed, but the lock had held. Another good push or two and it would have given, though.

'I'm the Constable of Leeds,' he said, loud enough for whoever was inside to hear. 'You're safe now.'

There was no response. He tried the handle but it wouldn't give.

'Can you let me in? There's no one here to hurt you.'

Again there was nothing and he waited. He needed to know who was beyond that door.

'Please, let me in.'

When no one answered he knew he had no choice. Standing back he raised a leg and brought the sole of his boot down hard just below the lock. The door shuddered but held until he did it again and finally everything gave.

Gently, holding the cudgel loosely, he pushed the door open and walked in. A girl was crouched in the far corner, shivering uncontrollably and trying to make herself small, tears coursing down her face, small fingers attempting to hold the torn bodice of her dress together.

'Don't worry,' he told her softly, 'I won't hurt you. Those men have gone.'

She looked up at him. He squatted, looking into her eyes and giving an encouraging smile.

'You're Nan, aren't you?' he said.

Eighteen

'A lot of people have been looking for you, love.'

He reached out to take her hand and she pulled fearfully away. Instead of grabbing her, he left his hand there, as he might with a beaten dog, patiently waiting for her to decide.

'You've been hiding a few days, haven't you?'

She nodded, eyes wide, as if she didn't trust herself to open her mouth and speak. He had a chance to look at her properly, and saw dark unkempt hair hanging in loose rat tails, grimy skin, fingernails bitten all the way down.

'Don't worry,' he told her kindly, 'Amos Worthy can't get you now. You didn't know about him when you took the job in his house, did you?'

'No.' Her voice was a bare croak, quavering even over one word.

Nottingham took off his coat and passed it to her. 'Button that up and you'll be decent. There are some clothes at the jail you can wear.'

She placed her small fingers in his and he pulled her upright. The skin on her palm was callused, and she wiped the tears from her eyes. He helped her up and she put on the coat, far too large on her tiny body; she looked like an absurd doll. The Constable smiled at her.

'That's better,' he said encouragingly. He kept one hand lightly on the small of her back as they left the house. It helped steady her, although the shaking was growing less, but also ready to hold her in case she tried to run. After the darkness inside the daylight seemed unnaturally bright as they emerged back on to Lands Lane.

'Tom was your brother?'

'Yes.' She looked at him curiously. 'How did you know that?'

'It's my job,' he told her.

'He's dead, isn't he?' she asked flatly, already knowing the answer.

'Yes,' he answered. 'I'm sorry. But you would have been, too, if we hadn't come. You'll be safe at the jail.'

She looked at him and shook her head, her eyes warier now. 'Until they hang me, you mean?'

'That depends on the judge.'

On Briggate he stayed close to her, ready for her to try to vanish into the throng of people in the street. But she stayed placid, letting herself be guided, glancing round fearfully, her arm linked through his as they walked. Yes, he thought, she'd be convicted by a jury and they'd hang her up on the Moor for her thefts. She knew that as well as he did, but it wouldn't happen for a while yet. He could give her a little more life.

At the jail he put her in a cell, and brought her

a mildewed dress from the chest of old clothes they kept, along with a mug of ale. When he returned, she'd changed her clothes and sat on the pallet, drinking.

'Are they here, too?'

'Don't worry, you're safe. They can't get you. Were they the ones who killed your brother?'

'No.'

'But you were there when it happened, weren't you?'

She closed her eyes for a few moments, squeezing them tight to try and keep out the memories and gave a short nod.

'They found us. We'd been in an inn to have something to eat and they grabbed us when we left. Four of them.'

'Where did they take you?'

'I don't know – a cellar.'

'Was Worthy there?'

'Yes.'

'Who else was with him?'

'The men who'd found us.'

She turned pale and put her head forward. He waited silently for her to continue.

'They made me sit on a chair in the corner. Tied my hands behind me. Then they started to hit Tom. Over and over.'

The tears began to roll down her cheeks. Nottingham wasn't even sure she was aware of them as she relived what had happened.

'What about Worthy? Did he hit him?'

'He used a stick, not his fists. Kicked him, too.'

'How did you get away?'

She snorted. 'The one who tied me couldn't make a knot to save his life. As soon as they were busy, I ran as fast as I could. I knew I couldn't do anything to save Tom, he was...' Her voice trailed away. Nottingham let quiet fill the room.

'And you've been running since,' he said eventually. She nodded slightly. 'You could admit to theft, you know. It might save you from the hangman.'

'Aye, and it might not.'

'If you don't it'll be the noose for sure,' he told her. 'Think on that.'

He closed the cell door behind her. The men were being held separately; they both stared at him defiantly through the barred doors.

'Did they say anything?' he asked in the office where Sedgwick and Lister were sitting.

'Not a word, boss,' the deputy replied with a deep, frustrated sigh. 'Mention Amos Worthy and they ask who he is. He must have paid them well.'

'He won't pay unless they bring him the girl,' Nottingham told him. 'They're just scared of what he might do if they peach on him.'

'You broke the wrist of the one you hit,' Rob said.

'He'll live.' He turned to Sedgwick. 'It's Nan.'

'I thought it must be.'

'She had to watch her brother beaten to death. Said Worthy was there.'

Lister grimaced at the thought. 'Would she say

that in court?' he asked.

'No point,' the deputy told him. 'Worthy has the Corporation in his pocket.'

'It's true,' Nottingham agreed. 'They use his girls, borrow money from him, and in return he gets away with murder. Literally.'

'So what are we going to do with them?' Rob asked.

'Keep them a while and then turn them out. Meanwhile I'll go and have a word with their boss. I'll tell them before I release them and we'll see how fast they run.'

Sedgwick smiled. 'What about Nan?' he wondered.

'She'll be for the Quarter Sessions. You'd better take her over to the prison at the Moot Hall. And tell the turnkey I want her watched.'

'Yes, boss.' He tousled Lister's hair. 'Come on you, escort duty for us.'

He waited until they'd marched her out, each holding one of her arms, and then he locked the jail and strode down Briggate.

In the heat the street was rank from the piles of horse turds and the waste that had dried in the central runnel or on the road. Worthy would be at the Old King's Arms, down at the corner with Currie Entry; it was where he always ate a late dinner. He might have owned the place for all the Constable knew.

He was sharing a bench with two of his men, his fingers greasy from the chicken leg he held, its flesh mostly gnawed away. Nottingham stood by the table until the pimp glanced up.

'You can leave,' he told the others. 'Don't go too far, mind, we'll take a walk after.' He put down the bird and wiped his fingers on his waistcoat, the stains joining hundreds of others on the fabric.

'Drink, laddie?' he asked, pouring himself a fresh mug of ale.

'I hear you were there when Tom got killed, Amos.'

Worthy looked at him guilelessly. 'Tom? Who's that, Constable?'

'Nan's brother.'

He nodded as if he'd just added an interesting new fact to the store in his mind.

'I heard you used your stick on him, too.'

'Did I?' He took a long drink. 'People have been telling you things, haven't they? Shame they're all lies.'

Nottingham stared firmly at him. 'Nan got away, though,' he continued. 'Whoever you hired to find her almost got her. Except we got them. And she's safe in prison now.'

'Is that so?' Worthy raised an eyebrow.

'Going to press charges against her, Amos?'

'No need. She'll hang without anything I say.'

'Gall you a bit, does it? That you didn't get to make an example of her?'

Worthy shrugged. 'I'm just glad to see you doing your job and catching thieves.'

'I'll be letting the two men who were after her go. Funny, they don't seem to have heard of you.'

'Strangers, mebbe, then. I'm sure if they stay

here long they'll know my name.'

'I'll tell them that, shall I?' the Constable asked.

'Up to you, laddie. Doesn't matter either way to me.'

He appeared completely unconcerned, but Nottingham knew that inside the pimp was seething. He'd caught Tom and made him pay, but he needed the girl, too, needed her more than her brother to show that no one could cross him in this city.

'I doubt if the lass has your money any more.'

Worthy smiled, showing the meat stuck between his teeth. 'There's always more to be made, Mr Nottingham. In my business, at least.' He stood, pushing himself away from the bench, and with a mocking bow swept out of the inn. The Constable followed, watching from the doorway as Worthy and his men strolled down Briggate.

Thoughtfully he ambled back to the jail, enjoying the afternoon sun on his back, not too hot, just enough to feel comforting. Inside he unlocked the cells of both men, told them they were free to go and relayed Worthy's none too cryptic message. He let them scurry away, one still clutching his broken wrist, then went over to the Moot Hall.

The prison was in the cellar, a frozen pit in the winter but pleasantly cool in this weather, well shaded, the walls solid and thick. The heavy stones of the floor resounded to his boots.

The prisoners there were waiting for the

Quarter Sessions, when their fates would be decided. A few might go free, but most knew they'd end up dancing in the air, transported, or serving their sentences elsewhere. As the court date neared the cells would fill up. At least they were treated better in Leeds than in other cities. Weatherspoon, the turnkey, was a fair man. He saw his charges fed, there was straw to sleep on, sometimes even clean, and the slop buckets were emptied every few days to cut down on the chances of jail fever.

Even so, Nottingham held a handkerchief to his nose as he entered. The temperature might have been pleasurable, but the smell of unwashed bodies and slops was acrid.

'Afternoon, Constable.' Weatherspoon was at his desk, oblivious to the odours after so many years. He was at least sixty, a small and wizened man with cramped, arthritic fingers and a shiny, hairless skull. He'd been here since Nottingham was a boy, looking after his underground kingdom with meticulous care. His clothes were old but well cared for, his suit of light wool sponged clean, shoes polished so their metal buckles shone, hose always the same spotless white.

'Mr Weatherspoon.' He gave a smile. 'The girl they brought over a little while ago. I need to talk to her.'

The man hefted a large, heavy ring of keys from the desk and made his way down the corridor. Nottingham waited. He could hear Weatherspoon fetching Nan – 'You! Not you, you stupid baggage, her in the corner. Yes, you, someone to see you.' – then the shuffle of feet as he returned with the lass.

She'd been in the place less than an hour but she looked older, careworn, as if she'd begun to fully understand the depth of her fate. There were fresh stains on the worn dress and already the stench of the prison was clinging to her skin and her hair.

'Hello, Nan,' he said. She smiled tightly in return but said nothing. 'Not the loveliest place to stay, is it?'

'No,' she agreed. 'Not been in worse than this before.'

'You're lucky,' he told her truthfully. 'Another city and this might seem like luxury.'

She looked at him in sullen disbelief.

'You're going to be here a month or more until the Quarter Sessions. You'd better get used to it.'

'And then the noose?'

'Maybe not.' He dangled the idea before her and this time her gaze sharpened with his words, hope flickering behind her eyes. He waited until he had her complete attention, then continued, 'Amos Worthy won't be pressing charges. If you admit the others, you might be able to escape hanging.'

'Why do you care?' she asked suspiciously. 'What do you want?'

'You managed to get away from Worthy. That's reason enough for me by itself.'

She kept looking at him. He knew she didn't believe him, but he held her gaze and said no more.

'So what do you want?' she asked finally.

'Nothing,' he told her, 'except to know how you and your brother started on all this.'

She looked at him suspiciously. 'Have you ever been hungry?' she asked.

'Yes.'

She snorted. 'You've been late for a meal?'

'I know exactly what you mean,' Nottingham said soberly, 'and I've been hungry.'

Nan eyed him for a moment, then continued. 'You live like that for a while and you'll do what you need to do. Me and Tom, we were on our own after me dad died. Me mam died when I was born.'

'Not everyone does what you did.'

'We're not all saints,' she said wearily. 'Tom had fast hands. I'd distract them, he'd take the things.'

'Picking pockets. That's still a long way from what you've been doing.'

She paced around the floor, measuring out the space.

'That all started with me,' she explained with a brief smile. 'I just wanted to live somewhere I wasn't cold all the time.'

'What happened?'

'Money, plate, lace...' She smiled wanly. 'I saw all that and thought I could live well from it.'

'So you took it and left.'

'Yes,' she admitted. 'I gave it to Tom to sell. Bought us three months off the street, that did.'

'And you thought you could do it again.'

'We did. Again and again. I persuaded Tom to do some servant work, too. It was worth it for a few days, especially if we kept moving around and didn't get too greedy.'

'You should have moved on from here sooner,' the Constable told her.

'Too late for should haves,' she answered with resignation.

'Maybe not. You might not get your neck stretched.'

She stood still. 'Can you promise that?' she asked finally.

'No,' he told her truthfully, 'I can't guarantee anything, but I'll put it all in a report. That will help. You'll still be transported. Seven years, maybe more. But you'll be alive.'

Nan smiled grimly. 'I'll think about it.'

She turned to walk back to her cell, and Weatherspoon rose from his chair to escort her. When he returned, the Constable had a soft word with the man. He wanted the girl kept alone. Worthy's reach could go below stairs as well as above in the Moot Hall. Better safe than sorry.

'You've got a strange look on your face,' Mary said cautiously as he sat down in his chair with a mug of ale. 'I'm not sure if you're pleased or not.'

He smiled at her and gave a soft laugh. 'I'm not sure myself, really.' He watched her hands move rapidly and gracefully with the needle and thread. 'How's the dress coming along?'

'It'll be finished in time,' she assured him. 'Emily's upstairs practising how to be a teacher.'

'What?' he asked in surprise. 'How do you practise that?'

'I've no idea,' Mary said tiredly. 'But our daughter seems certain she can. From what I've seen it mostly seems to be how to stand and look at people.'

He chuckled. 'The only teacher I remember seemed to enjoy beating people.'

'I don't see her doing that,' she said and he grinned.

'No,' he agreed, 'not unless all that power turns her head.'

'Better watch out – give her a month and it might. She might turn into a right little miss.'

'She'll learn fast enough.' He finished the drink. 'Do you want to go for a walk?'

'I've—' she began, then stopped and pushed the needle into the fabric. 'Yes,' she said decisively. 'I need a change from this; I feel like I've been sewing all day.'

'Knowing you, you probably have been,' he teased as she flexed her fingers slowly. The knuckles were swollen, the skin red. Tenderly he took her hand and kissed it, watching her blush like a girl, the colour rising up her throat and face.

'I love you.'

'Don't be silly,' she said, but her grin was wide and happy. Laughing, they left the house together, hand in hand up Marsh Lane and into the country.

'The fresh air feels good,' Mary said, breathing deeply. 'Do you know, I haven't even been outside today?'

'Then it's time you were. We were walking out most evenings until Emily came home,' he reminded her.

'I know, but everything's been a whirl since then. And you're as much to blame, you've been working until late, too.'

'I know.' He frowned. 'It's not been easy.' Nottingham wasn't going to say more that that; he'd always kept his work distant from home, as much as he could.

'That job'll be the death of you.' She pulled at him, bringing him close, and gave him a quick kiss. 'They work you too hard. You're not twenty any more.'

'I'm not thirty, either.'

'I know, Richard, it shows,' she told him teasingly, then put out her tongue, and for a second he saw the young girl he'd married in her face.

He watched her as they walked, thinking how good it was to have this Mary back, playful and full of spirit. After the winter he'd wondered if there could ever be lightness in their lives again, or if the ghost of Rose would always drift too close by them.

But she was right, he wasn't a young man any more. All too often he felt every single day of his forty-one years. He couldn't be like Arkwright, the old Constable, and do this job for

239

another two decades. The hours were too long, the demands on his body too high. He could see the day, not too far ahead, when he'd let Sedgwick take over and find something else to do. A job to eke out the small pension the city would grant when he left.

They walked on in a comfortable, companionable silence born from years together. Occasionally Mary would point something out, a flower or a bird, and they'd exchange a few words before returning to the quiet and the warmth of the time together.

Nottingham felt contentment seep through him, all the nagging cares and annoyances of the day vanishing. He'd needed this as much as Mary had, some small time away that they could share where none of life's realities could intrude. Even the ache in his thighs from riding was fading, although God knew it would return tomorrow after another trip to Horsforth.

An hour or more later they slowly made their way home. He put his arm around her as they walked, a small gesture of his feelings, the way he'd always relished the contact, the texture of her skin, and valued it now all the more.

He was awake with the earliest light, when the sky was hollow with dawn and the stars were still bright above. He moved quietly, dressing in yesterday's clothes. He'd save his good suit and shirt for church tomorrow.

There was a small chill in the dawn air, the stir of a breeze, welcome and refreshing after so many days of heat, and he breathed it in deeply as he walked towards Timble Bridge. He'd show Rob what to do at the morning cloth market then leave with Sedgwick to see Godlove.

It was going to be another long day, that was almost certain, but he felt rested and ready to tackle it. As he crossed the bridge a boy careered towards him down Kirkgate, small legs pumping and kicking up plumes of dust behind him.

He stopped and waited, one hand on the railing, knowing inside that the lad was carrying a message for him.

'You're looking for the Constable?' he called when the boy was a few yards away. Panting hard, the boy stopped and tried to catch his breath.

'There's a girl dead at the Moot Hall,' he said.

Nottingham was running himself before the sentence was over.

Nineteen

Sedgwick was waiting at the jail, pacing fretfully, his mouth set hard, hair wild and uncombed.

'It's Nan?' Nottingham asked and the deputy nodded slowly. 'How?'

'Hung with her own dress. It was torn into strips. Looks like she killed herself but I'm damned sure she didn't.' His voice was flat, his eyes showing nothing. 'Weatherspoon found her when he arrived this morning. The night man had vanished.'

The Constable ran the back of his hand across his mouth, his mind working furiously.

'Is she still there?'

'Yes.'

'Have you told the coroner?'

'Not yet. I wanted you to know first.'

'Good. Let's go and see her. Send someone for Mr Brogden,' he said with distaste. 'I'm sure he'll call it suicide.'

On the street the deputy gave a coin to a small lad who was up and curious, sending him scarpering off down Briggate. Then he joined Nottingham and the pair walked without speaking up to the Moot Hall.

Weatherspoon was at his desk, his face full of anguish, standing as soon as they entered.

'When did you find her?' Nottingham asked.

'About an hour ago.' The man's voice was anxious and cracking. It wasn't the first death here and wouldn't be the last, but he knew it shouldn't have happened. 'As soon as I saw the night man wasn't here, I checked on her straight away.'

'Let's take a look at her,' the Constable said and the turnkey led them down the shadowy passage to the cell and pushed the door open.

'Was it locked when you arrived?' the Constable asked.

'Yes,' Weatherspoon said.

She was hanging from a thick beam that supported the floor above. The old dress he'd given her at the jail had been ripped into ragged strips, knotted one to the other. As they entered, the draught caused her body to turn slightly so she was facing them.

There was a puddle beneath her where she'd pissed herself and a joint stool kicked over on the flagstones. Nottingham reached out and touched her hand. The skin was cooling, but there was still the faint warmth of a lost life there. The tongue lolled from her mouth, and there was a heavy, livid bruise on her cheek. One more fragile soul lost to the noose, he thought sadly.

'The coroner will be here soon. Leave her up until he's seen her,' Nottingham ordered.

Without a word they moved back to Weather-

243

spoon's desk. At the other end of the building the prisoners were raising a clamour, demanding their breakfast.

'Who's your night man?'

'His name's Wilkie. Came about two months ago,' the turnkey answered. 'He seemed fine. It's hard to find someone who's willing to be here all night...' He pulled out a piece of paper with the man's address scrawled on it.

'Go and see if you can find him, John. If he's around, take him to the jail.'

'Yes, boss.' Sedgwick ran up the stairs and into the growing day.

'She was very quiet after you left yesterday. You must have given her plenty to think on.'

'Yes,' the Constable agreed slowly. 'But nothing to make her kill herself.'

Weatherspoon stared at him. 'Are you sure it was murder? In my prison?'

'It probably was,' Nottingham replied. 'I'll tell you that she stole from Amos Worthy, and we stopped a couple of men from attacking her.'

'So you think he's behind it?'

Nottingham brushed the fringe off his forehead. 'Yes,' he said firmly. 'But proving it's going to be another matter altogether.'

Before he could say more, he heard the rasp of sharp heels on the stone of the steps and turned. It was Edward Brogden, the coroner. He held a withered orange studded with cloves inside his handkerchief, and pressed it close to his nose to fight the smell. With his eyes, the Constable indicated that the jailer should show him the body.

Brogden was in the cell less than a minute before hurrying back out in quick strides, confirming suicide in a single word then climbing back to the clearer air of Leeds.

'He disagrees with your verdict, Mr Nottingham,' Weatherspoon said.

'Let him,' the Constable said. 'This night man, has he ever left early before?'

The turnkey shook his head. 'He's always been very responsible up to now. Hasn't missed a day, respectful, good with the prisoners.'

'He didn't leave any kind of message? Not taken ill?'

'Nothing,' the jailer said.

Nottingham studied the layout of the prison.

'That door that goes to the main cells, was it locked when you came this morning?'

'Yes,' Weatherspoon confirmed. 'Always locked at nine, every night when the church bell sounds. It's good and solid.'

In other words, the Constable thought, the prisoners wouldn't have heard anything useful, and they'd have seen nothing.

'You can cut her down now,' he said. 'I'll send some men over to move her.'

He walked down Briggate, his steps fast. As he'd told Weatherspoon, he knew Worthy was behind all this, but he'd never prove it. Nothing would stick to that bastard. He'd lay a penny to a pound that the night man had already vanished, taking his possessions with him, a richer

245

man than when he'd begun work the evening before.

There was nothing he could do. He could feel the rage building. The pimp had won again. He wanted to do something, hit a wall, anything to relieve the fury and frustration, but instead he balled his fists and pushed them hard into the pockets of his coat.

Lister was at the jail, waiting. Nottingham had forgotten he was supposed to show him how to watch the cloth market this morning.

'I'm sorry, Rob. That girl, Nan, died in the Moot Hall cells.'

'What?' He began to stand up.

'She was hung. The coroner's said suicide, but you can guess for yourself what happened. The night man's gone missing.'

'What?'

The Constable let out a long, slow breath and made a decision.

'Look, enough people have seen you around by now for them to know you're a Constable's man. Go and walk up and down where they're selling cloth. The word'll spread quick enough, don't worry.'

'And if I see something?'

Nottingham smiled. 'Just do your job. Bring them here, put them in a cell and we'll deal with them later.'

'Yes, boss.'

He'd barely left when Sedgwick arrived, giving a quick shake of his head.

'Room's unlocked, just the furniture left in it.

Neighbours said it sounded like he left in the middle of the night. They thought he must have owed on his rent and was doing a flit.'

'He did that, right enough. Bought and paid for,' Nottingham said.

'Sounds like it.'

'I'm going down there,' the Constable announced, 'and then we'll go to Horsforth.'

'Boss,' the deputy warned, and Nottingham raised his hand placatingly.

'I'll let him have his moment of gloating. And then I'll warn him. Nothing more, John, I promise.'

'Do you want me to come with you?'

'No. We've a history, Amos and me. Better just the two of us. If you want something to do, go and keep an eye on Rob, he's looking after the cloth market. I won't be long.'

He strode along Boar Lane, the fury like a lump in his gut. He made his way down Swinegate and pushed open the anonymous door of the house. But the way to the kitchen was blocked by a big young man. The Constable had seen him before, tall and blocky, always dressed in a jacket and breeches that appeared too small for his huge frame. Today he wore new clothes and a short wig that looked ridiculous on such a large head. He didn't move, but stood filling the passage.

'I'm the Constable.'

'No one goes in until they hand over their weapons. Mr Worthy's orders.'

Nottingham took the knife from its sheath on

his belt as if to hand it over. As the guard's eyes followed the movement, the Constable shoved his knee hard into the man's cods and he dropped on the floor, clutching himself.

'You don't make demands of the law,' Nottingham told him and opened the door.

There were two more of Worthy's men in the kitchen, lounging against the far wall, but he didn't dismiss them. Instead they stood by the back door, hands resting idly on the hilts of their daggers, eyes fixed on their employer. He was sitting at the table, a mug of ale by his hand.

'What's wrong, Amos? Looks like something's got you scared.'

The procurer tilted his head and calmly pursed his lips. 'Just looking after things, Constable. A little protection never goes amiss.'

Nottingham raised his eyebrows.

'So what brings you here?' Worthy asked. 'Checking on my well-being?'

'The girl who robbed you killed herself at the Moot Hall last night.'

The pimp shrugged. 'Saves the cost of a trial and a hanging, anyway. You should be pleased, laddie.'

'The night jailer's disappeared, too. Left in the middle of his shift. Gone from his room, too.'

'Nowt so queer as folk. You ought to know that by now.'

'You must have paid him plenty.'

'Nothing to do with me.' He grinned. 'Nice idea, though.'

'I don't believe that.' Nottingham's voice

248

turned hard and the two men by the door stood straighter.

Worthy waved the suggestion away. 'Believe what you like, Constable. There's nothing you can prove, is there?'

'You know the answer to that.'

The pimp pushed his face forward, his features set like flint. 'Aye, laddie, I do. If you knew it was me, you'd be hauling me off to your jail now.'

'Oh, I know well enough,' Nottingham told him. 'I just can't prove it, that's all.'

'Then don't come bothering me with it until you can.' He turned back to the ale. 'You've said your piece and salved your conscience. Now you can bugger off.'

He returned to the jail deep in thought. Sedgwick was there, ready to leave, his face showing how much he was dreading the ride.

'You're safe from horseback today,' the Constable told him. 'There's something going on and I want you to get to the bottom of it.'

'What's that?'

'Worthy's keeping his men close and he's hired a new one. You remember that lad who used to haul carcasses around for one of the butchers at the Shambles?'

'The one who looks like a walking mountain? Aye, I remember him. He could stop a cart.'

'Well, he's working for Worthy now. It looks to me like Amos is worried. I want to know what's going on so we can stop it.'

'You think it's Hughes?'

'Very likely.'

Sedgwick picked at a fingernail. 'We could just let them kill each other and get rid of them all.'

'I doubt the mayor would like that too much,' he answered with a dark smile. 'He wants us to try and keep the bodies off the streets, remember? You know who to talk to. Find out what's happening.'

'What did he say about Nan?'

The Constable screwed his face up in disgust. 'What do you think? He doesn't know a thing about it, of course.'

'Of course.'

'I'm going to see Godlove. Get on it, John. Take Rob with you, he can see what makes the city tick. It'll open his eyes a bit.'

The deputy was relieved that he didn't have to ride. He always felt awkward and fearful on horseback, scared that he might fall off at any minute. He was much more comfortable on his own two feet, surrounded by the familiarity of Leeds, the faces, the streets that had been his life.

He found Lister at the bottom of Briggate, watching as the weavers took down the trestles and packed up. Some were already hauling the cloth they'd sold over to the warehouses.

'No problems?' he asked.

'Nothing.'

'There never are, really,' Sedgwick told him. 'They're an orderly lot. They're just cut-throats on prices, most like. Come on, we've work to do.'

He led the younger man over Leeds Bridge and into the streets south of the river. They had a different flavour, a little more spacious, closer to the country, the smell sweeter. The deputy ignored the wealth of Meadow Lane and moved instead into the hovels huddled tight against each other along Hunslet Lane and Bowman Lane.

The house he wanted was cleaner than its neighbours, windows shining, soot proudly scrubbed off the brickwork so it glistened as if it was new. The deputy knocked on the door.

'We're going to be talking to Joe Buck. He's one of the biggest crooks you'll ever meet,' he explained. 'And one of the richest. He looks mild enough, but don't let that fox you. Let me do the talking.'

'He's got money?' Lister asked.

'Plenty of it.'

'So why does he live in this place?'

'Some people don't need to flaunt it. He's a man of surprises, is our Joe. You'll see.'

The servant who opened the door was as tall as the deputy and more muscular, in a shirt so white it seemed to glow in the sunlight, tailored black breeches and a waistcoat the same shade of bright blue as the sky. A pale powdered periwig sat on top of a head as dark as Middleton coal.

'Master in?' Sedgwick asked casually, as if this was a conversation the two men had experi-

251

enced often in the past.

'In't back,' the servant answered, the accent local but underlaid by something else that gave the words a rich musicality. 'Tha knows where.'

Sedgwick winked at Rob and they made their way down the small passage that opened into a well-decorated parlour, light beaming through the windows, the furniture all in good taste and polished to a sheen, a thick Turkey carpet covering gleaming floorboards.

The man rose as they entered. The deputy had never seen him when he wasn't immaculately dressed, even for just resting at home. Today the suit was deep, sober blue, the stock and shirt white, and waistcoat a vivid shock of contrasting colours that somehow managed to suit him. In his early forties, he'd not yet run to fat, and lines barely aged his face.

'Mr Sedgwick,' the man said, extending his hand in greeting. The deputy didn't take it, but glanced admiringly round the room.

'The thieving business must still be good, Joe.'

He enjoyed watching the man wince, but the reply was calm and even.

'Business keeps going. Gentlemen, sit down.' He waved them to a pair of chairs by his own, gathered around an empty hearth.

'You must be Mr Lister,' he said, glancing at Rob and idly letting him know how well informed he was. 'I've met your father a few times. He's done well since he took over the *Mercury*.'

'Run into Amos Worthy lately?' the deputy cut in.

'As little as possible,' Buck answered with a small, pained smile.

'Not planning on trying to take over his interests?'

The man looked as if he'd been insulted. 'Mr Sedgwick, he deals in girls, you know that.'

'And other things. Besides, people expand their empires.'

'Not into those areas.' Buck shook his head in distaste. 'Mind you, there's been some bad blood between him and someone else from what I'm told.'

'Edward Hughes,' Sedgwick said and Joe nodded. 'We've already come across him. Have you heard of anything big building between them in the last day or so?'

'No,' he said, then spread his hands. 'But I stay out of that.' He paused. 'You should have a word with Bessie Hardcastle. She always knows what's going on.'

'Aye, that's a good idea. Always one to collect gossip, is Bessie. Thank you, Joe. Just make sure you watch yourself.'

'Don't you worry about me, Mr Sedgwick.'

Back outside, the deputy looked at Lister. 'What do you think?' he asked.

'I'm not sure. What does he do?' Rob wondered.

'Joe? He handles stolen goods, a lot of them. I know he looks like a molly, him and that servant, but don't be fooled. He's a tough man

253

under it all.'

'Who's Bessie Hardcastle?'

'An abbess,' Sedgwick said, and grinned at Lister's confusion. 'A bawd, she runs a brothel. Been doing it since God was a lad. Half the time I think she hears about things before they happen. I should have thought of her before. It'll still be early for her, mind. The lark's her nightingale.'

The house stood on Vicar Lane, just down from the corner of the Head Row. It was a nondescript place, with nothing to mark it out, fitting tidily between its neighbours. The deputy knocked lightly on the door and stood back, staring at the upper storeys where shutters were closed tightly behind the glass.

Finally the maid answered, a girl who would have looked demure except for the saucy twinkle in her eyes. She showed them through to a parlour hung with the fug of old smoke and stale beer.

'Are they all like this?' Lister asked, gazing around.

'All what?'

'Brothels.'

'You mean you've never been in one?'

'No,' Rob admitted with a deep blush.

Sedgwick laughed. 'Well, there's all sorts. This one's respectable, looks like any other house and there's plenty of decorum.' He indicated the good furniture and the painting hung over the mantle. 'This is where the merchants and the men from the Corporation come. It seems like home. They feel comfortable here.'

Before he could say more a woman bustled into the room, still adjusting a cap over her hair. She was in her forties, hard hawk-faced, her skin still puffy from sleep.

'The girl said it was you, Mr Sedgwick. What can I do for you so early?'

'Hello, Fanny,' he said with a broad smile. 'Business good? I was hoping for a word with your mam.'

'She's still sleeping,' the woman told him. 'She's been poorly lately, she doesn't do as much as she used to.'

'I'm sorry to hear that. How old is she now?'

'Seventy-eight, as close as we can reckon,' Fanny Hardcastle said with pride. 'Remembers everything, too, even Charles coming back after Cromwell.'

'So are you looking after things at the moment?'

'I am.'

'And getting the same gossip as her?'

The woman sniffed and stood straighter. 'I'd better be or I'll want to know why.'

'What's happening between Amos Worthy and Edward Hughes?'

'You mean you don't know?' she asked in astonishment. 'I thought it was all over everywhere by now.'

'If I knew I wouldn't be asking, would I?' the deputy asked patiently. 'They've been at it a bit, but I mean in the last couple of days.'

'Well,' she began slowly, 'yesterday evening

255

someone told me that Hughes has threatened to kill old Amos.'

'You think it's true?'

She nodded. 'The man who told me has always been right before. Why are you asking?'

'Just that Worthy's hired someone new and he's keeping his men very close.'

'That's not like him. Amos has never been the worrying sort.'

'Aye, I know,' Sedgwick agreed. 'He must be taking it seriously.'

'It's going to come to a head soon, that's what I heard.' She looked at the deputy. 'What are you going to do about it?'

'We'll make sure it doesn't happen,' he told her and she raised her eyebrows in disbelief.

'You're going to keep Amos Worthy from a fight?'

'If it comes to that, yes.'

'I'll believe it when I see it,' she said. 'Now, gentlemen, if there's nothing more...?'

'Give my best to your mam. I hope she's well soon.'

Back out on Vicar Lane the deputy led them to the White Swan and they sat with mugs of ale.

'Are we going to stop them?' Lister asked.

'I'm trying to work that out,' Sedgwick said with a deep sigh. 'The problem is Fanny's right. If the pair of them are really set on a scrap we'll be hard pressed to keep them apart.'

'Worthy's been a pimp for a long time?'

'Yes.' The deputy took a long drink.

'But Hughes is new here? He could be the

weak link,' Rob said thoughtfully.

Sedgwick looked at him. 'How do you mean?'

'He won't be sure of his ground here yet.'

'He's cocky enough to challenge Worthy.'

'Yes, but what if the city pushed back hard at him?'

'It won't work. The boss and I were already there. It didn't seem to do much good.'

'That was talk. What if it was more than just a word?' Lister suggested. 'Make sure he knows exactly where he stands.'

Sedgwick gazed down into his mug, swirling the dregs.

'I suppose it's worth a try,' he decided finally. He drained the ale and stood up. 'Well, are you coming?'

They strode down to the Calls, stepping between puddles of waste in the street as the deputy glanced among the broken, dilapidated houses.

Finally he banged on a door that looked the same as all the others on the street. The girl who opened it looked barely fourteen, her face still young and unlined but eyes deep and full of sad experience.

'Hello, love,' the deputy said kindly. 'How are you?'

'Fine, thank you, sir,' she replied, confused by the question, and tried to sketch a brief curtsey.

'Is Mr Hughes around?'

'Yes, sir.'

'Tell him the deputy constable wants a word, will you? There's a good lass.' He gave her a warm smile.

'Yes, sir.'

She closed the door again and they heard her footsteps. Sedgwick shook his head sadly. 'Poor girl has probably never had a kind word spoken to her in her life.'

'Was that why you did it?'

The deputy laughed. 'Always be nice to people until they give you a reason not to be. That's what my father told me. He was right, too. She's done nowt, there's no need to treat her anything but politely.'

Lister looked at him with curiosity and respect. 'And her pimp?'

Sedgwick grinned. 'Wait and see.'

When the door opened again, Hughes was standing there, drinking from a chipped mug, dressed in an old, darned shirt, his stock loose, breeches and stockings stained. The deputy watched him carefully, seeing the way he tried to mask the anger in his eyes.

'It's early,' Hughes complained, running a hand over his shaved scalp. 'What do you want?'

'Just another word,' Sedgwick told him. 'Here or inside?'

The man shrugged and led them into the house and through to the kitchen, as slatternly kept as the parlour. Dishes sat on the table caked in dried food, hosts of flies buzzing as they fed on them. Scraps littered the floor, rotting and slimy underfoot, and runnels of damp bloomed mould on the walls. God help the coroner if there was ever a dead body here, the deputy thought. The poor bugger would choke.

'You like your luxury, don't you?' he asked, gazing around. Hughes looked blankly, missing the irony. 'Planning a run in with Amos Worthy, are you, Edward?'

The man spat on the floor. 'You can call me Mr Hughes if you want to ask me any questions.'

'Can I?' Sedgwick said. 'That's very generous of you, Edward.'

The two men stared at each other for a long moment.

'Aye, we've had some words,' Hughes admitted finally.

'People are saying you've threatened to kill him.'

Hughes laughed, showing discoloured teeth. 'That's what they're saying, is it?'

'It is.' The deputy's voice was hard and dangerous. 'And the people who told me don't lie.'

'So what if I did say that?'

Sedgwick shook his head slowly. 'Threatening murder. That's a serious business.'

Hughes snorted. 'He's been warned, that's all.' He began to raise the mug to his mouth. The deputy reached out calmly and in a single, flowing move snatched it from his hand and threw it against the wall.

'So have you. You've been warned twice now. Edward.'

Hughes crossed his arms over his chest. 'So

259

he's paying you off as well as your master, is he?'

In a swift moment Sedgwick had him pinned against the wall, a forearm tight across the man's throat.

'Don't you ever suggest that,' he said coldly. 'Ever. You got that?'

Slowly he applied more pressure, staring at Hughes as the man's face reddened, increasing the force until the man nodded his understanding. Sedgwick moved back, leaving Hughes to rub his throat. 'I don't care what you were thinking, Edward,' he told him. 'It's over. Do you finally get that?'

'Yes,' he answered in a croak.

'Run your whores like a good boy, no one's going to quibble about that. We already told you, didn't we?'

Glaring, humiliated, Hughes croaked agreement.

'If you want to go beyond that, find somewhere else to do it. Next time I come back here it won't just be for a friendly word. You've had your second warning now and it's your last.'

The deputy turned on his heel, gesturing at Lister to follow him. He slammed the door loudly, pushed a hand through his thick, wiry hair and said, 'I need another drink after that. Christ, that place smelled foul.'

'Do you think it'll work?' Rob asked.

'I don't know.' Sedgwick sighed loudly as they walked up Call Lane, back towards Kirkgate. 'Maybe for a day or two. He thinks he's a

260

tough one, does that lad. He reckons Worthy might be weak so he's going after him. But he'll get a shock it if really comes down to it.'

'Worthy's still strong, then?'

'Oh, aye. Have you ever met him?'

Lister shook his head.

'He must be well over sixty by now, but he's still big. I wouldn't want to go up against him. Got a temper on him, too. Hughes wouldn't stand a chance. The boss hates him, but he seems to like him, too. It's strange; doesn't make any sense to me.' He pushed open the door of the White Swan once more and sat on an empty bench in the corner. 'You can get them,' he told Rob.

Twenty

The Constable nudged the horse into a canter, holding tight on the reins as he jounced up and down in the saddle. He wondered grimly what the deputy had found and hoped against hope that Hughes and Worthy wouldn't collide. He needed to be out here, on his way to Horsforth, but he needed to be back in the city, too, taking care of his business there.

He'd made good time, but felt his legs tremble as he dismounted, the animal snickering with the pleasure of the exertion as he turned it over to the stable boy. Well before he could reach the door, Samuel Godlove was coming out to him, dressed in his country clothes, once again a suit of sturdy brown cloth, woollen stockings rather than hose, his head bare, and worn, scuffed, working boots on his feet.

'Mr Nottingham.' He extended his hand and the Constable took it, seeing no sign of guile and deception in the man's sad eyes. 'Please tell me you have some news.'

'Not yet,' he apologized. 'I'm sorry, I know you need answers, but I do have a few more questions.'

Godlove's face clouded momentarily but he

262

said, 'Yes, of course, of course. I need to check a few things, would you mind walking with me?'

Nottingham agreed and the pair set off together.

'You went to Bradford that last time your wife left to see her parents.'

'Yes,' Godlove answered, sounding a little surprised. 'That's hardly a secret. I have some friends over there. I go and see them often.'

'Might I ask who?'

'Charles Deane and his wife. He trades in wool there; I've known him since we were boys.' He scratched his cheek. 'Are you trying to suggest something?'

'Not at all.' The Constable smiled reassuringly. 'I just need to know where you were.'

'I stayed there overnight,' Godlove offered. 'I do that regularly, have done for years. We played cards and drank quite a bit. I had some business out towards Halifax the next day and then I came home.'

'Quite late?'

'Yes, I suppose it was,' he answered slowly. 'I never thought about it. I didn't imagine I'd have anyone asking me questions on what I'd done.'

'No, of course not.' Nottingham paused, changing the topic warily. 'Tell me, did you know your wife went into Leeds every week?'

'Leeds?' he said in astonishment. 'She went there sometimes, to see a dressmaker or buy things, and we'd go to the assemblies on occasion, but it certainly wasn't every week.'

263

'She and her maid went out one day each week.'

'Yes. I told you that before.'

'That's when she went into the city.'

Godlove was silent for a long time.

'I don't understand,' he said eventually, his confusion evident. 'She always told me she could only tolerate Leeds in small amounts.'

'I can assure you, she went there every week,' the Constable said again. 'We have proof of it.'

The man raised questioning eyes. 'But why would she go there?'

This would be the test, he thought, to see how Godlove reacted when he heard. So far he seemed perfectly honest, his sorrow completely believable. God knew he didn't want to have to say it; if the man was innocent it would break his heart. But there was no other way.

'Well?'

'She had a lover there.'

He watched carefully, studying the man's face. For a moment Godlove was completely still, as if the world had stopped, and then his mouth started to move, but no words came out. If this was acting, Nottingham decided, he was the best player in England.

'I don't believe you,' he said finally, his voice stretched tight with hope. 'She had everything she could want here.'

Except the man she really loved, the Constable thought. And that was worth more to her than an estate.

'I'm sorry,' he said with a sigh. 'I really am,

but it's true.'

It had only taken a few seconds, but whatever life and fire had remained in Godlove had evaporated. For all his wealth and stature, all his lands and goods, he looked as empty and broken as a beggar on the road.

'Who was he?' he asked bleakly.

'He's dead.'

'Dead?'

'He killed himself,' was all the Constable would say.

'Did he kill her?' He heard faint hope in Godlove's question.

'No, I'm almost certain he didn't.'

'What was his name?'

Nottingham shook his head.

'What was his name?' The question came out like a desperate plea. 'Please, you've just told me that my wife had a lover and you won't tell me who he was.'

The Constable hesitated for a moment; perhaps the man had a right to know, and the knowledge could do no more harm.

'He was called Will Jackson. He was part-owner of a cloth finisher.'

'How old was he?'

'He was young.'

Godlove nodded once, as if this was the answer he expected.

'When did they meet?' he asked.

He didn't really want to know, Nottingham understood that. It would simply be salt placed on a gaping wound. But at the same time he had to, needed to. Not knowing, to wonder always, would be even worse. And he'd been cruelly deceived, he had a right to the truth, at least some of it. Some things were better kept in the dark of the grave.

'It was before you knew her,' he said gently. The man opened his mouth but the Constable held up his hand. 'She stopped seeing him for a while. I don't know how or when it all began again.'

'They met every week? You're sure?'

'It seems that way.'

'Did he love her?'

In the man's position he'd have asked the same question, needing the answer however much pain it caused.

'Yes,' he answered, without any doubt. Jackson had killed himself because he couldn't have her.

Godlove sighed, running his hands through his hair over and over, as if he didn't know what else to do. He seemed to grow smaller and smaller before the Constable, as if a breeze might eventually lift him and carry him away.

'I'm sorry,' Nottingham said. He reached out to touch the other man on the arm but Godlove pulled back, turning his face so that he wouldn't have to show the tears in his eyes.

'I didn't kill her.' His voice was quiet. 'I couldn't. I loved her.'

'I believe you.'

'Can you go now? Please.'

The Constable left the man in the field and

walked away. At the stable he collected the horse. When he reached the end of the drive he glanced back to see that Godlove hadn't moved. At times he hated this job. He'd broken a good man whose only fault was to love a faithless girl.

And even then, the blame wasn't all hers, he thought. If her parents hadn't been so greedy for money she could have had the man she loved. He wasn't sure which of the pair had more of his sympathy. There was no beauty in any of the love he'd seen here, just pain, hopelessness and death.

The bachelor who'd bought his bride was alone again, everything he'd believed about his wife shattered, the other two were dead. There were no happy endings, only dark ever afters.

Nottingham was still brooding after he'd reached Leeds and stabled the animal. He pushed his way through the crowded streets, glancing quickly at Worthy's door as he passed and made his way to the jail.

He still didn't know who'd killed Sarah Godlove.

'Anything, boss?' Sedgwick asked as the Constable sat down and poured a mug of ale. The day had grown hot and he was weary.

'He's innocent, no doubt about it. What did you find out here?'

'Hughes again. I went round and had a few strong words.'

'You think it'll work this time?'

'Not for more than a few days. There's going to be trouble soon.'

'His fists are bigger than his brain,' Nottingham said. 'It's Saturday. You'd better have more men out tonight, just in case he decides to start something. Rob, you can go out with them. If there's any trouble at all, crack some heads hard and fetch Mr Sedgwick. Carry a cudgel. I don't want this getting out of hand.'

'Yes, boss,' Lister answered.

'Right,' he told them, 'go on home, the pair of you. Rob, come back about eight. Get some sleep, you'll be out late tonight. You spend some time with that family of yours, John.'

'Yes, boss,' Sedgwick replied with a grin.

'Honest, he told me to go home,' he explained to Lizzie when she wouldn't believe the Constable had released him early from work. 'I don't know why, but I wasn't going to say no.'

She still looked at him sceptically before letting her mouth curl into a slow smile.

'Go on, I'll buy it, John Sedgwick, but thousands wouldn't.' She stood up, smoothing down her old dress. 'Well, since he told you to spend time with us, we can go out for the afternoon. Isn't that right, James?'

The boy took her hand and nodded firmly. The deputy knew he didn't have a chance against the pair of them.

'Where do you want to go?' he asked with a loud sigh and a smile.

'Kirkstall Abbey,' Lizzie answered quickly. 'I

268

haven't been there in years.'

He agreed with just the slightest reluctance, the memory of Sarah Godlove's body as it had looked at the jail flickering through his mind.

'We'd better get going, then,' he said, then wondered, 'Are you sure it's not too far in your state?'

She shook her head sadly at him.

'John, I'm having a baby, I'm not dying or ill, you know. People have been doing it for centuries. Now stop mithering me. It's lovely out, let's enjoy it.'

They strolled along the riverbank, following the path out of the city. James kept running ahead, gathering an oddly shaped twig, a grub on a leaf, and bringing his finds for them to inspect.

The afternoon sun was warm, not too hot, perfect for a slow amble together. He held Lizzie's hand, proud to be out with her, to have his small family around him. They passed others, exchanging polite greetings.

'Have you asked the Constable about more money yet?'

'No,' Sedgwick admitted. 'It's been busy.'

'The sooner you do it, the sooner we'll know. And we're going to need it, John.' She rubbed her stomach lightly, a reminder he didn't need.

'I will,' he promised. 'Soon. I mean it.'

'Has James ever been out here before?'

'Once, not that he'd remember it. He was just a baby then, couldn't even crawl.'

'Do you ever miss her?' Lizzie asked casually.

The question took him aback. 'Miss who?'

'Annie. The one you were married to.'

'God, no,' he answered fiercely. 'Good riddance to her. You know, even her father warned me not to marry her, and he was right. James is the only worthwhile thing to come out of that.'

'Well, he's ours now.' She squeezed his hand tightly. 'And the new one will be, too.'

'So what do you want to call this one?'

'Not yet,' she told him, the lightness and merriment suddenly gone from her voice. 'It's bad luck to think of that before they're born.'

He nodded and kissed her cheek, then ran off after James, roaring like a beast to scare the lad and chase him until they fell in a tangle. They drew closer to the ruins of the old buildings, the tower rising tall and stark against the sky.

'Is it very, very old?' James asked. He looked up, his voice full of awe.

'Aye, it is,' Sedgwick told him. 'It's been here a long time.'

'Was it a castle?'

'No, it was like a very big church, I think. But I'll take you to a castle one day, if you like.'

'Yes, please,' the boy said eagerly and his father laughed, tousling the lad's thick hair. 'You go and explore. We'll be sitting over here.'

'And don't get into any trouble,' Lizzie warned.

'I won't, mam,' he said, and he ran off to climb the old staircases and delve into the cellars.

'Mam,' the deputy said with a grin.

270

'The best word in the world.'

They sat on the remains of a low wall, watching the river swirl lazily by. After a while Lizzie stretched then lay down on the grass.

'I'm just going to doze for a little while,' she said. 'Do you mind?'

'Of course not.'

He took off his coat, folding it to give her a pillow. As he knelt she reached out and took his hand. In a soft, contented voice she said, 'Why are you so nice to me, John Sedgwick?'

'Because I love you, you daft thing,' he told her. 'Why do you think?'

As she drifted away, her face caught in the sunlight, he sat, watching over her, giving out a low whistle every few minutes to summon James. The lad was relishing the freedom to run and play unchallenged, his face and hands already mucky, his smile a mile wide. It looked as if he'd found some older boys to follow, and he was determined to show he wasn't any kind of baby, fearlessly jumping off arches taller than himself and clambering along treacherous pieces of masonry.

Sedgwick saw himself at that age, full of the same indestructible spirit. He'd broken a few bones and knocked out one or two teeth, but it had never stopped him. It was better than caution; there was far too much of that around. Boys needed a bit of adventure. Soon enough they'd be grown and the world would close in around them.

But not for him. Sometimes he thought he had

the best of everything. There was his family, and the job gave him enough rough and tumble, too much of it at times. He'd been beaten, he had scars, but it hadn't put him off. The money kept them fed and paid for their room. Lizzie was right, though; with another bairn on the way they needed something a little larger. He'd talk to the boss on Monday. He was a good man, he'd understand.

They stayed out at the abbey until the shadows were lengthening. After the other boys had wandered off, Sedgwick and Lizzie entertained James, running hither and yon with him until he was exhausted.

They followed the road back to the city, stopping at an alehouse close to the Kirkstall Forge, an old, small cottage made over with benches and old, dry rushes on the earth floor. The ale was good, quenching the thirst that he'd built up during the long afternoon.

'You look like you enjoyed that,' Lizzie said wryly as he drained the mug in one long swallow. 'The way that went down anyone would think you'd got no clack.'

'I needed it,' he told her, and started to signal for another.

'We'd better get home,' she told him, tilting her head towards James, his eyelids sagging. 'He's dead on his feet, poor lad. We've worn him out.'

'I'll carry him, don't worry.'

The boy stayed nestled in his arms, soft sleep-

272

ing breath on his neck as they neared Leeds, the air ripening with the smells of the city.

'I might be called out tonight,' the deputy told her.

'It's Saturday, you usually are.'

'This is something different,' he explained. 'There's someone thinks he can put Amos Worthy out of business.'

She sneered in disbelief. 'What's his name, Death?'

'Just someone new who runs a few girls and has big ideas.'

'Same as the rest, then. You think he'll succccd?' Lizzie asked.

Sedgwick shook his head. 'Not a chance. He doesn't have a clue what he's going up against. I can't stand that bastard Worthy, but at least he can use his brain.'

'So why hasn't Mr Nottingham put you in charge if there's going to be trouble?'

'He's letting the new man handle it.'

'Do you think he's up to it?'

'Only one way to find out. He'll come if he needs me. He's been good so far, though, I'll give him that. I wasn't sure about him, but I'm starting to think he'll work out very well.'

Rob Lister had been waiting at the jail for half an hour before the night men arrived, loud and rowdy. He'd tried to rest during the afternoon but had spent the time shifting around in his bed, a mix of excitement and nerves coursing through him and chasing sleep away.

He'd dressed in his oldest suit, threadbare at the elbows, the knees worn, the seams resewn several times, and an old shirt that should probably have been torn for rags. At least if there was a fight, nothing good would end up ruined. Compared to the night men, though, he was wearing royal robes. Some had clothes held together with little more than faith, and the best of them wore ripped shirts and patched breeches.

They knew the routine, and he was happy to simply follow them. They split into three pairs, patrolling the streets and glancing in on the alehouses and inns. The noise in each place dropped whenever they walked in, rose again as the door closed behind them.

For two hours he moved between the groups. When working none of them spoke much, and a couple cast him resentful looks, this youthful outsider the Constable had put over them. He was very aware that he'd yet to prove himself. The brief scuffle the other day had been nothing, he'd barely landed a blow before it was over.

The cudgel was in his pocket, close to hand if he needed it, but so far there'd been no sign of trouble. That would arrive later, when people had drunk down the week to forget about how little they had. Saturday night was their opportunity to find oblivion on gin or ale, the chance to laugh and love, to argue and fight.

The whores worked their corners on the street, flirting with old paper fans, exchanging banter with the men as they passed. One of the girls whispered in his ear, offering herself for a penny, but he smiled with a blush and turned away. The others laughed at his embarrassment, the girl loudest of them all.

'Never mind, love,' she told him in a warm voice, husky from cheap drams, 'you can come back when those two aren't around.'

The men were friendlier after that; he'd become one of them. By eleven they were breaking up brawls as grudges that had been held for days began to boil over. Everything was dealt with quickly and efficiently, the offenders dragged off to the jail to sleep it off.

With midnight the worst of it was over. A few drunks still staggered around, some had passed out on the street, curled in nooks or around corners like babies.

'Quiet night,' one of the men told Rob as they walked down Briggate. 'Often gets bad on a Saturday.'

'When do we work until?' he asked.

'While four.' The man coughed, hawked and spat on the street. 'Often it's Mr Sedgwick out with us, but happen he deserves a night off with that girl of his. You have a lass, do you?'

'No.'

'Should have gone with Essie, then,' the man winked. 'She'd have seen you right. Lower rates for a Constable's man, too.'

'I'll remember that when I get paid,' Rob answered with a smile. 'She wasn't bad looking.'

'Clean, too. That's the important part,' the man advised sagely. 'Allus remember that.'

275

One o'clock came, then two, rung out by the bells of the Parish Church. Everything was quiet; the people were in their beds. Once they ran after a shadow that scurried down the street, but lost him in the tangle of courts off Briggate. They'd resumed their walking when one of the men stopped.

'Wait,' he said, listening intently. 'I can hear summat, sounds like it's down by the bridge.'

Lister and the two men set off at a run. He slipped the thong of the cudgel over his wrist. As they pounded down Briggate he began to make out voices yelling, and felt the fear rise in his belly.

There were about ten of them in a mêlée. The night men forced their way into the throng, cudgels flying. Lister hesitated only a second before joining them, his blood rushing.

He saw Hughes, a knife in his hand, going after another man. Rob tried to fight his way through to them, pushing hard, bringing the wood heavily down on arms and heads.

A fist caught him in the face and rocked him. He shook his head to clear it, tasting blood in his mouth. Hughes was still there, his eyes wild, the blade of his knife red. Rob lowered his shoulder and charged through the crowd. There were fewer of them now; some lay on the ground, others were starting to run off.

A large older man was facing Hughes, a knife in one hand, a silver-topped stick held in the other. A cut on his arm oozed blood on to his coat and drops of sweat stood out on his face, but he still stood tall, mouth set, a burning look of hatred on his face.

'You stay out of it, laddie,' he warned, not even turning his head to the Constable's man. 'This is between me and him.'

'No,' Lister said. He was breathing hard and his heart punched in his chest. He was the Constable's man here. He wanted to prove himself, to bring order. He raised his voice and shouted, 'This stops now.'

The older man looked at Hughes then stared at Rob, shaking his head slowly.

'I told you to stay out of it, laddie,' he said sternly, as if he was addressing a child. 'You're not Richard Nottingham yet.'

Rob came to in one of the cells, his vision bleary, flames of pain in his head. He began to sit up, but a gentle hand on his shoulder kept him still.

'You stay there,' the Constable said. 'Rest awhile.'

Lister tried to clear his sight, blinking until he could make out the soft, blurred outlines of Nottingham and Sedgwick standing over him.

'What happened?' he asked. His voice was thick, as if his tongue had grown too large for his mouth. He tried to remember, but could go no further than a brawl of some kind.

'You were knocked out,' the deputy told him. 'You were trying to stop a fight.'

He tried once more to recall it, but nothing

277

came, no details, just a deep smudge of figures and vague voices without words.

'You got between Edward Hughes and Amos Worthy,' Nottingham explained.

It meant nothing. Very carefully he raised his hand, gingerly running the fingertips over his head until he felt the lump above his ear, the wound crusted heavily with blood. As soon as he touched it, it began to throb and he drew in breath sharply.

'Cudgel,' Sedgwick said. 'You went straight down, the night men said. They brought you back here. The apothecary says you should be glad you have a thick skull. Nothing's broken.' He smiled. 'Don't worry, it's happened to us all. You'll be fine in a couple of days.'

'That was brave, though, facing down those two,' the Constable said. 'Try and sit up slowly now and have a drink of this.' He steadied Rob's arm as he sat, and handed him a mug. 'It'll help you sleep in a while. One of the men will see you home.'

Lister drank, the liquid foul enough to make him gag at first but then welcome in his dry throat, washing it down with some small beer. He stood, taking care to hold on to the bed for balance, and then tried to walk a short way. His skull hurt, his eyes could only make out shapes, and there were still waves of agony, but after a minute they started to gently recede.

'You might never remember any of it,' Nottingham told him. 'There's a few times I've lost an hour or more. Don't worry about it. You just

278

go and rest in your own bed. It's Sunday, you can sleep it off.'

'Yes, boss.'

They waited until the door of the jail had closed before they began planning.

'You want Hughes?' the Constable asked.

The deputy nodded, not needing to say a word.

'Right, let's have him in one of the cells until tomorrow. You need any help?'

'No, I'll do this myself.'

Nottingham sighed. 'Maybe it's as well someone cracked Rob like that and they all ran off. They probably thought they'd killed him. There would have been some real blood otherwise.'

'What are you going to do about Worthy, boss?' the deputy wondered. It was the question the Constable had been asking himself since he'd arrived, dragged from his rest by one of the men hammering on his door.

'I'm not sure yet,' he answered thoughtfully. 'Let him stew for a while. The men said he'd been cut.'

'You're not going to let it go?'

'No, I'm not,' he replied with certainty. 'One of my men could have died because of him.'

Sedgwick said, 'The lad had me worried for a while there. He was out for a long time.'

'He seems fine now, that's what matters. We'll never find out exactly who hit him. Go and get Hughes. I need to go home and then to church.'

'Yes, boss.'

* * *

279

The sun was up, the sky clear and a pale, even blue. In the grand houses servants were already working, cleaning, preparing for the day, kitchen fires burning, a haze of smoke rising above the chimney pots.

Mary greeted him with a kiss and some bread and cheese, enough to take the edge off his appetite. Emily was still upstairs, making sure she looked just right in her new outfit, calling urgently for her mother every few minutes for an opinion on this, that or the other.

Finally he heard her stepping lightly down the stairs and he waited in the living room to see her. The dress was modest, as befitted a teacher, not cut too low, and merely a peek of snowy petticoat at the hem, her hair tucked primly under a clean, pressed cap.

'You look a picture, love,' he told her proudly and meant every word. He took her hands and kissed her forehead. 'You'll make a grand teacher.'

'Assistant,' she corrected him, but her eyes sparkled as she skittered back to her room.

'You've done a lovely job on the dress,' he said to Mary.

She smiled with weary satisfaction. 'It was worth all the effort to see her happy. You'd better go and change, Richard, we need to leave soon.'

They paraded into town, Nottingham flanked by the women in his life, smiling happily as they walked up the path to the Parish Church. For today at least he hoped to leave all the problems of work behind, to simply enjoy living.

The Reverend Cookson was preaching, the usual drone that won him praise but always sent half the congregation to sleep. Filled with people, the church was drowsily warm; several times the Constable found himself drifting off and Mary poking him in the ribs with her elbow to bring him back. Somewhere behind him he could hear a man's gentle snore, cruelly interrupted by the order from the pulpit to stand for the end of the service.

The congregation clattered out, eagerly breathing in the fresh air after the stuffiness inside, exchanging greetings and gossip. Emily stood talking earnestly to Mrs Rains about the work she'd start the next day, bobbing her head and smiling.

'There's no need to wait for her,' Mary said quietly. 'If I know Mrs Rains she'll be talking for at least fifteen minutes. And then she'll give Emily exactly the same instructions tomorrow morning.'

'No excuse for her forgetting, then,' he answered with a laugh. Slowly they strolled through the lych gate and down Kirkgate, Mary's arm through his, finally free to relish the tranquillity of Sunday. Church never lifted his spirit. He'd seen too much of the inhumanity of man to believe in a loving God. But he went because it was expected of his position, to sit and be seen, to doff his hat and bow in all the right directions. And, he admitted, there was something restful and even comforting in the familiar litany of prayers and hymns.

For all he tried to keep them at bay, the thoughts of work wouldn't vanish entirely. He knew that tomorrow he'd have to confront Amos Worthy, to do something to make sure the fighting between him and Hughes didn't flare up again into outright war. But he had no idea what.

He despised all that Worthy stood for, the way he exploited his girls and used his position and contacts to make himself invulnerable to prosecution. Yet since he'd discovered that the man had long ago been his mother's lover, protecting her after her husband had thrown her and her child out, he'd come to see the man in a slightly different light.

It wasn't a bond; it wasn't even something he could put into words. There were only wisps of feeling which eluded definition. They were opposites in almost every way. But somewhere, he knew, Worthy had some sense of honour, however twisted it might seem, and he could respect that.

The night before he'd crossed a line, though. Lister was a Constable's man, and that meant he had to be obeyed. He was untouchable. For what they'd done, Nottingham had no alternative but to stamp on both the culprits, to remind them who had charge of the city. He didn't imagine Hughes would be a great challenge, but Worthy would be a tougher proposition.

'Penny for them,' Mary said, touching his arm.

'Sorry,' he apologized, knowing she was used to this by now, never prying when he turned quiet, but always understanding. She pulled herself tighter to his arm and smiled up happily at him.

'It doesn't matter. I just like being with you.'

They continued in companionable silence, relishing the small joy of togetherness as they walked up Marsh Lane and he put the key in the door. While Mary bustled in the kitchen, he stared out of the window, looking out to the fields. Maybe it was time to give Sedgwick more responsibility, he pondered. To think of spending less time at work and more of it here. Who knew how long he'd live?

Maybe he and Mary really would grow old and bent together, but in his heart he knew it wasn't likely. He'd seen too many die, men and women his age and younger. It could happen at any time, in any way.

Twenty-One

He heard Emily moving around even before he pushed off the bedsheet. Quietly, he dressed and washed then tiptoed down to the kitchen. She was waiting, all prepared, her books gathered in a parcel, her face shiny and eager for the day to start.

'Can I walk in with you, papa?' she asked, and he could hear the excitement in her voice.

'Of course you can, love. I'd be proud to be seen with the best teacher in Leeds.'

She came and hugged him, something she'd rarely done in a long time, just once after Rose had died and she'd needed the comfort.

'Thank you,' she told him.

'For what?'

'Making Mr Hartington write that letter. I was so scared when I came home that day.'

Nottingham stroked her cheek. 'All I did is what any father would do. Me being Constable carries a little more weight, that's all.'

He poured some small beer and pulled some bread from the loaf. 'Do you want something to eat?' he asked her.

'I can't.'

He understood. She was nervous, pacing the

floor, impatient for him to finish. She'd arrive far too early at the school, but that was what she needed today. Give it another fortnight and she'd be dashing down the road to reach the place in time.

After they left the house her feet moved quickly, and he laughed silently to himself as he kept up with her; any quicker and she'd be running to school. As they approached the jail he took her arm.

'You need to be ladylike, you're in town now.'

'Yes, papa,' she said, then giggled like a little girl when he grinned.

Lister was waiting outside the door, soberly dressed, a tricorn hat perched high on his head. He bowed to Emily, showing a bandage wrapped neatly around his skull as he doffed the hat. The Constable smiled as she blushed beetroot.

'You'll do fine,' he told her, placing a small kiss on her forehead. 'I'll see you tonight and you can tell me all about it.'

He watched as she walked away, and he sensed that she was trying not to run.

'Your daughter, boss?'

'Yes,' he said proudly. 'She starts teaching at the Dame School today. How's your head?'

'I feel like I've spent three days drinking, but without any of the fun,' he replied wryly.

'It'll wear off.' He looked in the cells and saw Hughes sleeping on a bench. Give him one more day, he thought. Tuesday would be soon enough for him. 'You're in luck, there's not much to do, Rob,' he advised. 'Look after things here. I'm

285

going up to Roundhay with Mr Sedgwick, if he ever arrives.'

'Yes, boss.'

'Your friend Edward Hughes is locked up. Give him a little food and ale when he wakes. Don't tell him how long he'll be here.'

'What about the other man?'

'I'll be dealing with him later. If anything comes up, find one of the men. There shouldn't be much.'

He was finishing his instructions when the deputy pushed the door open.

'Morning, John,' Nottingham said. 'I see you got him. Did he give you any trouble?'

'Nothing to worry about.'

'Good. Now you can come with me. We're off to Roundhay.'

He took the knife that had killed Sarah Godlove from the drawer and handed it to Sedgwick. 'See if there's a match for this when we're there.'

For the first mile as they rode out, Sedgwick complained. The Constable had expected it, a list of objections about the animal, the saddle and stirrups, even the feeling of being on a horse. He listened patiently, knowing it would trail away in time.

'Why are we going to see the Gibtons again?' the deputy asked finally.

'Too many unanswered questions,' Nottingham told him. 'I've let this Sarah Godlove business drag on too long. There's something very

286

wrong with the Gibtons. I'm going to push them and see what happens. I want you with me since we're dealing with people of quality.' He uttered the words in a cutting, sardonic tone.

A full five minutes passed before Sedgwick spoke again.

'Boss?'

'What, John?'

'Is there any chance of more money?'

'More money for what?' He suspected he knew the reason but he wanted to be certain.

'For me,' the deputy said hesitantly. 'It's just that with the baby coming we'd like to be able to afford somewhere bigger.'

Nottingham turned in the saddle. Sedgwick looked ill at ease.

'I think I can manage that. It won't be much, mind, but a little more each week. Would that help?'

Sedgwick grinned widely, and for a moment he looked just like a young boy who'd been given an unexpected treat.

'Thank you, boss. Lizzie'll be happy now.'

'You'd better keep her sweet. You're going to be with her for a long time.'

'I bloody well hope I am,' the deputy said.

'She's a good lass. She's certainly got the measure of you, no mistake.'

They left their horses tied in the shade of a tree, panting and wanting water. Nottingham knocked on the large front door and waited until it was answered by a maid, different from the one he'd seen last time.

'You're new?' he asked.

'Yes, sir.' She coloured and gave a full curtsey. 'It's my first day, sir.'

'What happened to the other girl?'

'The master let her go, sir.' The blush on her face grew deeper.

He smiled at her, but wondered why the other girl had been dismissed and whether it had anything to do with him.

'I'd like to speak to Lord Gibton. I'm the Constable of Leeds.'

'Yes, sir.' She scurried away, glancing nervously over her shoulder several times, a questioning look in her eyes.

Within a minute Gibton was striding down the hall. This time he was wearing clothes made for a country man, but certainly not for work; the material was fine, the riding boots lovingly polished to a high shine. His mouth was set, eyes hard.

'What do you need now, Constable?' he asked dismissively.

'Some more questions, sir.'

Gibton stood and waited. 'Well?'

Nottingham smiled and inclined his head. 'Perhaps we should go in the drawing room, sir.'

The man snorted but agreed.

'Can my man go and get some water for the horses while we talk?'

Gibton gave a curt nod. 'Go round to the kitchen,' he instructed.

The Constable raised his eyebrows at Sedgwick, then followed the baron.

'Now, what is it? I don't have time to keep talking to you.' He was standing by the fireplace, the portrait of him and his wife over his head. The picture caught the man's arrogance well, Nottingham thought, the haughty, upturned jaw, the innate, unquestioning sense of superiority. There was no trace of the grace, the goodness and looks they'd had when younger.

'When your daughter had intended to visit that last time, I gather you sent the servants away.'

The baron gave a small grunt. 'I knew that girl must have talked to you.'

'Is that why you dismissed her?'

'Not really,' Gibton said casually. 'She wasn't good at her job. There's no point in paying servants who won't do the job properly.'

'But she did tell me the truth?'

'Yes,' he admitted reluctantly.

'You didn't mention that before, my Lord,' Nottingham said impatiently. 'I'm looking into a murder. The murder of your own daughter. That means I need the truth, and all of it, please, however painful it might be.'

Gibton waited a moment before answering. 'Would it have made any difference, Constable? It's a very private, delicate matter. And I told you, Sarah never arrived here.'

Nottingham said nothing, but stared at Gibton. Outside, the rooks cawed loudly in the trees. Finally the man gave in and shook his head.

'When my wife has an episode it can sometimes be easier with no one else around. She can become very difficult.'

The Constable sensed how much it had pained him to make that admission, especially to a social inferior.

'And how bad was this attack?'

'Very bad indeed,' he answered gravely. 'It was the worst she's ever been, in fact, and that's in many years. That's why I needed to send the servants away for a few days. As soon as I could see what was happening and how severe it was likely to become I told them to go. I didn't want them seeing her like that. They'd have lost all their respect for her.' He said it as if that was the most important thing in the world.

'What happens to her?' Nottingham asked.

Gibton looked at him, and the Constable guessed he was assessing how much to reveal. Finally he shrugged.

'My wife has never had the easiest of tempers,' he began. 'She doesn't suffer fools well. But with one of these episodes it usually begins with a bad headache, so bad she has to take to her bed. Then she'll become loud and sometimes she'll be violent.'

'Violent?' Nottingham hadn't expected that.

'Yes. She lashes out. She doesn't know what she's doing, and she doesn't remember it afterwards. She's hit me before and she's very strong then, she's out of control. So perhaps now you see why I told the servants to leave.'

'How do you treat it?'

'I've learned over the years. I've had doctors in.' He sighed in resignation and for a moment looked like a lost, ordinary man. 'Nothing they've given her has helped. About the only thing I can do is tie her to her bed when it happens.'

'I'm sorry,' the Constable told him.

The baron raised his head, and for a passing moment Nottingham could see all the years of pain in his eyes. Then Gibton gathered himself, straightening his back.

'I'm trusting that none of this will go beyond these walls,' he said.

'You have my word,' Nottingham promised. 'How long does an episode last?'

'Sometimes an hour or two, sometimes longer. This last time it was a full day. She didn't recall a thing.' He paused, considering. 'Maybe that's a blessing.'

'How is she when it's over?'

'She sleeps for hours and when she wakes up it's as if nothing had happened. It just takes her some time to come back to herself.'

The Constable walked over to the windows and looked outside. The day was still, the sun shining and peaceful, but inside the house the atmosphere was gloom and darkness, and always would be.

'Where's your wife now?' he asked.

'She's in her room,' Gibton said.

'I'd like to see her, if I might.'

'I don't think—' he began, but Nottingham was shaking his head.

'You have to understand, my Lord, anyone can say anything. I'm not doubting your word, but I need your wife to confirm it.'

291

The man tightened his mouth then agreed.

'I'll have the girl call her,' he said, and left the room.

Nottingham returned to the window and sighed. What he'd heard had been heartfelt and sad. But he knew it wasn't the complete truth.

There was enough of it in there to try to keep him off the scent. But Gibton was hiding something, and it was more than just embarrassment and pain at his wife's madness.

And madness was certainly what it sounded like. It bore out all the tales about the woman. He sighed, not relishing the idea of meeting her but knowing it was necessary. Through the glass he could see Sedgwick ambling lazily towards the stables. He tapped on the window. When the deputy looked his way, he tilted his head questioningly and received a nod in return. Nottingham smiled.

Gibton returned, his hand supporting his wife's elbow. She was a small, thin woman with a pinched face and eyes like gravestones, looking at the Constable with a dark suspicion that verged on outright hatred. It was hard to believe that she'd once been a beautiful girl. All the grace and loveliness she'd supposedly possessed when she was young had been chiselled away by bitterness.

'My Lady,' he said with a small bow.

'My husband says you need to talk to me,' she addressed him in a voice as cold as last winter. 'I assume you have a good reason for this disturbance.'

'I do.' Nottingham gave an easy smile. 'Would you sit down, please? And you, too, my Lord.'

They glanced at each other but did as he asked, arranging their clothes carefully to avoid creases.

'Now,' she said through thin, tight lips, 'what is this?'

'First, I'd like to remind you that all these questions, all this inconvenience, have a purpose,' the Constable began, a new fire in his voice. 'I'm trying to discover who murdered your daughter.' He paused, watching the couple, hoping for a reaction. But their eyes never left his face, hers burning, his quietly attentive. 'I've been shocked by the way you've taken her death so calmly. If my daughter had been killed I'd have done everything in my power to find out who did it.'

'You're not us,' Gibton told him, the haughtiness back in his voice. 'Don't presume to try and understand what we feel. Just because we choose not to show it doesn't mean we don't grieve. And unless I'm wrong, finding the person who did this to Sarah is your business. As the mayor has reminded us every time we've asked, you're supposed to be good at your job.'

'He doesn't look as if he could be good at much,' Lady Gibton commented, eyeing him up and down with distaste.

Nottingham took a deep breath.

'Tell me, my Lady, did you know that your daughter was planning on leaving her husband and running away with her lover?' He let the

293

question hang a moment before plunging on. 'That's the same lover she had before she met Mr Godlove, the one you made her give up.'

Laby Gibton stood up and came near. She needed to look up to talk to him.

'You're a liar.' The words hissed from her and he felt spittle warm against his face. She drew an arm back to slap him, but the Constable reached out and took a light hold of her wrist.

'No,' he said quietly, 'I'm not lying. I told her husband two days ago and the news almost broke him. There's one thing I didn't mention to him, though. Your daughter was pregnant with her lover's child.'

She tried to move her arm, to bring it round to hit him, but he kept his grip tight on her. Her eyes flamed, and her husband stared at the floor. He had them. Nottingham released her wrist and stepped backwards. 'But then, you already knew that, didn't you?'

Neither of them replied, but he could feel the guilt in their silence.

'I'm sure you really were ill,' he told her, 'although I'll never be able to prove it one way or the other. The timing was fortunate, though, wasn't it, with the servants dismissed?'

'You've been told before, she never came here,' Lady Gibton said.

The Constable smiled. 'I've been told many things in the last few weeks. A few of them have even been true. But that wasn't one of them. Sarah arrived here that Thursday after the servants had gone. You hadn't been expecting her but it turned out well. There were only the four of you in the house when she gave you her news – you two, your daughter and her maid. I haven't forgotten about Annie.'

Gibton stood and began to walk out of the room.

'Are you leaving, my Lord?' Nottingham asked. 'I've not even sketched an outline yet.'

The baron stopped, then turned. 'I won't stay to listen to this,' he announced.

'Your wife doesn't seem to want to leave yet,' the Constable said. 'I think it would be better if no one went. After all, so far I'm not sure which of you killed your daughter.'

Twenty-Two

This time Lady Gibton's open hand came up before he could move and cracked him hard across the cheek. He felt the hot, sharp sting on his flesh.

'Get out,' she screamed. Her face had turned wild and feral, and he had to reach out and pin both her arms to stop her hitting him again.

'No,' he told her. 'You're both going to hear this.' He waited until the tension in the room dropped slightly.

'You'd better have extremely good proof that we killed Sarah,' Gibton said threateningly. 'She was our daughter. We loved her.'

'Of course you did. You loved her enough to keep her away from the man she wanted to be with, and sold her so you could have all this.' He glanced around the room, taking in the portrait and the new furnishings. 'I'll tell you one thing I can prove – that the knife which killed Sarah came from here. One of the servants recognized it and said it went missing during those few days you sent them all away.' He paused again, hoping they would fill the silence. 'That should be damning enough for any jury, I'm sure you'll agree. They'd have no choice but to hang you both – unless the mob dragged you out of jail and did it themselves. It's happened before. In my experience, people hate those who kill their own children.'

He looked from one of them to the other.

'Hanging can either be fast or slow,' he continued, his voice low and hypnotic. 'Did you know that some people going to the gallows pay the hangman to make it quick, so the neck breaks and it's over?' As they watched he brought his hands together and made a snapping motion. 'Like that. The people who die that way are the lucky ones, so it's said. If no one will do that for you, or the drop isn't long enough, you choke. It takes up to twenty minutes; I've timed it. That's all those long minutes when the pressure grows on your neck and you feel your life slowly leaving you, and the mob watching everything. I'll wager you a penny to a guinea that no one would take your money to speed it up. They'd be gathered on Chapeltown Moor for you two. Minor aristocracy, killed your own daughter. It would even be in the London papers. You'd be famous.'

'You've ranted and threatened, but you still haven't said why we're supposed to have killed Sarah,' Lady Gibton said icily. 'Tell me, Constable, why would we kill our flesh and blood?'

'Money, plain and simple,' he replied. 'If she'd run off with Will Jackson, Godlove would have cut you off. All this would have gone.' He gestured to take in the house. 'You'd been waiting all these years until Sarah had grown up and you could arrange a marriage for her that would leave you well off. Now she was going to take everything away from you, and all for something as trivial as love. So you killed her.'

'Do you really think anyone will believe that?' she said.

'I know they will,' he answered confidently. 'We have proof of Sarah's visits to Will Jackson every week. He was selling his business. You'd be surprised what we've discovered.'

'Facts you've twisted,' she sneered.

'You know, you should have encouraged her with Will,' he told them. 'He went on to do very well indeed. And he's the one she wanted.'

'Her husband loved her,' Gibton said.

'Yes, he did,' Nottingham agreed sadly. 'He was besotted with her. It's just a pity she could never return that. She was a lucky girl in a way, having the love of two men. But there was only one for her.'

'She was better off with Godlove,' Lady Gibton said firmly. 'I told her so.'

'No, *you* were better off when she was with Godlove,' the Constable corrected. 'She wouldn't deny her heart, though, would she? She couldn't give Will up.' He paused. 'You know, I should have concluded all this earlier. But I simply couldn't believe that parents could cold-bloodedly kill their child for money. I refused to think it was possible. I should have known better.'

Gibton pushed himself away from the wall and walked towards the Constable so that both husband and wife now stood close to him.

'And do you honestly think you'll obtain a conviction in court?' he asked disdainfully. 'You'd do well to remember who sits on the bench. It's not the likes of you, Constable –' he spat out the title '– in your rag bag of clothes. It's the kind of people who'd dine here, people who send us invitations, people who understand what life is like for us.'

He didn't need to say more; Nottingham understood. Money could build thick walls against justice. A title could make them impregnable. But he wasn't going to be cowed now.

'My guess is that it was Lady Gibton who wielded the knife,' he said. 'Let's be generous and say she was still in her madness, and perhaps she didn't know what she was doing.' Her eyes gave nothing away, her stare flinty. 'You still had to kill Anne and get them away from here to finish the job. That was calculated. I don't know what you wanted people to think when you left Sarah at Kirkstall Abbey. I can't even guess at that. If you'd dumped her the way you did Annie I'd never have suspected a thing. Just two young women killed by robbers.' He inclined his head in the direction of Roundhay. 'You know, I can leave here and ride into the village. The Taylors are desperate to know who killed their daughter and why. I can tell them who was responsible and why. If I do that do you really believe you'll last until the end of the day?'

He gave them time to consider that. He might

299

not be able to put them on the gibbet but there were other kinds of justice.

'I'm giving you until Friday to decide what you're going to do,' he told them. 'That's when I tell Annie's parents and Mr Godlove what happened. You will let me know what you plan to do before then. And if you believe my threats are all bluster, then I suggest you wait and do nothing. I'll warn you now, though, that I'm not a man to say things idly.'

Gibton reached out to take his wife's hand. As his fingers began to curl around hers she pulled away sharply. 'You won't do it,' she said.

Nottingham raised an eyebrow. 'Won't I?'

She smiled coldly. 'You're a little man. All you can do is bluff.'

'You'd better wait and see, hadn't you? Even we little men can keep our word.'

He left them standing in the room and walked out into the sunlight. It felt bright and clean on his skin.

'I thought you were going to arrest them after I gave you the nod,' Sedgwick said as they rode back down the long hill towards Leeds.

The Constable let out a long, deep breath. 'I was,' he began. He was glad to be away from the house. 'Then Gibton reminded me that all the magistrates are from his class. They'd never let him or his wife swing. They can read, so they'd be able to plead benefit of clergy, if nothing else; they wouldn't even receive a real sentence.'

'Aye, I suppose so,' the deputy agreed reluctantly. 'So what did you do?'

'I've told them they have until Friday.'

'To do what?'

'To decide what they're going to do to make amends.' He looked at the deputy. 'They're going to punish themselves,' he explained. 'Christ, killing your own daughter to keep on receiving money for her. Who could do something like that?'

'And if they haven't done anything by Friday?'

'Then I tell Godlove, and Annie's parents.'

'They'd kill them.'

'I know,' he answered flatly. 'I'm not sure they believed me when I said I'd do it, though.'

'They have a few days to stew on that. Which one do you think did it?'

'Her,' Nottingham replied without any hesitation. 'He told me about her. She really does have bouts of madness. She was in the middle of a very bad spell when Sarah arrived. My guess is Sarah had only come to tell them she was leaving with Will. The mother saw everything collapsing and lashed out with a knife.'

'Then why did they take her out to the abbey?'

'I don't know. They just didn't want her anywhere near Roundhay. Maybe they weren't thinking straight. Or they decided that if Sarah was found over there, it would look like she'd never been here. I can't even pretend to grasp it, John. I'm not sure I want to. Who can understand how they think?'

'There's something wrong with folk like that.'

'True,' the Constable agreed with a sad shake

of his head. 'One thing about this job is that you find some people who aren't normal. But I'm not sure I've ever come across a pair like these before.'

'You should have just told Annie's parents and left it at that.'

'I thought about it,' he admitted. 'But then we'd have more mess to clean up. And those people wouldn't have judges for friends.'

'Aye, that makes sense, I suppose.'

They rode on quietly, passing through Harehills, a few cottages and a tavern huddled close round a crossroads.

'I've been thinking. Can you wait until September for more money?' Nottingham asked.

Sedgwick looked at him quizzically.

'We'll have a new mayor then. I've met him a few times. He started small, he was apprenticed to a draper. I think he'd give us more to spend.'

'If he hasn't gone all high and mighty.'

'He doesn't seem to have. Don't worry, I'll find you something.'

'Thanks, boss.'

'I have to look after you,' he said with a grin. 'After all, you'll have my job one day.'

From what the Constable had said, Lister had expected a quiet day. He didn't know enough about the job to do much, just to sit, look through papers, and have his thoughts return to the boss's daughter. She was a pretty girl, with real warmth and joy in her eyes.

It was stupid, he knew that. He shouldn't be

302

thinking about her. He'd barely even caught a glimpse of her face. But that didn't stop his mind drifting back to her every few minutes. It would pass, he told himself. He'd take a walk, see another lass with a pretty smile and then she'd be in his head instead.

An hour grated past and he wished he was with the Constable and Sedgwick. They'd said little about why they were going out to Round-hay, but there seemed to be a sense of finality about it, as if they were preparing to settle things.

He was casting about for something, anything to fill the time when the door flew open and the men walked in. There were three of them, all tall and bulky, all of them armed with swords. One turned the key, locking them in, another drew his weapon and gestured Lister to a chair. No one said a word. Rob sat down, watching the blade that was straight and unwavering, the point held close to his chest.

He gazed up at the man's face for a moment. He was in his twenties, eyes showing nothing, his mouth just a straight line. His clothes were old, the nap of the jacket worn, seams fraying, collar worn smooth, the elbow of his sword arm threadbare.

Rob watched helplessly as the other two took the cell keys from the hook and disappeared down the corridor. He heard the rattle of iron while the third man kept the sword pointing at him. He waited, breathing slowly, trying to memorize everything he saw. If they'd wanted to kill him, he reasoned, they'd have done it immediately. As long as he stayed still and quiet he was probably safe. The man facing him appeared completely calm, his concentration easy and absolute. He was a professional, unafraid.

Had they come to kill Hughes or to free him, he wondered? That was the only question. There was no noise from the cell. He listened carefully for a voice, then caught the scrape of boots.

They came back, the two invaders and Hughes, grinning broadly. He paused, pushing the man's sword arm away, then hawked and spat in Lister's face before laughing.

As silently as they came, the men unlocked the door and left.

He sat for a full five minutes before moving. His heart was thumping and sweat trickled cold down his spine. He couldn't have done anything, he told himself over and over, hoping against hope that the Constable would believe him when he returned.

He walked down the corridor, a prickle of fear on his neck. The keys were still in the lock, the door to the cell gaping open.

It seemed impossible that anyone would have dared do this, to walk into the jail and free one of the prisoners. He sat in the chair again, each moment sharp and fixed in his mind. Only now, as it all played through again in his head, did the terror really begin to rise.

The boss wouldn't keep him on after this. He'd think that he'd helped them take Hughes, that he couldn't be trusted. But if he'd tried to stop them, he'd have died; he knew that. They'd have killed him without a second thought. He looked down at his hands and saw they were shaking violently. The tremor began to move through his body, beyond his control, unstoppable.

It had only just passed by the time the Constable and Sedgwick came in. He'd drunk a mug of ale, spilling part of it on the desk, and was beginning to feel a little calmer.

'By God, you look pale, lad,' the deputy said jokingly. 'That blow the other night must have been worse than I thought.'

'Hughes,' Lister began, then hung his head. He could feel shameful tears beginning to form in his eyes and he tried to blink them away.

'Rob?' Nottingham asked with concern. 'What has happened?'

Sedgwick dashed down the corridor, and he looked up to see him return, shaking his head.

Slowly he recounted it all, every detail, feeling ashamed, the image of the big, cold man with the sword growing larger in his mind and Hughes's spittle still burning on his cheek so that he tried to paw it away.

'I couldn't stop them, boss,' he explained desperately.

'You did exactly the right thing,' the Constable assured him. 'There's a difference between bravery and stupidity. John?'

'Yes, boss?'

'Go and get as many of the men as you can find and bring them back here. Make sure

305

they're armed.'

After the deputy had left, Nottingham put a hand on Lister's shoulder.

'I meant it, Rob. They were going to take him either way, and you're a lot more use to me alive than dead. If you want some revenge, you'll have it in a little while.' He pulled a pistol from the drawer, checked, loaded and primed the piece before sliding it into his coat pocket. 'Have you ever used a weapon?'

'I had a fencing master for a few months when I was younger.'

The Constable raised his eyebrows.

'I wasn't very good,' Rob admitted wryly. 'My father decided it wasn't worth the cost.'

Nottingham chuckled. 'That's a real Yorkshireman for you, always after value for money. Never mind, at least you know how to handle one of these.' He brought an old sword and scabbard from the cupboard. 'Just a word of advice. With this lot you won't gain anything by just wounding them. You understand?'

'Yes, boss.'

He strapped the blade on to his belt, its weight and shape awkward against his body, and saw Nottingham use a whetstone to hone the blade of his knife. He felt strangely serene; all the dread that had left him quaking just a few minutes before had passed. He brought his hand down to rest on the hilt of the sword, wrapping his fingers around the grip.

'You remember what he looked like?'

'Yes.' He was certain he'd never forget the

man's face.

'Watch out for him. Don't get your blood up and go looking for him. He sounds like he knows what he's doing.' Nottingham primed another pistol and sharpened a second dagger, leaving them lying on the desktop.

They had a few minutes to wait before Sedgwick came back, a clamour of voices behind him outside the door. The Constable gestured at the weapons and the deputy took them.

The men spilled into the road on Kirkgate, looking to him for instructions. He heard the deputy and Lister follow him out and the sound of the door closing. The afternoon sun was high and hot, making him squint awkwardly. He thought how ridiculous it was to have to do this on a summer's day when everything should have been peaceful and placid.

But he had no choice. Hughes believed he could flout the law in Leeds, and Nottingham had to show him he was wrong. Hughes had challenged; the Constable's reply would be swift and absolute. He glanced at the men. Some of them had bright eyes, eager for the fight. Others kept their faces blank, hands dug into their coat pockets. He waited until they were all quiet and expectant.

'Right,' he shouted. 'This is what we're going to do. Half of you will go with Mr Sedgwick. You'll be at the back of the house. The rest of you are coming with me to the front. When I give the signal we'll go in. Smash the windows and the doors. Create confusion. I don't know how many there are there, probably seven or eight. They'll be expecting us, so it's going to be nasty.'

'What's the signal?' someone asked, and Nottingham gave a shrill, two-note whistle.

'Any questions?'

'Do we get extra pay for this?' another man yelled from the back, accompanied by laughter that grew louder when the Constable answered.

'We'll pay for your funeral if they kill you. How about that?'

They marched down Briggate and turned on to the Calls, a loose, ragtag group of men, looking dangerous enough for folk to keep out of their way. A couple of the men laughed and joked, but Nottingham remained quiet and alert. He was certain that Hughes would have someone looking out for them, giving him warning.

Why had they broken the man out of jail? It was a reckless, pointless thing to do. They'd invited this. The Constable rarely picked a fight, only when there was no other way, but when he did, it was always to win.

Sedgwick took five of the men and vanished into one of the courts. He'd need a few minutes to find the house and set everyone in position. Nottingham looked around his men, all of them silent and tense now. Lister rubbed nervously at his chin with the back of his hand.

Nottingham felt the dampness of sweat under his arms and down his spine. The knife was in one hand, the pistol in the other. Finally he raised a hand and nodded. The men gathered around the front of the house, clustered behind him. He gave the whistle and his boot crashed hard against the door. The wood splintered but the lock just held.

The Constable quickly brought his foot quickly down a second time, then a third, and the door finally gave, flying back against the wall in the hallway.

'In there,' he yelled, gesturing at the parlour. 'Rob, with me.' He started to climb the stairs, glancing upwards. Hughes would be there, he thought, where he'd be safer.

The man guarding the door at the top had no chance. Nottingham pulled the trigger, the sound of the gun deafening with the walls so close, the smoke dense and choking. The body fell with a short cry.

Nottingham kicked the door open, held back for a moment, then dashed in. There was one room, with a pallet in the corner. Hughes and two of his men stood together in the middle of the room, all of them with swords drawn.

He heard Rob behind him, the sliding metallic scrape as he drew his weapon.

'Think you can take me?' Hughes asked. The Constable said nothing, his gaze flickering between three sets of eyes, trying to anticipate how they might move. 'Think you're better than me?'

Lister circled to his left, alert, watching. The man closest to him made a feint and he drew back slightly. The other guard slashed at Nottingham. The Constable moved aside, slicing his blade down swiftly on the back of the man's hand, cutting deep across the skin. He dropped the sword with a scream. Nottingham moved in quickly, his boot connecting with the man's balls, already looking at Hughes as the bodyguard fell.

Lister and the other man were exchanging blows, the sound ringing through the room. The lad seemed to be holding his own, from what the Constable could judge. In front of him, Hughes held his blade in both hands like an amateur. His eyes were manic, a wide rictus grin on his face.

Somewhere in his head Nottingham heard footsteps running up the stairs. Then there was the violent thump of a pistol and Hughes crumpled to the floor, his gaze blank now, red spreading across his colourful waistcoat. The deputy loomed in the doorway, smiling.

'Give it up,' Nottingham ordered the last man, his voice hoarse, holding his breath until he dropped his sword and raised his arms, a cut above his wrist dripping blood. 'Take him downstairs,' he said. He'd done almost nothing, but he was panting hard, his throat dry, the fury surging through him. 'Did we lose anyone?' he asked.

Sedgwick shook his head. 'A couple of them cut, nothing serious. Three of theirs dead, two more to go off and hang. Not even a good fight in them.' He spat.

The Constable nodded. It was better than he'd hoped. He realized he was still holding the pistol and knife and put them away. He left, easing his way around the body on the stairs.

How long had it taken? Two minutes? Three? No longer than that, he was certain. The men had gathered outside, forming a tight ring around their prisoners. The two in the middle lowered their heads, knowing they'd be doing the hangman's dance up on Chapeltown Moor soon enough.

'Good job, lads,' he told them. 'There's a mug of ale for each of you at the Ship.' He waited until the last of the defeated had been brought down and thrown in with his companions. 'Take them to the jail,' he ordered.

Lister was standing, still looking dazed, the dull sword hanging by his side, his fist clenched so tight on the hilt that the colour had left his knuckles.

'You can put it away now, lad,' Sedgwick said with a grin, tousling his hair. Blushing, suddenly aware, Rob sheathed the weapon.

'You did a good job there, you even wounded him,' Nottingham praised him. 'Was that the one who held you earlier?'

'Yes.'

'I'd say the fencing master was worth his money, then. I've seen that one before. He's a nasty piece of work.'

'Honestly, boss?'

Nottingham nodded, and it was no less than the truth. The man had been around the city for a year or more, working for whoever offered enough. He was one of the hard men, good with his fists, good with a blade, fearless if the price was right. Leeds would be better with him on the gallows.

He glanced up at the sky, scarcely believing it was still only afternoon. Between this and the encounter in Roundhay the day seemed to have lasted a lifetime.

'What about Worthy?' the deputy asked, and Nottingham sighed wearily.

'Tomorrow, John,' he said. 'He'll keep until then. Let him feel that the competition's gone before I bring him crashing down. All I want now is a drink and to go home.'

He led them to the White Swan and settled a pitcher of the landlord's best brew on the table with three mugs.

'To Rob,' he said, offering a toast. 'You're a real Constable's man now. You've drawn first blood.'

They drank deep, throats parched from the brief fight. Lister was smiling as broadly as a lunatic and Nottingham understood exactly how he felt. He remembered the first time the old Constable had taken him out and bought him a drink. It was as if he'd grown up, blossomed into a man after so long as a child.

Part of him could happily have stayed here drinking until the late evening, enjoying the company and the banter. But the tiredness was catching him up. He felt it deep in his bones as the thrill and shock of the violence drained out of his body.

He stood up, arching his back to stretch it, and wished them good night. Let the young stay carousing, he'd done it often enough himself when he was their age. Outside the air was still. As he walked past the Parish Church the shadows loomed longer in the shank of the evening. A few birds still sang and the smell of flowers from the woods by the beck was strong.

He stopped and inhaled deeply, hearing the languid burble of the water and feeling the quiet settle around him. He rested a few minutes, drinking in the air as he'd drunk in the ale and letting it fill his soul. Then, smiling, he strolled on home.

Emily was waiting, sitting upright and alert, her face eager, unable to hide the joy in her eyes.

'It must have gone well,' he said to her. Had it really just been that morning that he'd seen her off for her first day of teaching?

'Oh, papa,' she replied contentedly, 'it was perfect. This is what I should always have been doing.'

He hugged her close before holding her at arm's length. 'I'm glad.'

Mary was in the kitchen and he went through. He wrapped his arms around her waist, pushing his face against her hair.

'She sounds happy.'

'She is. I think she must have relived every minute a hundred times since she came back.'

'Let's hope it stays this way.'

She turned and nuzzled against him. 'I think it might. That business in Headingley affected her more than she's said, you know, especially coming after Rose's death. She needs something like

313

this, something safe.'

He closed his eyes, relishing the familiar scent of his wife, feeling as if he could stay this way forever until she tapped him playfully on the arm.

'You're falling asleep on your feet, Richard. Go to bed.'

She was right, and he knew it; she was always right. He was as drained as an empty barrel, hollow and useless. Rest was the best thing for him now. He kissed Mary tenderly, hugged Emily and started up the stairs.

'Papa?' his daughter asked quietly.

'What is it, love?'

'That young man at the jail this morning? Who was he?'

Nottingham had to force himself to think back. It seemed too far in the past.

'You mean the one with the bandage on his head?'

'Yes.'

'He's just started working for me.'

'What happened to him?'

'He was cracked on the head when he tried to break up a fight,' he explained, then added darkly, 'but he had his revenge for it this afternoon.'

'What's his name?'

'Rob Lister.'

She nodded and he was laughing silently to himself as he entered the bedroom. So she had eyes for Rob, did she? Well, he thought, if she did the poor lad wouldn't stand a chance. And she could do a lot worse. He stripped, folding his clothes, and finally settled himself, the sheet thrown loosely over his body.

But for all his exhaustion, he couldn't fall asleep. His mind was like a spring pushed too tight, unable to wind down, and he knew he'd have to suffer it, forced to let the thoughts run and run through his head until they were finally ready to fade away.

Mary came to bed, and he heard her breathing change as she quickly fell asleep. Finally, perhaps an hour later, he started to doze.

Twenty-Three

He woke as usual before first light. A thin band of pale blue just touched the eastern horizon, and there was a hint of dawn through the open window. He splashed water on his face to rouse himself, dressed and let himself out as quietly as possible.

In front of him the city was still asleep. It would stir soon enough, with the bustle of kitchens and laundry, the carters on their early deliveries, then the weavers arriving for the Tuesday market.

At the jail he checked the cells. Hughes's men had been moved to the Moot Hall prison to await their trials and death sentences. Everything was quiet as he sat and began to write his report for the mayor. He recounted the swift attack on the jail and his reprisal, trimming carefully to make each statement as bald and matter of fact as possible.

He accounted for the deaths and wounds, taking time to praise his own men, Sedgwick and Lister in particular. That was only fair; they'd been fearless.

By the time he'd finished, the sun was well up. He sealed the paper, then walked down Briggate, stopping at the Old King's Arms for the Brig-End shot breakfast they served on market days. The beef was dry, but it made no never mind, he was hungry. The pottage was fresh for once, and the ale tasty, ample to renew him for the day. It was always tuppence well spent, the same price it had been as far back as he could recall.

The trestles were set up, just one row on each side today; most of the weavers already stood behind them, displaying the lengths of cloth they'd brought in to sell. In the middle of the street the merchants chatted quietly, waiting for the chimes of the Parish Church to call seven so trading could begin.

The Constable exchanged brief greetings and nuggets of gossip until the first peal of the bell took the men's attention, then he strode off down the middle of the road, leaving them to make their deals in the whispers that had always been part of the cloth business.

He turned on to Swinegate, sliding between the men and women barking wares from their shop fronts, around maids exchanging their tittle-tattle in moments of freedom from the houses, and avoided the piles and puddles emptied earlier from upstairs windows.

He walked through the door where the paint had peeled and the wood faded, footsteps firm on the flagstones in the hallway. The parlour door was closed tight, a key in the lock, but the entry to the kitchen was open as ever, no towering guard in front of it this time.

317

Worthy was standing by the table, a full mug of ale in front of him. He faced the window, luxuriating like a cat in the patch of sun. Without turning, he said, 'You must think this is your home away from home, laddie.'

'Why's that, Amos?' Nottingham leant against the table and poured himself a drink from the jug.

'You seem to come in here anytime you please without a by your leave. You'd ask any honest man for permission to enter.'

The Constable drank slowly. 'If you were an honest man I'd treat you honestly, Amos.'

The pimp turned to face him. He'd seemed thinner since the winter, but now, with dust motes in the air and the bright morning light harsh on his face, Nottingham felt he could have been seeing a different person. Worthy's skin had taken on the hard, polished texture of vellum, and his ancient clothes no longer bulged against his flesh. He looked old.

'I heard what happened yesterday.'

'All of it?'

'Aye,' Worthy nodded. 'That Hughes is no loss. If that boy of yours hadn't stopped me I'd have saved the trouble.'

'And then you'd have been the one in jail.'

'Not me, laddie,' he answered with an enigmatic grin.

'You've been there before.'

'Only for an hour or two. And I won't be there again.'

'Don't tempt fate.'

318

Worthy stared hard at the Constable. 'Nowt like that,' he said firmly. 'Look at me. Go on, take a long look.'

Nottingham did as he was bid, fixing the picture in his mind.

'Now, tell me what you see.'

'Someone who's starting to show his years.'

The pimp chuckled softly. 'At least your mam brought you up to be polite. But save it for the Corporation. You don't beat around the bush with me.' He waited. 'Well? What do you see?'

'You look old, Amos,' Nottingham told him.

'I'm dying, laddie.' It was a simple statement and the Constable didn't know how to respond. He watched the other man's eyes and saw it was the truth; the time for dissembling and deception had passed.

'I'm sorry,' he said finally, and meant it.

'Don't be. You're not immortal yourself. It catches us all in the end.' His voice was matter-of-fact, as if he was talking about someone else. 'It's cancer, that's what they say. Been growing inside me for a while now, and there's bugger all anyone can do about it.'

'Who knows?'

'Just the doctor in York who told me. And you.' He raised his bushy eyebrows. 'You didn't think I'd be stupid enough to tell anyone in Leeds, did you?'

'You've told me.'

Worthy shrugged. 'That's different. I know you, you'll keep it to yourself. You won't even tell that tall drink of water who works for you.'

319

He grinned, and for a passing moment the ghost of a younger man sparked in his face. 'And telling you keeps you off my back.'

'You think I won't arrest you?' Nottingham asked.

'I know you won't, laddie. What's the worst you can charge me with? Fighting in the street?' He turned his head and spat on the floor. 'Not worth your time, not for the ten minutes I'd be there.'

'I suppose you're right,' the Constable conceded.

'If you really believed you could have had me for something, you'd have had me in a cell. We both know it.'

'I would,' Nottingham agreed. 'Did the doctor say how long you'd live?'

'Why, want to be rid of me? Aye, I suppose you do, really.' He shrugged. 'I don't know, laddie, I'll go when I go.' He lifted an arm to show a wrist, the skin loose on the bone. 'Probably not long, by the look of it.'

'Do you have much pain?'

'Sometimes,' he admitted. 'That doctor sold me summat, but I can't be doing with it, all it does is make me fall asleep. That's just what I want, isn't it, to sleep my way into death.'

'So what do you do?'

'Bear it, of course,' he said, as if it was the most obvious thing in the world. 'What else are you going to do? A few drinks help. So does a girl here and there, or breaking a few heads.' He paused. 'Anyway, my problems will be over soon enough. Yours are going to start after I've gone.'

That was true, Nottingham realized. Worthy had controlled most of the prostitution and much of the other crime in Leeds for years. He was a known quantity, smart in his own twisted way, with the Corporation neatly folded and tucked into his pocket.

With his death there'd be a space, and a hundred men all eager to battle each other to assume his crown. All the skirmish with Hughes had done was give them a very small taste of the future.

'You see it now?'

'I do.'

'You're going to be a busy man, Constable.'

Nottingham nodded sadly.

'Happen you'll end up thinking I was the lesser of two evils.' He started to laugh, which turned into a wet cough, stopping only when he drew in a deep breath and spat again. 'Better,' he said, wiping his mouth with his sleeve then taking a deep drink.

'How long have you known, Amos?'

'Since the start of spring. And for God's sake, get rid of that long face. I'm only telling you because you need to know. I don't want sympathy. If you start acting like a lass I'll knock you into next week.'

'I should be happy. God knows I've wished you dead often enough.'

'So now your prayers have been answered.'

'Are you ready for it?'

'What, shriven and penitent, you mean?' He snorted in annoyance. 'What sort of bloody stupid question is that, laddie? You die, it's all over. It happens when it happens.'

'No heaven or hell?'

Worthy shook his head with conviction. 'If you're going to have those you need to believe, and I haven't done that in a long time.' He poured more of the ale. 'There's plenty I've stopped believing in over the years.'

'You'll die a rich man.'

'Aye,' Worthy agreed with a sigh. 'Not as rich as everyone thinks, though. Still, better than begging on the streets.' He paused. 'I've made my will, and it'll prove without a problem. There's something for you in it.'

'No,' Nottingham said quickly, but the pimp held up his hand to stop him.

'Hear me out. It's not meant for you, I've got more sense than that. It's for that daughter of yours. It'll bring her an income so she won't ever have to depend on anyone. I heard she's just started teaching at the Dame School.'

'Yes,' Nottingham answered tightly, angry that the man should follow his family so closely.

'There's no money in that. She'll only earn pennies.'

'Honest pennies.'

'Like a Constable's pay?' Worthy taunted.

'It's more than you can say for your money.'

Worthy sat back. 'I earn my money then I invest it in London. Did you know that? It grows down there, and that's quite legal. So how do you know which bit's honest and which isn't, Mr Nottingham?'

'I'm not going to let Emily take money from you.' He stated it as a fact, not a challenge.

'The money's there,' Worthy said calmly. 'Why don't you let her decide when she reaches her majority? She's a clever girl, isn't she? Must be, to be a teacher.'

'Yes.' The Constable curled his fingers tightly around the mug.

'Then let her make up her own mind. You tell her your tale and let the money speak for itself. See what she wants to do.'

'No, Amos.'

Worthy smiled. 'It's too late, laddie. The will's made and I'm not paying any more to a bloody lawyer to change it now.'

Even in death the man would vex him, the Constable thought. He'd have thought it through and done it deliberately; it was his way. He finished his drink.

'Don't worry, I won't be causing you any more trouble, unless some other mad bugger starts to think he's better than me.'

Nottingham stared at him.

'Just do me one favour, will you, laddie?' Worthy asked, his voice suddenly serious.

'What's that?'

'Come to my funeral. I don't think it'll be a crowded do.'

'I wouldn't miss it, Amos. If only to make sure you're really dead.'

'Better,' Worthy said with a small grin. 'But

323

what you don't realize yet is how much you'll miss me.'

Nottingham stood up and looked at the other man again. He wasn't frail yet but he'd be close to it, much of his hair gone, the rest wispy, lank and grey. Quickly he turned away and walked out of the house, closing the door quietly behind him.

Twenty-Four

Wednesday passed quietly, just the petty routines of crime, a purse cut here, a fight there, a few stolen coins. The Constable sent Lister out patrolling the streets with Sedgwick to learn his craft. He was waiting, knowing he'd hear from Gibton soon. The man might be arrogant, but he wasn't a fool.

The note arrived on a cloudy Thursday when the air was close and the heat pressed down. The animals felt it, carters' horses unwilling to move, and the people were ill-tempered, parading sluggishly in the streets.

A farmer from Roundhay, in Leeds to purchase a few items, delivered it, his eyes casting nervously around the jail. He thrust it into Nottingham's hand then left abruptly.

The Constable weighed it in his hand before tearing open the heavy red seal. The paper was elegant, thick and heavy, but the words were a hurried, awkward scrawl: *Friday at nine, Gibton's Well*.

It wasn't so much a request as a command, he thought drily. That certainly fitted with the man. But he didn't really care what it was as long as the couple admitted their guilt and made their atonement.

The storm came early in the afternoon; thunder roiled briefly overhead, rain pelted for a few minutes, turning the dirt to clinging mud, then it passed on, leaving the air fresher and cooler again.

He watched it all through the window, saw people dashing into houses and shops, heard two girls scream at the loudness of the thunderclap. Once it had all gone he walked outside, drawing in deep breaths. Tomorrow the Godlove business finished. It had taken too long. He should have discovered the truth more quickly, but who could have imagined parents doing such a thing?

Yet he knew there was more to it than that. It had taken place on unfamiliar ground, outside the city he knew so well, among people with wealth and titles. The merchants in Leeds didn't worry him, no matter how rich they might be. They were people he saw every day, ordinary because they were so familiar. But Samuel Godlove, with his countless acres, or Gibton, the man who would have gleefully pawned his soul if it brought a good price; these were people he could never understand. They lived in a manner far beyond his ken. He'd fumbled in the dark all through the business.

In the end he decided to go alone.

'Don't, boss,' Sedgwick said. 'What if he wants to kill you out there?'

'Then he'll have a fight on his hands. Come

on, John, you've seen the man. Do you really think he'd be a danger?'

'You don't know the place,' the deputy objected.

'I'm not discussing it,' Nottingham told him flatly. 'Everything will be fine.' He pulled the pistol from his pocket and showed the knife in its sheath on his belt. He left, amused at the old woman the deputy was becoming.

The horse was waiting at the stable. Gentle as it was, he hoped he wouldn't need to mount it again for a long time. He rode out past Sheepscar, taking the path to Harehills before finally turning on to a cart track along the valley where a sign indicated the well.

It was only a short distance, perhaps a quarter of a mile, before he saw the stone building standing back in the woods, a small area in front of it roughly cleared.

A horse was tethered there and he rubbed its flanks. The flesh was already cool; whoever it was had arrived some time before. He glanced at the well, just a small square carved out of the woods around a spring. The stone wall surrounding it was taller than a man, offering privacy for bathing. A wooden door stood ajar, leading into a tiny building at the side.

Cautiously, he came close, then drew the pistol and used it to push at the wood. It swung open slowly with a loud squeak. Nottingham waited, listening closely, but the only sounds he could hear came from the trees, the soft rustling of leaves and the cries of birds.

As quietly as possible, he walked in. There was a single high window, leaving just a faint light, the corners full of deep shadows. He stood still, letting his eyes adjust, gradually making out the shapes of benches and pegs hammered into the wall to hold clothes. One set hung there, peacock proud, a pair of polished boots neatly below them on the floor.

There was another door, closed tight. He lifted the latch as quietly as possible, barely daring to breathe, careful to stay out of sight as he pulled the handle back.

Nothing. He strode out into the bright shock of morning light. Flagstones formed a walkway, and rough steps led down to the small, square pool where Gibton lay naked, face down. His arms were splayed, his body a pale, ugly colour.

Nottingham squatted and reached out to touch the dead wet flesh, his fingertips rocking the corpse in the water, small ripples sparkling in the sun.

The Constable returned to the changing room and riffled through the pockets of the man's clothes. Gibton was certain to have left a letter; the man couldn't kill himself and not mark it in some way.

He found it in the inside pocket of the jacket, a roughly folded sheaf of papers. He took it outside, into the woods, found a stump a few yards from the horses, and sat to read.

By now you will have seen my body and have your proof that I am dead. If you go to my house you will see that my wife is also dead. I gave her poison last night after the servants had gone to their beds.

I shall explain what happened. It is true that Sarah arrived with her maid, as she did on occasion. She was going to leave Leeds with that man she loved. She was carrying his child. She enjoyed every word she told us.

It is also quite true that my wife had been ill, the worst I had seen her, with her ranting and raving. By the time Sarah arrived she had begun to recover. I was tending her, and had taken the knife and cut the bindings I had used to tie her to the bed.

The words put my wife in a red rage once more, not to be contained. If she left, Godlove would want all the money he had given us, and we would be paupers again. Had the girl thought of that? As Sarah walked away, she stabbed her.

With her dead, I needed to kill the maid. Early the next morning I put their bodies in the cart. I found a quiet spot for Anne, for no one would care if she was ever seen again.

For Sarah, though, I had to think. Kirkstall Abbey would be close enough to her home to bring questions. But I rushed the business and botched it. If I had taken the knife you would never have known with certainty.

The only death I regret is that of my wife. She was a good woman, faithful to me and to my name. But perhaps even that is a blessing, for she was growing worse and we had been told

329

there was no cure. In all things, maybe, there is some good to be found.

He folded the sheets and forced them into his pocket. Who was the more insane, he wondered with a deep sigh, Gibton or his wife? Neither of them had cared for Sarah's happiness, for her joy in life. And when she'd tried to take it, to be with the man she loved, they'd killed her to hold on to their comfort.

With more cunning they'd never have been discovered. But now they were dead, like Sarah, like Will, and awaiting the judgement. Only Godlove was left, his own life like purgatory now.

He sat for long silent minutes in the wood, feeling inexplicably sad. Then he took a deep breath and climbed back on the horse. In the village he could tell them about the body at the well.

Twenty-Five

Nottingham stood by the grave as the vicar himself recited the service for the dead. Worthy had spent enough to ensure the best, no mere curate to preside over the burial, and a lengthy eulogy that transformed him into an outstanding citizen. His corpse lay in the best of coffins with its wood buffed to a high gloss.

There was a sharp bite to the autumn wind in the churchyard. Already the leaves were beginning to tumble, swirling and spiralling across the grass and crunching underfoot.

The voice droned on, intoning the prayers for the dead.

'Thou knowest, Lord, the secrets of our hearts; shut not up thy merciful eyes to our prayers: but spare us Lord most holy, O God most mighty, O holy and merciful saviour, thou most worthy judge eternal, suffer us not at our last hour for any pains of death to fall from thee.'

The Constable pulled the collar of his coat close about himself. He was almost the only mourner, exactly as the pimp had predicted. His men had abandoned him in the end, his friends on the Corporation had forsaken him. The only one left, so he'd heard, had been the old woman from the parlour, who'd tended him like a baby in his last days. She stood a few yards away, a bent crone covered head to toe in deep black.

Worthy had died two days before, gently, in his sleep. The old woman had discovered him early Sunday morning, her banshee wailing dragging the neighbours from their rest.

The Constable had heard of the death as he left the morning service. Lister had been waiting outside the Parish Church, his face eager with the news and the chance of seeing Emily for a few brief minutes. Nottingham had sent him to find Sedgwick, and the three men had spent the afternoon at the jail, making their plans.

The procurer had been correct. Once he'd gone the fighting would begin in earnest and they needed to be ready. Everyone who thought himself a hard man would be on the streets, threatening the whores and trying to become king. They had to make sure all the pretenders were knocked down.

He hadn't spoken to Worthy since the man had told him he was dying. There seemed to be nothing more to say, no farewells to be made; they'd come quite naturally to the end of words.

The vicar finished his litany, closed his prayer book and lowered his head. Nottingham bent to pick up some of the dirt piled by the grave. He raised his hand and spread his fingers, letting the dust and clumps fall loudly on to the wood six feet below.

'...through our Lord Jesus Christ, who shall change our vile body that it may be like to his

332

glorious body, according to the mighty working, whereby he is able to subdue all things to himself.'

A time had ended.

He turned away and walked across the churchyard to the spot he knew so well, where his older daughter, Rose, had lain since February. He stood and looked down at the sinking mound of grass. Another few months, once another winter had passed, and they'd finally be able to put up the headstone for her.

In the beginning, after she'd died, he'd come here often to feel close to her, to talk to her and say all the things he felt he couldn't tell anyone else. Now, although he still loved her so much, he no longer came regularly. He'd allowed her memory to grow fainter, relinquishing her rather than trying desperately to hold on to her.

He sighed, knelt, and plucked away a few weeds. He was sick of death, of the bodies he'd seen, the people he'd had to tell, the faces he'd known who were no longer there. Too many of them over the years.

Slowly he pushed himself upright, his knees tight and aching as he rose. He was growing older himself, and he hoped that this winter wouldn't be as bad as the last one. Bye, love, he said softly to Rose and made his way to the lych gate where Sedgwick was waiting.

'He's finally in the ground then?'

The Constable nodded.

'He is. And it's where we'll all be in the end, John. Think on.'

Afterword

For many centuries arranged marriages were commonplace. They united powerful families, brought together wealth and land. At many social levels they were the norm. If a marriage also brought love, that was good fortune, but it was certainly never a consideration.

The dowry, also known as the bride portion, was also common. It was what the bride brought to the marriage, and its amount would vary with the status of the couple. Although a bride price – what a man might pay to the bride's family for his new wife – is long established in the East, where it's seen to recompense them for her services and value, it has no real mention in the West.

That doesn't mean it never happened, especially in the lower echelons of nobility, and baron is the lowest. The respectability of society – of aristocracy – was a great draw to those who had money and no title, and wealth attracted those who had title but little money. It was a match made, if not in heaven, then somewhere. It's worth remembering that all too often in this period women had next to nothing in the way of rights and were treated like chattel. This takes that premise and builds on it.

These days both Horsforth and Roundhay are suburbs of Leeds rather than the outlying villages they were in the 1730s. The 'old Roman road' is Street Lane, any traces of Rome now myth, not fact. But the ruins of Kirkstall Abbey remain, more ancient and fragile now, yet still imbued with a very deep sense of spirit. To be there, sitting on the banks of the Aire on a summer's day is to feel a powerful connection to history.

Gipton Well (not Gibton), otherwise known as Gipton Spa, is still extant, hidden away at one end of Gledhow Valley Woods, not far from Roundhay Road. It was built in 1671 by Edward Waddington and for a time it was favoured by some of the great and good of Leeds. It's been fenced off since 2004, but the Friends of Gledhow Valley Woods have been restoring it.

I rely on a number of books when writing about Leeds. Chief among them are: *The Illustrated History of Leeds* by Steven Burt and Kevin Brady (Breedon Books, 1994) which remains my most valuable resource; *Leeds: The Story of a City* by David Thornton (Fort, 2002); *The Municipal History of Leeds* by James Wardell (Longman Brown & Co., 1846); *Gentleman Merchants* by R.G. Wilson (Manchester University Press, 1971) and *1700* by Maureen Waller (Sceptre, 2000). Additionally, there was wonderful information to be gleaned from *The Merchants' Golden Age: Leeds 1700–1790* by Steven Burt and Kevin Brady (self published,

1987), *Old Leeds Inside Out*, compiled by Steven Burt (no publisher listed) and the *1989 Centenary Edition Miscellany of Publications of the Thoresby Society, Leeds in the Seventeenth and Eighteenth Centuries* (Thoresby Society). And nothing would be complete without the mighty *Ducatis Leodensis* by Ralph Thoresby himself, the first historian of Leeds and its surrounding areas.

I'm grateful to many people who've contributed in different ways to make this a much better book than it would have been if I'd worked alone. There's Kate Lyall Grant at Severn House/Crème de la Crime, my agent Tina Betts, and Lynne Patrick (to whom I still owe a huge debt).

Linda Hornberg's maps always bring the book more alive, and Thom Atkinson's critiques are invaluable; a truly brilliant writer himself, if these novels shine, much of the credit lies with him.

And this book wouldn't have happened without Penny or August (who slept through most of it), or thoughts of Graham.